WILDCAT DREAMS in the DEATH LIGHT

WILDCAT DREAMS in the DEATH LIGHT

REAGAN M. SOVA

Michigan City, Indiana: First To Knock

First To Knock
432 St. John Rd. #101
Michigan City, Indiana, 46360

Copyright © 2022 First To Knock, LLC

All rights reserved under Pan American and International Copyright Conventions. No part of this publication may be reproduced, stored in a retrieval system, or transmitted in any form or by any means, electronic, mechanical, photocopying, recording, or otherwise, without prior consent from the publisher.

This is a work of fictional poetry. Names, characters, businesses, places, events, locales, and incidents are either products of the author's imagination or used in a fictitious or satirical manner.

Cover painting: Edward Lasala
Book design: Nick Ferreira
First To Knock logo: Edward Lasala

First Printing
Printed in the United States of America
ISBN: 978-1-7349060-4-2
Library of Congress Control Number: 2021952470

Contents

ערשט	9
צווייט	21
דריט	35
פֿערט	49
פֿינפֿט	67
זעקסט	71
זיבעט	79
אַכט	87
נײַנט	107
צענט	121
עלפֿט	131
צוועלפֿט	139
דרײַצנט	147
פֿערצנט	161
פֿופֿצנט	175
זעכצנט	181
זיבעצנט	193
אַכצנט	201
נײַנצנט	215
צוואַנציקסט	223
איין און צוואַנציקסט	231
צוויי און צוואַנציקסט	237
דרײַ און צוואַנציקסט	245
פֿיר און צוואַנציקסט	251
פֿינף און צוואַנציקסט	261

ערשט

my 11th summer
Aunt J borrowed her step uncle's catboat
and sailed us to the middle of
the big lake where her husband had drowned
she plopped anchor
and leaned back over the stern like she
was being baptized in a river of ghosts
the splashing men from afar yelled
help us help us
save us save us
i pointed and said they're there
Aunt J hoisted anchor i steered to them
closer we came they cried our boat
sunk please rescue us
we helped the six of them aboard
all small enough to surprise me
with worn faces of grown men
but the bodies of boys none taller than me
Aunt J passed the jug of hobo honey wine
we all drank like
Snow White and the Seven Dwarves of Death
the man with the ace of spades tattoo on his
chest said we are all horse jockeys except Frank
Frank is not a rider
he is just a midget who shovels horseshit
they guffawed i
would have been pulling my blade
if i was Frank

but he chuckled and said i just like horses
well that put the twinkle in Aunt J's eye
for nearly two years Frank came around
he took me to the pumpkin patch
the day i became a Bar Mitzvah
he said i got something for you
rummaging in his wagon
from the gunnysack he lifted
and said this was my father's guitar
spirits have been strumming it
at night i hear them
Frank handed me the instrument
moon moths fluttering
my eyes moistening as i gripped the neck
never had i received such a gift
through thin trembling lips i said i like it
when he married Aunt J
i sang one of the handed-down songs
he had taught me
Gypsy Davey
except i changed the words
it was late last night when the boss come home
he's askin' about his lady
the only answer he received
she's gone with the Gypsy Frankie
gone with the Gypsy Frank
the crowd in the orchard that day
all hundred really got a kick out of that
rollicking joyfully
many horse people among them
they cheered the next part
go saddle for me my buskin' horse
and a hundred dollar saddle
point out to me their wagon tracks
and after them i'll travel
after them i'll ride
all day people said
there is that singer there he is
for weeks and months after

songs of my own poured
from me i wrote them in my sleep
everywhere i went more people kept
saying there is Sloman there is the young
Jew who plays guitar we want that song you
sang that goes *i didn't reinvent the wheel i*
just rolled and rolled and rolled snake eyes
Bob who owned the country store
let me play there for a small revolving cast
always coins jingling my jar
women and men would see me
sitting and sipping and say
take up that guitar
of the dead unknown poets
and sing their spirit words we will
meet them in time
except one day i was strumming songs
when two of the jockeys who had
almost drowned with Frank
rode up to the country store on a mule
hopping down stumbling crumbling
to the earth like two tiny Towers of Babel
speaking nonsense
i knew they had had half the wine in town
they got up dusting themselves
the one with the ace tattoo
said you're Frank's new son the
adopted orphan of a shit-shoveling midget
they cackled all over themselves
i said from the chair Frank is a good man
the other jockey said good for chasing mice
from the barn
a cat could replace Frank
they tittered i rose i
said you want to get your asses whupped by
a man of 13
the tattooed one said you want me to
uppercut this mule
they cracked up

the mule looked sweet but
he actually punched him they laughed
i barked hey now you want me to put
this guitar on the ground
get out the great tree knife and
set the blood spraying from your necks
the other jockey said you want me
to blow this mule's brains out
they did not laugh
he pawed for his silver pistol i
sprung toward him i
smashed the guitar of spirits upon his head
the neck busted off the body i
fumbled for his sidearm we struggled with it it
fell to the ground and discharged into his foot
he toppled over crying Lord mercy
another pistol fired into the air it was Bob
who had stepped out of the country store with
his six-shooter and his son Luke who had a big
axe i had seen him grip the bottom handle and
slowly touch the blade to his nose one night the
only person in town strong enough to do that
Bob said you midgets better be on this
mule riding out of here in a jiffy or i am
coming to burn your homes and stables
Bob was once a Civil War soldier of 12
he had spilled the teeth of spies
the wounded jockey howled in pain
the tattooed one had his arms up
Bob advanced and cocked his
Samuel Colt saying and that is no threat
it is a fucking promise
the jockeys mounted the mule with their gun
and left a trail of blood dripping from his foot
i gathered the banged-up guitar in pieces
Bob holstered his Peacemaker and said to me
sorry son
say Luke pour him a shot of whisky
and a glass of sweet tea

i had my tongue in my cheek i would not cry
saying much obliged Bob
i shuffled home with the guitar parts
Frank and Aunt J from the porch had
never appeared more bewildered
what happened they said
i said Frank never stands up to
those rotten jockeys
they walk all over him
i went to the barn to sulk with Sweet Kiss
within an hour the shouting of the jockeys
reached my ear i
exited the barn there were five with
their poor mule quarreling with
Frank and Aunt J
one had his foot bandaged he saw me and
drew his pistol he said i ought to put a bullet
in this wild orphan's peculiar foreign face
the tattooed jockey said aw now
does the cockroach trouble the house
this young Jew hardly merits the
fuss of murder i have brought a railroad spike
we shall hammer it through his foot for
a suitable punishment
then we will be on our way
his fellow jockeys concurred
Aunt J stepped off the porch quaking
she said had i known your souls i
would have let every one of you but Frank
sink to the bottom of the lake now leave
but the wounded jockey aimed
his silver upon Aunt J and said Frank it is
time for you to control your woman and
punish your boy he needs to learn
Frank uneasy in the spotlight said lower
your weapon and everyone listen to my words
you will want to hear them i
have been studying you all for 17
seasons you are lousy jockeys i should have

been a rider but i lacked the courage to
whip the beasts i love but no longer
you all race me on Halloween and if one of
you win you shall have all my money
the tattooed jockey said how much
Frank said i have five dollars
they all guffawed knee-slapping
the tattooed one said to the wounded one
lower your piece Frank is too damn funny to kill
but in all seriousness here is the deal Frank
we will race and to the winner goes your life's fortune
all five big ones and the orphan gets his foot spiked
now take that deal or we get the spiking done now
i piped up saying i will abide that bet but if Frank wins
you all leave me be and we keep your mule
the tattooed jockey consulted the others
he said we agree to that
Aunt J buried her face and said oh no
Frank said i agree to all this but if
you ever pull a firearm on my wife again i
will find you and blind you in your sleep
the jockey tucked the sun-warm silver
inside his pants with no apology he spit
they ambled off
two riding the mule three walking
Frank cracked the whip upon himself
training hard the next couple months
there were times his face flushed so red
i thought he would die
he lifted medicine balls five hours a day
he danced wildly atop wine barrels screaming poems in dead languages
he downed brimming mugs of raw ostrich eggs
he jumped rope with the entwined hair of dead horses
he rode Sweet Kiss backward both of them blindfolded
he shot sharp blowgun darts into the ace of spades from 50 paces away
he lit the card afire and smoked the ashes
i fed Sweet Kiss and brushed him i
shoveled the shit i was proud to be Frank's Frank i
sang Sweet Kiss victory songs in the moonlight i

had no guitar only my voice
Aunt J fretted the entire time she spent dark days
in the bathtub with her wine
Halloween came and the crowd did assemble
at the grand horse track the stands packed
they were all dressed in costumes of
sailors monks nuns bootleggers
several devils
a couple archangels
one as Lucy Parsons
and another as the mother of endless sleep
a woman in a fox mask tapped my shoulder outside
the trophy room the whole town filing past
she lifted her disguise it was the Locksmith
she whispered in my ear bet on Sweet Kiss
she kissed me passionately on the lips when
i opened my eyes she had vanished
there were those cloaked as newspapermen
the wolfish hog rancher could not disguise he
was a pig and not the curly-tailed good kind i
rendezvoused with Frank and Aunt J
in the jockeys' changing room
Frank in a silk jockey's shirt of violet and a black cap
shaved with short hair he smelled of barber's lotion
he said sheepishly do i even look like a jockey
i had grown a half-foot taller than him i
said you look like a king i would follow into battle
we embraced Aunt J was crying with roses upon her hat
Frank gave me the five dollars he said if i lose
you take this money and you run son you buy a gun
or do what you will but you ramble i will take the heat
i said no chance in hell Frank i will not leave you
he said you must or i will be one more jockey
with a mind to spike your foot you hear me
i said what if you win
he said then that money ain't for your keeping
we chuckled even Aunt J too as she dabbed a tear i
made a hot beeline for the betting window i
pushed all my country store coins across plus Frank's dead

presidents i said seven dollars on Sweet Kiss to win please
the old woman inside choked on a bite of rhubarb pie
she said wow are you sure he is quite a long shot 30-to-1
i said yes ma'am everything is riding on Sweet Kiss
the bugle boy played the tune
Aunt J and i had a ground-level spot
in the stands
near the finish line
among the incognito masses
the banker with the blood of
the newborn lamb in his mustache
the mayor's advisor with her nose full of goof dust
the shopkeeper smoking navy-cut cigs with her eyes closed
the diplomat dreaming falcons fucking in the Balkans
the old gray priest cussing the stray Dutch bitch
the sea captain who had killed a man for salt
the migrant who had gathered crops with a cracked skull
they all cheered they
had their bets placed too
the moon blotted out the sun
the type of solar eclipse that only
happens once every ten thousand years
the man aimed the pistol skyward
at the forehead of God
right between the eyes he pulled the trigger
they shot off
the pacesetter was Big Sleep
rode by the tattooed jockey he was whipping him
the wounded jockey mounted upon
Collapsed in the Street after Taking Opium
nipped at their heels
i could not see Frank in the back
32 charging legs
flinging dirt with the furious step
of stampeding hysterical buffalo angels
fleeing heaven in fear
Sweet Kiss sprinted forth as if
swept by gale-force spirit winds of hope
i did not know Frank's strategy

but he had one
Aunt J cheered in a frenzy
the roses rolled off her hat
the sun's brilliant face shone again
i destroyed my throat and burst
a blood vessel in my eye
they exploded across the line
Frank first by the length of a horse head
the champion jockey
draped upon Sweet Kiss like a lifeless
velvet cloth obscuring the magician's hand
he tumbled from his steed into the dirt
i yelled Frank
and hopped the barrier i dashed to him the
ancient trouble drums pounding in my head i
slid onto the earth on my knees he
was turning violet as his shirt he
beckoned my ear to his lips and pushed words
faintly through labored breath
make a good funeral for me
make it at dusk
play a song as night falls
you will find another guitar of spirits if you so seek it
my ghost will guide you
tell Aunt J in my heart for her
there was only love now fare thee well
Sweet Kiss nuzzled him i said you will
be ok Frank i love you you are a champion
i hollered into the huddle around us
who among you is a doctor
but Frank had already crossed the natural bridge
Aunt J fought through the tumult to see him
i attempted to console her as she fell upon the dirt
in grief she ripped her dress
a newspaperman took a picture with a pop
and the smell of flash powder
reporter pencils scribbled fevered shorthand
shredding commotion among the spectators
dragonflies in their throats

some jockeys ashamed of themselves
even the tattooed jockey wept on the track
they loaded Frank onto the big wagon Aunt J
jumped up and laid next to him wailing
the track crew harnessed Sweet Kiss to the wagon
and there were four men with colorful pointy-toed shoes
costumed as the kings of each card suit
heart diamond club and spade
the heart said we will lead Sweet Kiss to the funeral parlor
the crestfallen tattooed jockey said i will be haunted
by this until i die Frank was a good man he has bested us all
i collected my winnings
210 dollars with the darkness of
guilt myself but it was all i had on earth
the only inheritance i would ever know i
fetched Frank's fine suit of clothes from
the locker room for the funeral i
rode out on the tattooed jockey's mule i
did not find sleep in the night
there was a storm with thunder like
God's dark laughter sidewalks
flew into the air a giant tulip poplar
crashed into the governor's outhouse
killing him instantly
the banker's buggy drawn by a zebra team
was sucked up in a twister thank heaven
the zebras were not harmed
in my room at Aunt J's i struck a match
in the dark of a thousand midnights i
saw my sister dancing the ghost dance she
sang of all the homes she had haunted she
sang of all the horses she had spooked she
sang of all the books she had filled she
sang a future tune
a tornado song from the day i was born as
a wildcat howling in the dark and in the fog
she showed me the book of the dead whose
words are glowing embers with a dusklight song
for Frank's funeral i sang it with her

Frank and Aunt J appeared briefly by the window
and everyone vanished with the final lightning strike
i kept singing 'til sunbeams gave chase to the clouds
the blue sky morning of peace had arrived
a beautiful day to bury Frank if Aunt J was ready
my people do not delay the rest of the dead i
prepared breakfast for Aunt J and me
the radiant sun spurred bird songs i
checked Aunt J was not in her room i
poked my head in the barn Aunt J had shot herself
the shotgun aimed into her heart
i was startled again when
a bluebird flew from the hole in her chest
she had died with her eyes open i
kneeled shut them and kissed her forehead
there was a letter on the ground with my name on it
i am sorry to cross the bridge so soon
but take comfort i feel no pain
my step uncle Horace
will help you find work and lodging
you are a man
i trust you will make a
good funeral for Frank and me
with lights in the dark
i have written below the story
a traveling peddler did tell me
when i was a little girl
this to me is the story of life
fare thee well J
i read the story she did write about a man
who had been pursued by a pack of bears
and their claws of death i
wept forcefully upon the grass i
dimly recalled my family's lifeless funeral i
consecrated unto myself the sacred mission
the ceremony of light to honor Frank and Aunt J
i had the song in hand but i
could not do it without the right guitar
nor the Locksmith keys

not even the rabbis have them
my head wobbled and throbbed as if struck by a cannonball
the barn door had been wide open
Sweet Kiss must have bolted
i mounted the mule i
fell asleep upon his back and woke deep in the forest i
saw two dalmatian horses running wild i
saw the librarian sunbathing bare-chested i
saw the wild boar swarmed by a buzzing blanket of yellow jackets i
saw the argument about smoked hickory i
saw the rabbi limping with a knife in his thigh i
saw the mercenary for the Sultan of Yogyakarta breaking wind i
saw the pair of grandfathers lovingly fucking 'neath the windmill i
saw the woman with my mother's eyes cutting tomatoes
and talking to the dead i
saw the Scotch immigrant whittling arrows i
saw the dwarf hugging the trunk of the great tree
pretending it was his dead son i
saw the cobbler's ghost
driven into the ground with stomping incantations i
saw my father as a collapsed bridge i
saw the grave they had dug me before i was even ever born
i hopped the train in Kalamazoo
hobos helped hoist the mule aboard
we changed boxcars now and then
chunking our way
for a few days and nights

צווייט

when the train stopped i got out
and journeyed atop the mule again
through the wood
bound for alluring sounds i heard
the violin of the Chinese emperor's
armless great granddaughter
i had no idea where i was
i had to have crossed several state lines
my hands shaking in hunger
the unmistakable smell of popcorn
and candy conquered the air
i told the mule follow the scent exiting the forest
nothing i had ever seen to that point could
have prepared me for the circus
like a village laid before me
more precisely a kingdom
there were preachers at the gates railing
against the temptation of women i tied the mule
to the makeshift board fence around
the outside the young Gypsy jingled coins
in a metal mug i had never seen anyone with
the jitters so bad his head bobbing uncontrollably
one arm twitching
the other upon a crutch
he was dragging his crooked foot behind him
hauling a wagonload of sadness in his eyes
the money Frank and Sweet Kiss had won for
me had never left the bottom of my pocket i

gave the trembling Gypsy a whole dollar i
slid past the preachers and took my ticket i
galloped to the food tent not even the clown
on the penny-farthing bicycle with the monkey
on his shoulder and them both juggling
tiny tangerines could distract me
i wolfed waffles and popcorn with root beer
at the picnic table under lantern light
the woman dressed as Mona Lisa suckled
cotton candy across from me the whole time
a newspaper on the table got the story wrong
it said Frank was the first dead man ever to win a horse race
but i knew he was a living jockey when he won
he had lost so much weight before the race
they said that plus the thrill of overtaking
his rivals was the Sweet Kiss of Death
for his champion's heart
with my knife i sliced a good chunk
of quality hay from outside the menagerie
i borrowed a bucket of water lying around i
said to the Arab at the gate what is your name friend
he said Fat Ali
i said i am Sloman i
just have to feed my mule then i will return i
will remember you if you remember me
he said deal
i gave the mule the hay and water i
pet his ears and said your name shall be Leonardo
after the Mona Lisa painter
you really are that magnificent
Fat Ali gave me no quarrel bless him i made
my way back to the menagerie inside it was
like Noah's Ark rambunctious Satanic goats
lambs lions a bear playing around with a dog
scorpions of the Arizona Territory snoozing peacefully
a rhino giving birth i
was one of dozens of awestruck grubby onlookers
Dorothy the elephant could have crushed
us and all the animals and rivers of lions

and strong men but with her loving trunk
she plucked a peanut smaller than a dime off
my hand i was surprised when
the gentleness of it made me cry
i slipped into the sideshow tent
there was the bare-chested lady with
pythons cobras and sand snakes coiled around her
the albino man beating the drum of reptile skin
the Negro woman Bessie of a 107 years of age quoting
the Bible from memory
with her Hebrew name she had known wilderness she
was speaking Deuteronomy when i
shuffled along to the Chinese emperor's
great granddaughter who had no arms
playing the violin with her feet
the sound of it had reached me in the forest
there was the world's tallest man twice my height
also the skeleton man of skin and bones i
bought cards off every one of them
why not i had the money i knew that might
never be the case again
outside their tent i was swept into the big top
everyone yelling the show is starting
inside they had electric lights a thousand people
around the ring i had weaved my way
to the front the show kicked off
with the French man lifting a tractor with his teeth
the Ukrainian woman who walked a tightrope while
bending solid metal bars there was the man
with the long mustache juggling silver rings
his dozen dogs jumping through them
the tramp clowns did a skit before the world's smallest
man rode an Arabian horse and did backflips on her
there too was the Russian knife thrower
but the Gypsy aerialist
she took the trapeze and
flew and flipped and twisted in the air
dancing with death
it was silent

Wildcat Dreams in the Death Light

when she dangled upside down
her eyes locked upon mine they were
one emerald
one amethyst
she the rose that opened in dusklight
she flung herself skyward as if
summoned by Hashem himself i
tensed expecting she would break her neck
but she grabbed the trapeze one-handed doing the splits
her dark legs born of mountain beauty
and untold miles of hard Gypsy traveling
with music and dancing
her smile wide eyes sparkling i
could not cheer with the crowd i
could not even draw breath
the mass exodus swept me from the big top
that was ok i went along i knew i
could not speak to her that night i
needed to prepare i
bumped into a clown beneath the night sky
he was a young Negro man
my age wearing a wig of women's snow white hair
backward blue jeans and big cracked glasses
i said pardon me friend do you know where in America we are
he said Denver
i said no shit
he said yep
Leonardo and i had in fact traversed four states
i said how much longer will this circus be here
he said we have one more night
then we shove off for Pueblo at daybreak we
are doing five nights there as well
i said do you happen to know
the Gypsy aerialist who performed last
he said yes that is Nadezhda
i said my oh my
he said yes the girl is a maestro in the air
i said say you do not act like any clown i have known
he said well i reckon my heart is not much with clowning

i said that is fine by me i appreciate you being knowledgeable
i handed him a dollar coin he
said hot damn i thank you generous fella
i left without going inside the fourth and final tent
it had a tiger painted on the outside with the words
FEROCIOUS BABOU AND HER WHISKERS OF MAGIC
but she would have to wait i
untied Leonardo i said to the preachers by the entry
i do solemnly swear to accept Christ as my savior if you
tell me where in Denver i can find chilled muskmelon
i made headway under the moonlight i
slept off the road in the bramble thicket
my mind racing i dreamed faster than the
baseball that had knocked my sister's tooth out
i bought a basket of fine food plus
some garments and a surprise for Nadezhda
i washed up in the river i
returned to the circus camp a shade past noon they
must have just finished rehearsal i saw a dozen performers
leaving the kingdom heading for the cluster of caravans over
yonder my heart kicked like a spooked horse when i
saw her open the door to that red caravan and step inside
i brought Leonardo we rapped outside
she opened and stared us down
those multicolored eyes had me choking
on my tongue but i got it together i
said hello there Nadezhda i am not sure what you have
planned for lunch but i would like to invite you
to a picnic with me and my mule Leonardo
she said how do you know my name
i said well there was a Negro clown well he was
a young man he was not too keen on clowning
but he did seem an alright feller and everything
under the hot spotlight of Nadezhda's attention i
got to awkward yammering and stammering and
an object inside her caravan leapt right into my eye
a very fine guitar leaning in the corner between the wall
and the cupboard but Nadezhda snapped me from the
momentary distraction saying no thank you i am busy

she shut the door oh my did my mouth hang loose
i was nearly rocked off my feet i had blown my chance i
took up the braided rope around his head i
said c'mon Leonardo but i was not more than five steps
on my way when a Gypsy woman with a scrub bucket
and a scarf over her hair passed me by
blazing a path to Nadezhda's caravan
with her hand upon the door handle
i said ma'am
she whipped her gaze to me
i said i would be much obliged if you told Nadezhda i
have her kitten
the woman with some dubious shock said her kitten
i said yes ma'am
she went inside and a jiffy later Nadezhda came out
not looking too friendly
i said i thought you would want to meet this feller
i scooped the real live kitten from the basket atop Leonardo
i said and i got us smoked salmon and chilled muskmelon i hit
pretty good on Sweet Kiss my Aunt J's horse
but contrary to what you might have read in the papers
my uncle Frank did not ride that horse when he was dead
Nadezhda had a nice long gander at me i did have a new black
fiddler's cap and the long sleeve marinière i
had the kitten in my arms aw he is purring i said
she said hold on a second
she went back inside i thought i
will abide here 'til the end of time if need be but
there she was only after a minute she had a quilt under
her arm i attempted to wrestle my wide grin back into
a poker face she did flash a reluctant smile when she
registered my excitement we strolled along in silence
with Leonardo the breeze was cool and good
i said i know a grass patch at the edge of the woods
Nadezhda laid her blanket there we
sat i said how old are you
she said 12 what about you
i said i was a Bar Mitzvah
even the stallion Sweet Kiss attended the ceremony i

am a man of 13
she said you are a Jew
i said yes are you a Gypsy
she said does my caravan roll on four wheels
i said both our people have known exile and hard traveling
there should be a union between them
she said so you have big dreams
i said my dreams ride the victory horse across the natural bridge
my dreams strum the guitar of the dead unknown poets
she said i had guessed you were crazy
i had to grin again i was the moon
her smile cast sunlight on the darkness of me
in my time my heart had pumped graveyards
of rage on the brink of rebellion
hordes of peasants lynching their landlords
ancient scores settled after a thousand years of rancor
i have been the three-legged hog wandering
the warlord's garden only ever in my suffering did God
send the patron saint of dirty looks and
smoldering embers of longing in the eyes of the dead
i sliced smoked salmon with my knife and gave
Nadezhda some
the kitten licked a small piece and fell asleep
i said how about you what do you dream
she said do you mean at night or what do i want in my life
i said maybe there is no difference
she said at night sometimes i
close my eyes and i am still flying through the air i
dream i am a ship whose crew has gathered the courage
to sail with no hope or i am a train never stopping
the hard-luck conductor has my father's eyes
i ceased sawing muskmelon so struck was i
i had to ask is your father alive
she said no
the czar's soldiers pulled his teeth out for no reason
he died of an infection in the gums
my nervous tongue caressed my gold tooth before
i said may his memory be a blessing i am sorry
she said thank you the first good memory i have is of

balancing on his hand he taught me to backflip he
taught me how to find water in the sands of the desert
i said what did he do
Nadezhda said everything
coppersmithing blacksmithing bladesmithing silversmithing
liquorsmithing hunting fishing riding climbing trees he
could find honey anywhere he played many
musical instruments strangely and beautifully
i said i spied a guitar in your caravan
she said yes that was his
i said how about your mother does she do everything too
Nadezhda said yes
she reads cards
she heals
she roasts chestnuts
she took me to Paris when i was a baby
i had a magic day there playing in a field before
we came to America now what about your family
what are they like
i said well i was four
when i stayed the week with my Aunt J
we went down to the station
for my family's homecoming
but we saw the train afire in the distance
i was taken in by my Aunt J
she married Frank he was nice to me
he was a champion jockey
they crossed the bridge only a few moons ago i
swore i would have a good funeral for them i
will when i have learned how but now some
tornado swirling has swept me away i
could not sit shiva still i had to ramble
Nadezhda said i am terribly sorry
it seems as with me
death has undressed in your midst a time or two
i looked at Leonardo being such a good boy i
said yes i reckon that is the truth but i
am a hoper i like the sunny side for example
praise Hashem there is still good mules

and sweet sleeping kittens in this world
she said yes and trees and gardens
i said and wine
she said and whales
i said and muskmelon
she said and walnut cake
i said and carving pumpkins at Halloween
she said and singing in a field
i said and singing on the mountain
she said and dancing by the river
i said and kissing at the picnic
she stopped cold i scooted closer
i said 'neath the tall trees
we smiled into our eyes i
pecked her a quick one on the lips
i dreamed on my back like
i had caught the Holy Ghost
she laughed and lay next to me we
held hands gray sky gazing with all the spirit winds
of our ancestors whooshing through those trees
we walked the field of grass to the kingdom
me her the kitten and Leonardo
i said do you know the young
Gypsy with the jitters at the circus gates
she said yes he is my brother Ahimoth
i said my God how does he fare
she said not well
i said here please give him this he
need not know from where it came
i forked over another whole dollar poor feller
when we got back to her caravan i said there can be no
better way to pass an afternoon than on a picnic with you
she said i actually had a pleasant time myself i
was reluctant at first but it appears you turned out
to be a gentleman
impishly grinning adjusting my fiddler's cap
i said yeah appears so
she said now what is your name
i said Sloman

she kissed my cheek
with a frenzy of work in the near distance
to match my stomach butterflies
men and animals rushing around i
said can i maybe see you again tonight i
know you are leaving on the morrow i
can sing you a moonlight song
the precious stones of her eyes glinted in mine
she said maybe
if you find me again i
can show you my Clydesdale Scotch Castle
her mother who had been eavesdropping
threw open the caravan door with words of
Nadezhda you will not see this boy again he
is not our people he has already tricked me once
i said ma'am that was no trick i give Nadezhda
this kitten free and clear if she wants it
do you
she said yes
i handed her that soft furry tiger-striped guy i
said may he be half as good a traveling companion
to you as Leonardo is to me
Nadezhda downcast said goodbye Sloman
she went inside with him the mother drilled me a look i
had not seen too awful much on account i did not
attend school regularly and had skipped a bunch of stuff
but i did not need the meaning of it explained to me
she slammed the door i trundled off with Leonardo i
scrounged us a dinner of catfish for me hay for him
there was a woman on 40-foot-high stilts i could see
from outside the board fence they unloaded a damn
sea lion from the wagon a man arrived by zebra
shirtless covered in tattoos with horseshoes dangling off
his nipples a falcon tried to steal my hat i saw what i
could not believe the young Gypsy man with the jitters
lugging a bale of hay for the menagerie he was in fine
form i said to myself oh you must be shitting me
he ran in and out of the gate barking orders working
with others he jocularly whipped the world's smallest

man's ass with an arrow
all my compassion for him had been chased away
Leonardo and i spied him from the nearby grass patch
as the sun sunk into dusklight
the people streamed through the gate
the preachers gathered and out that jittering Gypsy came
i had no doubt my two dollars would be returned unto me
or he would not appreciate this moonlight blade
he got going more than ever
his head spinning like a whirligig
his left arm flapping like a baby eagle
his leg stomping and trembling like Dr. Frankenstein was
jolting him with electricity like he was an experiment
gone haywire sure enough his right arm stayed
plenty steady to hold the metal mug for his audience
they paid him no mind
the darkness brought a chill i
was the cold-blooded cobra anticipating the instant
his act would slip my fangs deadly ready i
waited ten minutes 20 40 minutes
he kept right on bucking and twitching in his unending
seizure the strangest thing happened as people passed i
found myself rooting for their alms he sure was putting
in the work c'mon just give him a penny
he provoked in me three strong turns of feeling
beginning with deep sympathy
secondly roaring spirit winds of revenge but finally it
rose up in me the begrudging admiration the hat tip of
the rival who cannot deny the dedication and craft of his
adversary even Nadezhda who had taken a dollar off me on
his behalf they had played the game to perfection who is to say
there was not the anguish in his head to match the
staggeringly consistent bodily act he cultivated across the land
in that moment i killed my enemy and ate his
eyeballs i saw the world as he did i would need to
find the goof dust man for my plan i
fed and tied Leonardo i paid Fat Ali for admission
and with a dollar tip he told me i should see
the British man with the Turkish opium powder by

the sideshow the Brit eyeballed me from above in his
tall top hat he said are you not a little young for this vice
i put on an air of hard traveling
i said sir it is not for me
it is for my mule he is so old i
aim to grant him all the pleasures he
requests of this world 'til he departs
for the one we cannot see
he sold me a tiny glass vial i
next procured a puff of cotton candy i did not eat i
imbibed the show under the big top there was the
fat man playing the fiddle he stuck his head in the
lion's mouth there was the crusader knight in full armor
walking the tightrope
before the trapeze act i got curious and sniffed some
of the goof dust i was flying wild like the aerialists
Nadezhda did a double flip and a grown man
caught her legs he performed with two other girls
slightly older than Nadezhda i was guessing
they too were Gypsies
though none could compare to Nadezhda
she lit up my world all over again i did not meet
her when the big top cleared out for the night i
had my plan it required several hours of waiting
with Leonardo in the field we drank wild water
off leaves the moon was a silver stallion
stirring ghosts around me i shut my eyes i
saw Frank the spirit rider
the hour came i brought Leonardo to the circus camp i
tied him to the back of the red caravan
where Nadezhda and Ahimoth did sleep
also therein was their mother i walked around to
the front i rubbed the remaining goof dust on
my upper lip beneath my Hebrew sniffer
i drummed loudly upon Nadezhda's door moaning i
did stuff some cotton candy into my mouth i
did tumble upon the ground knowing
the mother was a healer and when she appeared
at the door in night clothes with a lantern

it was me she did find bucking in a seizure
rabid animal cotton candy froth at my mouth she rushed
out with Nadezhda and Ahimoth close behind they
kneeled above me the mother gripped my head with
both hands i fixed my gaze past them to the moon i
thrashed the mother detected goof dust 'neath the
snout she shouted a command in the Gypsy tongue
Nadezhda scurried into the caravan the mother
slapped my cheek she said stay alive boy or i
will kill you at the silent party myself you stay awake
Ahimoth gripped my jittering legs ha ha Nadezhda
returned posthaste with a candle flame under a
metal mug held with a rag
the mother took it and said drink
she flooded my mouth with what
i will say was no Bob's country store sweet tea
within two minutes i had vomited half my life away
my collapse upon the earth was most sincere
the mother and brother hooked their arms into mine
they dragged me toward the caravan
never had a plan of mine gone so perfectly they
laid me on the floor next to the table
Nadezhda draped our picnic quilt over me the
mother and Ahimoth retired to their respective bunks
my eyes were shut with my fists crossed over my chest
Nadezhda in a bitter mournful whisper said
when you sleep like this you look like a dead king
she climbed into the bunk above Ahimoth's
the kitten i had given purred at my side
a solid hour must have passed before i
took her father's guitar and crept out the caravan window
Leonardo there to receive me we rode by moonlight
i could not sleep with my excitement i played the dead
Gypsy's guitar deep in the woods 'til the morning light
by noon i had made my way back to the site of the
circus all the wagons caravans tents animals food
workers and performers the giant miracle had vanished
it must have been the saddest empty field in the world
nothing is darker than the shadow of fun

i bought up some victuals a coat and a compass before
quitting Denver the road unfurled ever long in
my weariness i was lost with night closing in

דריט

the sounds of a wild flute beckoned my ear the last
time i had no direction the music delivered me so i
followed it to a ramshackle cottage in the woods i
would not have been surprised to meet
Old Mother Hubbard living there i
was greeted at the fence by a wolf dog who definitely
had a cigarette dangling from his mouth and though i was
tired i squinted closer to detect in the dim evening light
the cherry glowed brighter as he inhaled
it did surprise me he was smoking
i left Leonardo outside the fence and strolled past the
dog i doubted he would bark or bite because that would
mean losing his coffin nail he followed me around back
where i startled the hell out of
a cross-eyed Indian woman playing the flute
i said i beg your pardon ma'am i am looking for
the town of Pueblo do you know it
she said yes i do but why should i give you directions
i am a Ute
your fathers who lust for gold have driven my people
from our lands killed my family i am a hermit now i
play a song to summon death and here you are
i said ma'am with respect i am Hebrew i
come from several states away
my forebearers have been exiled i
myself have known blood feuds so i do not
discount your rage only if you believe one word
of mine i beg it be that my brain is not

ate up with the rotten worms of gold dust lust
i seek the Gypsy aerialist
i seek songs of poetry
i seek dreams of the blade that was hidden in my mother's wheelchair
i seek chilled muskmelon
one day perhaps i will seek a garden though
i reckon then from your horrific trials
you will not tell me the way to Pueblo i
bid you and your smoking wolf dog adieu
i turned to leave she said wait
where did you get that guitar on your back
i said i stole it off a dead Gypsy
she said listen and try to play along
the guitar hung around me on a piece of
twine i pulled the instrument to my front as she graced
her Ute flute i joined her beautiful song the old
wolf dog had finished his cig and was howling the vocal part
i do not doubt Leonardo could hear our music coming
from the other side and that it pleased him
the woman brought me wild raspberries and a cake of
buckwheat with a mug of dream tea she said i thank you
for playing music with me i have missed that
in the morning i will tell you the way to Pueblo if
you are not too afraid to stay with me for fear of
having your throat cut as you sleep
i said ma'am the risk
with this arrangement is not squarely on me for i
have never been called slow with the knife
she laughed crazily and showed me inside
she made a spot for me with blankets
in her drawing room i
dreamed the Locksmith in the fox mask
we were walking the shores of Lake Michigan
she said did you know you and Nadezhda
belong to the same people
i said how is this
the Locksmith lifted her mask and hushing with the gentle waves
she whispered those you call Gypsy are born of a Hebrew tribe
they have scattered from Beersheba with Nebuchadnezzar's merciless reign

they have molted copper for the Etruscans
they have choked in their blood from Justinian plague
Nadezhda's people were an untouchable caste in India
they were forced to hunt wild blue cows
they refused
they rambled through the Ottoman empire
they have 19 buried in a mass grave outside Bucharest
they have been slaves
they have celebrated death with joyous singing and dancing
some have walked fields of thorns so sharp their feet have been pierced
some have dug wells and been snakebitten
some have been fired from cannons
some have lived and died and never once bathed
some have been born with ten siblings and been the last to die
some have floated downstream clinging to a violin i
hear your common heritage in the music
now do not lose that guitar
i awoke in the night to the dog barking and the bloodcurdling sounds
of the Ute woman like she was being attacked i checked on her hastily
she was screaming in her sleep
in the morning she wore a shirt full of elk teeth
she told me the way to Pueblo i thanked her
and said can i offer you some money
she said i do not ask it though i will not deny it
i gave her two dollars and she saw me off
i mounted Leonardo in front of her cottage
before i left she said did you dream good
i said yes though i heard trouble in yours
she said my dreams of death have been locked in battle for ages
i said i wish unto you that the good ones win fare thee well
Leonardo and i sojourned on i wrote
a song riding muleback for Nadezhda
the day had faded to night when Leonardo and i found the circus
the throng spilling from the gates
we waited a bit to work up my courage
the kingdom quieted to a handful of scattered bonfires outside the fence
among the caravans groups of ten or so gathered around each one
i led Leonardo among them i told him to make a noise if
he saw her we passed the clown fire the sideshow fire

the fires of workmen hobos they called them razorbacks
but in the end it was them who spotted me
the mother yelped you
the whole circus camp went silent
Nadezhda shrieked sneak thief you got me in a load of trouble
she was up high standing on Scotch Castle's back barefoot
Ahimoth was seated around the fire with the aerialist man
the two other Gypsy girls and Nadezhda's mother
the five of them stood in the manner of those who rise to fight
the attention of all the hushed fires crackled upon me
Leonardo did not budge a hoof he sensed the danger
but my eyes rested upon Nadezhda and never left
she was the only other person there with me
i knew i would not talk my way out of this
so i spun the guitar frontwards into my hands
i got to strumming
she came down off the horse listening as i sang
i was walking with the Locksmith
she asked the sounds i'll take with me
i spoke of the hum of the arrow
the wild unsheathing of swords
the dirt and the shovel the digging
the hobo in rags with his mouth harp
i had been dancing with death it was silent
i was the rose that got pressed in the book
i said unto the Locksmith
do you think that there's a key for me
she said yes in the sands of the desert
behind the crooked tooth smile of an orphan
riding on trains with the hard-luck conductor
among the union of men of all colors
they found it in France when you played in a field
inside the roses that opened in dusklight
i know that death has undressed before you
so it is lost but found in creation
i concluded into the same silence as when i
first struck up it could have been remarked the
family appeared somewhat disarmed especially Nadezhda
the tear skating down her cheek was to me more

sacred than holy water
i said to her
i know i have stolen your father's guitar
i know i have repaid your kindness with falsity
i know i have been swindled of two dollars
i know i have tricked the trickster
i know all i have is my songs
you know i am gathering my forces for
a proper ceremony for Frank and Aunt J
i know i must ramble and i must ramble
closely to you Nadezhda if you will have me
the fire danced behind her we gazed into each other
sparks shooting off in my soul she was not
giving that look to Leonardo behind me i knew that much
but before she had a moment to move or say anything
her mother blazed a warpath to me she pulled my arm
nearly out of socket leading the way around to the door
of the caravan she flung open
sternly saying inside
i said ok let us have it out then
i went inside she said sit
i sat on one side of the table moonlight through the window
she shut the door and struck a match
lit two candles on the table and sat across
the first time i was in there i was in such a sorry state i did not
appreciate the ornate carvings upon the walls nor the ceiling
much of the trim gold like my tooth
Nadezhda's kitten sleeping on her bed
even a little stove with a chimney her mother's stony illuminated face
said if you and your mule leave now and never return you may keep
my husband's guitar it is haunted by the dead unknown poets
i said yes ma'am that is partly why i stole it
she said well you may keep it
i said for Nadezhda i would burn it and smoke the ashes
she said you will not
i said i shall not
our stalemate festered a moment candles wobbling
she breathing frustrated air said
i know not from where you came

and i know not where you will go but my daughter's
past present and future resides with her people
from them her husband will be chosen
i said perhaps then the chosen husband will be me
she said now you speak nonsense
i said i sang of the Locksmith who
has revealed to me our heritage you and i
are descended of Jacob and the tribes of his 12 sons
your branch began their journey from Beersheba
Nadezhda's mother sprung from her chair toward the door
she said i have given you the chance to speak sensibly
but with this madness i must now
i said i know of your tribe's slavery
i know you were an untouchable caste who refused to slaughter cows
i know of the mass grave in Bucharest
i know of the one who has floated downstream with the violin i
myself have family flowing in a river grave
Nadezhda's mother froze with her eyes upon me
a stunned expression one might wear glancing a hoary ghost poet
or a relative who materializes long after his or her crossing
the mother said how did you learn this who told you
i said the Locksmith of my dreams she does not visit for tomfoolery
she speaks the truth we are of the same people
the mother's mind must have traveled through time
so distant and forlorn was her gaze
she said that was my father floating with the violin
without warning soldiers drew swords and attacked his band
they were playing in the town square they had not done anything
he was the only one to escape to the woods the river
he lost his band of friends they were mostly his cousins
he had been stabbed through the stomach
they found his body floating downriver
they buried him with the others in a mass grave outside Bucharest i
have never mentioned this massacre to my two children i
did not want them growing in fear i wished them to rise in light
i said ma'am in the darkest imperial night Nadezhda strikes me as a
lightning bolt yes Ahimoth and i have tricked each other but we will
make a good path we are after all of the same people
death is our brother

the mother rummaged in the cupboard
and retrieved the deck of cards
she shuffled at the table by candlelight i did not say
a word she overturned the first card it was the ace of spades
i said Frank has already defeated him i
am preparing to honor the victory
the mother said i see your time of dying you will pass at the foot
of a great mountain straddled by the bare-chested virgin with
the black eye patch there will be golden melon rinds all around
and a mule and a tiger it will be a good death
now if the next card is a spade
you may stay among us however
if i draw a heart diamond or club
you must agree to leave or you will live a life of fire
and the things you fear shall truly come upon you
i pulled my chair forward i
said the flames you describe have licked me in my youth
as a man i will meet them with my blade you have my word i
know the odds are not in my favor but destiny has its eye on me
i accept your terms ma'am now turn the card let us see it
she drew and jerked backward as if the card was a viper
it too was the ace of spades
the mother overturned the deck they were
every single one of them the death card she
gritted her teeth saying now how crafty are you never have i
encountered the likes of it among men animals or spirits
i said i suppose you have not yet met my Aunt J's stallion
the mother in a huff returned to the cupboard and replaced
the playing cards for a deck of the tarot sort
she emptied them from the box
she shuffled furiously but soon
she ceased and spread them upon the table
every single card was the number 13 with the horse and the rider
whose face was death
i said the papers said Frank was dead when he rode Sweet Kiss
but if you wish to know something strange look at this
i unsheathed my knife and showed her the bottom of the handle the
engraving was a rider identical to the one on the card same skeleton face
i said i found this knife in the woods stuck into the great tree i

Wildcat Dreams in the Death Light

pulled it loose and blood poured from the tree i drank some of it
the mother became still like she might actually weep
she softly said i do not know what you have done with my cards
i said ma'am perhaps someone has played a trick on you
but it is not me
surely you dealt your cards since the morning of my departure
there is a Ute woman a great distance away she
could tell you the night previous and all day today
the only place i could have been is riding to your door i
have no agents employed at this circus
the mother collecting her cards said how old are you
i said i am a man of 13
she flopped back in the chair
a handful of number 13 death cards over her heart
she cried i concede you may remain among the circus but you will
respect my terms or your good death i have foreseen will vanish
i said i am listening
she said until her 14th birthday you will not speak
to my daughter nor her kin
you may only write to her in letters
she may reply i want purity in distance
i want her to learn to write like i never did
she was taught by the sword juggler
she reads Walt Whitman
in all the years you know her you will observe
the three pillars of an honorable man toward his woman
the first you must protect her from those who wish to harm her
i said yes ma'am i will defend her on this side of the bridge
and the other i will never stop
the mother said good the second pillar
she has had a performer's heart since her first steps i have seen it
time will take her talents but if you should try to quell them you
should prepare for fire
i said yes ma'am her talents
are what did draw my eye in the first place
the mother said the final pillar i demand of you is that you
protect her always from yourself
i said if it rises in me the urge to touch her harmfully i will
march a beeline into the nearest ocean it will be my grave

the mother said good i only have one last question
who are your parents
i said they are the secret caretakers
of a 4,500-year-old bristlecone pine tree
Nadezhda's mother said i should have known
now how will you earn money
i said ma'am i have a pocketful of it
i will buy a guitar and make honest coins
the mother said it will not be enough
you must not burn through that pocketful of money
on the road money flies from you faster than you realize i
want to know you can work among us i
want you to see Alf Jackson in the silver caravan
he owns this circus i
will put in a good word
now you may go i do not know where you will lay your head tonight
nor the next but it will not be in here
i said do you happen to have some paper and a pen
she gave it to me i wrote
dear Nadezhda
may i follow you a while
sincerely
Sloman
i said my first letter to Nadezhda
i drizzled wax from the candle to seal it with my thumb
i left it upon the table
the mother did not share my cheer although with my hand upon
the doorknob she said what is your name
i said Sloman
she said Sloman no matter what becomes of you and my daughter
so long as you observe the pillars of honor
and these 18 epistolary months
you may keep my husband's guitar it is yours now
i said thank you i am much obliged good evening ma'am
i left i
slept upon the ground near the camp under the crab apple tree
Leonardo with me when i awoke in the morning
i took off my fiddler's cap like
a magician with a dove fluttering out except it was a letter

dear Sloman
yes
cordially
N
i marched to the silver caravan
i knocked
the tall gray-bearded man answered
he had a silver-rimmed monocle and a stovepipe top hat in his hands
he boomed you must be Sloman
i said yes sir are you Alf Jackson
he said indeed i am
he offered his rough hand i shook it
he gripped like he was trying to crush my hand bones
i said how do you do Mr. Jackson
he said call me Alf
come in have a seat
he showed me inside his caravan
he had a big roll-top desk full of documents
and a baseball signed by President McKinley
there were two chairs next to the desk we
each took one he said it has come to my attention you
would like to join our little world-famous outfit
i said yes i would Alf though i will need some time each day
to play my guitar i am preparing for a funeral of sorts
Alf said oh dear who went and bit the dust
i said my Aunt J and her husband Frank
perhaps you have heard of the rider
who won the race when he was dead
Alf said i have i read about him
my condolences when is the funeral
i said well i cannot yet say it could be years
it is a path locked to me i wish to join your circus
to follow my love and forge the keys
Alf said my my my
like he was impressed
he said now one thing i
must ask have you any prejudices
i said prejudices
he said yes against coloreds say or Gypsies or Irish

i said on the question of race i myself am Hebrew
my people have known brutality and exile i have rambled
once i left school and disappeared for a month after
the teacher kept trying to kiss me on the mouth i
stole the rich man's potpie with a Negro outlaw heading north
we ate the pie with our bare hands under the covered bridge
it was raining hard she told me of the evil fire
and the man who had violated her
and beaten her so severely the baby inside died
she walked into the barbershop one fine day when
he was leaning back in the chair about to be shaved
she said with his eyes closed he looked like he was
dreaming of a jug of wine she slit his throat
with her great grandmother's knife
the old barber stirring lotion with his back turned
was in for a big surprise
that is how she ended up an outlaw
but with all she had seen she still
spoke to me of the union of men of all colors
of living waters upon evil fires
i told her yes ma'am i do believe one day there will be a flood
Alf said oh yes oh yes i will be right there with you my good man
that is one thing men like the Ringling Brothers do not understand
the one who harnesses the strengths of all the races will be the one
on top of that mountain i am climbing it so hard some days i think
my feet will crumble off
he laughed knee-slapping
he said but before i go to my grave
my mother who calls me small potatoes
my brother who commands seven battalions
my cousins who jack off in dusty mansions
the Ringlings who scheme
and all those who have doubted me will know i
am the greatest showman ever to walk the face of the earth
now how can you help me ascend to such heights
what benefits can you bring to my circus
what is your greatest strength
i said my memory i remember everything
Alf said everything

i said everything i see
he said but what could you have seen with so
few years under your cap my good young man
i said well
i have seen the elderly monk gored by the giant falling icicle
i have seen the family of elk sleeping next to me in the moonlight
i have seen Bob's jar of brandy
i have seen the vial of goof dust i used to trick the trickster
i have seen the blood trickling
from my grandfather's ear when he died roller-skating
i have seen good luck without grace invite darkness
i have seen the Gypsy's vision of my death by the mountain
it was a good one
Alf said ok what about your greatest weakness
after a couple seconds of pause i earnestly said
damn Alf i had one but i forgot
Alf roared with laughter he stood in hilarity with his back to me
he hunched over guffawing
right when i thought to check if he is ok he whirled around
and pressed the dagger to my throat
the handle was a silver cobra
he gripped my neck with his other hand standing over me
he said you think you have seen things i
have seen snake attacks
wolf attacks
bear attacks
whole towns ripped to shreds i
have seen a 700-pound native man of the Hawaiian Territory
singing with a knife in his shoulder i
have seen Warchief Rain-in-the-Face blow Custer's brains out
from point-blank range i smelled the gunpowder i
have seen an arrow pierce my leg why the hell do you think i limp
i have seen Libby Bacon Custer riding me bare-chested
when the general was still warm in the ground i
own seven pairs of white alligator boots i
live in Hollywood i
bought Mable's marble mansion
so boy do not tell me you have seen things
only to run a cockamamie jest upon me

staring back at Alf i was thinking how easily i could have
pulled my blade and with the speed of hummingbird wings
stuck his guts 17 times before he had even blinked
but my love for her kept my head cool
i said Alf i intended no jest but i will abide whatever you say
Alf sheathed his dagger in the case inside his vest
he said good i knew you would be a good sport
now between you and me ticket sales have hit a tiny slump
out west here i need you to be the workhorse clean-up boy
and i need you to shine in my advertising brigade i need
you to plaster as many of my posters as humanly possible all
over town i have spent a small fortune on the artwork and printing
if you see posters for the Ringling Brothers you tear them down
you curse and spit upon them
you light them afire
you put eternal death hexes on them and their families
i said i can do that
who all is part of the brigade
Alf said well currently it is one colored boy
Frederick is his name
you can make sure he is not causing trouble once he
got a mob after him but i vanquished them i take care of mine
in the evening Frederick will be clowning you go see Fyodor
the knife thrower you will have a special role during the show
you work hard for 12 hours in a day i will give you 75 cents
and a hot dog i have met trapper boys who work the coal mines of
West Virginia for a chest full of soot they do not even get a quarter
i present to you a damn generous offer
any questions
i knew what i had to say i said no Alf i got you loud and clear i
appreciate you taking me aboard i am a workhorse

פֿערט

i asked around the kingdom and found Frederick i introduced myself
he was the unenthusiastic clown i
had spoken to previously
he was in regular clothes
we strolled into town with Leonardo and some posters
i had my guitar i
said how old are you Frederick and where are you from
Frederick said 14 i was born in Jesup Georgia but i have been
on the move a long time i am a river running
i said do you have parents
he said well how do you think a fellow comes into this world
we chuckled
he said in seriousness my mother is in Washington DC i
will see her at Christmas she is a cook and housekeeper
for P.B.S. Pinchback do you know him
i said i do not believe so
Frederick said he is the only Negro ever to be governor
of a state his mother was mulatto his father was white you
know sometimes they hate them more than full-blooded Negroes
i said who is they
Frederick said the poor whites the rich man uses
especially the White League
they are Democratic Party marauders
it took four of them to run my granddad through with their bayonets
he was murdered in the Colfax Massacre
that is when my mother first met P.B.S. as a young girl
i said how about your father
we passed some brick buildings getting closer to town

Frederick waited so long i did not think he would answer
but he said he died a few years back some tools fell on him
he was a craft metalworker he taught me some metalworking
the night after he died i dreamed he was training a falcon he
set it free yet it returned to perch proudly on my shoulder i
glanced the eyes and knew it was death
i said i do not doubt it Frederick
wherever i have been and gone i find the feathers all around me
Frederick said yes i have met some vultures too
Negro and white they were picking fights with me after he died
under the moonlight i have fought more than one
they get bold when they know no angry daddy
will be knocking their door the next day
some people have cruelty in them that is one big reason i
swam down the river i left some of my clothes on the banks
so they all thought i had drowned but i joined the circus i
wrote my mother she knows i will see her again
how about you Sloman where are you from
i said well like you i have origins back to Adam and Eve
but in more recent times
my mother's folks came from Odessa to London where she
was born and met my father who was from Gdańsk
they married and traveled to New York City
when i was hatched they were living on Fire Island i
do not remember it a wink i
was five months old when they heard
the thundering hoofbeats of war
the cholera riots
my kin had known pogroms i am Hebrew
they drifted west to Battle Creek Michigan where i
spent most my youth i
left the island but kept the fire
Frederick and i chuckled at this
he said yes i see it in you
i thought Frederick was going to be a good friend of mine
until we got to the main commercial strip of Pueblo horses and people
passing by i lifted the posters off Leonardo and tied him to a building i
dropped the stack on the dusty ground i
got my guitar with my jar out

i said watch this
i sang
Frederick cut me off mid-song
he said just what in the hell are you doing
i said making a living
he said but if Alf finds out we did not circulate these posters
he will keep our 50 cents he
might kick us off the circus
i said Frederick you know half the town saw the circus last night
he said well half the town i am not sure i reckon it was a few hundred
i said yes but you know they did not stay silent about it
would you if you saw for the first time what they do under the big top
he said no i suppose i would most likely be yapping about it
i said then why not call our work done
Frederick said i actually always thought
Alf puts too much stock in these posters
you know what i think he should do first night we get into town
i said what Frederick
Frederick said he should have a parade with performers
and animals like the other circuses do
have them come marching right through town
turning all the heads
you know what Alf said when i suggested this
he said why would they buy the cow when they can get the milk for free
hey what are you looking at
Frederick turned to see what had distracted me
the carriage rolling by under the overcast sky
i swore i
saw the Locksmith inside eyeballing me
the horse pulling her was a dead ringer for Sweet Kiss i
could never have explained it so i said nothing Frederick i
like the sound of your parade idea
i said wait a minute you said 50 cents
did you know Alf started me at 75 cents a day
Frederick's mouth dropped he said what
i said and a hot dog
his big betrayed white eyes bloomed wide
he kicked the dirt and plopped on the ground
leaning against the building

i said it is not fair Frederick that is why i told you
he said i know i am not mad at you i am just mad
i said how about we demand you a raise when we get back
Frederick said no that would just stir trouble for us both i
need this job so we will have to leave it be
i said i will give you some of my wage then
Frederick said i appreciate that but i do not wish to take your wage
besides it is an odd number so it would never be split evenly
and i am mainly mad he keeps having me clown
i said why do you not like clowning
Frederick said well the wig for starters
it is dead woman's hair i do not like how he
always tries to dress me like a woman
i am a man
i said do you play music Frederick
he said i have messed around with the mouth harp in my day
i said well let me get you a mouth harp so we can play together
Frederick looked up his eyes imparting surprised interest
i said and we can pass those fliers out
while we do some shopping i
am in the market for a good tent and bedding too
i got Frederick an old silver Honher for a dollar
he said hot damn awfully nice of you
i said think nothing of it this is a gift to myself as well i
believe us playing together making a bit more
racket we will see more money in my jar whenever
you play with me we will split it 50/50 i will not
pull the bullshit it seems Alf is up to
i bought a buffalo mummy bag a pen and papers
a sweater a few other articles of clothing
a used frameless army knapsack
who knows what became of the former owner
Frederick said damn you sure got a pocketful of greenbacks
i said well i got an inheritance thanks to a horse and the
champion rider they said was dead upon him
we wandered through town playing music
Leonardo sauntering with us my supplies on his back
i said here is your first parade Frederick
he laughed in a better mood we made it back to the kingdom

and ate an early supper around the fire with the sideshow crew
still daylight i
saw the world's tallest man wolf Lord knows how many hot dogs i
sliced off a piece of muskmelon for Frederick i had bought it in town
i said do you know Fyodor
Frederick said yes he is the Russian knife thrower
i said Alf told me to pay him a visit i
will have a role in the show tonight
Frederick said you are lucky you made friends with me i
know what they are fixing to do to you
they will William Tell you i bet
i said they will tell me what
Frederick said no they will William Tell you
that means he will throw a knife at the apple on your head
but they have not done this trick in seven months since shortly after i
came aboard Fyodor cut off a German's ear on accident
the woman in the green robe cackled nearby
she said sorry to overhear but the color drained
from that new boy's face when you told him
i snapped to reality i said ma'am for your information
i am a man of 13 i
have seen God killing angels on a whim
i laugh at death
she said you are adorable
Frederick's swift smirking glance lit my smile as well
i said well i am obliged ma'am
i eyed her trying to place her
the naked memory rung my bell the woman with the snakes
i foresaw William Tell and the spectacle of my foolishness
in front of the crowd most importantly Nadezhda and her kin
my own birth had tricked the trickster i devised the plan
i said i saw you with your snakes what is your name
she said Guinevere
i sat next to her and said how would you like to make
three whole dollars one now two when the job is done
she said for what
i whispered close to her she laughed
she said make it five and we have a deal
i went to see Fyodor

Wildcat Dreams in the Death Light

he was shaving outside his caravan with one of his knives
he spit into the bucket
and said there will be a seat for you in the front row
i will mark it with a rose you sit there i
will call you out of the crowd
i said i know you are fixing to William Tell me
he said be that as it may you should act surprised
when i throw my knife i want you to stay still and dream
the Statue of Liberty with sweat on her upper lip
i have never killed a man unintentionally you
will marvel at how alive you feel when
my knife is breezing past your blindfolded head
my knife will sever your attachment to the world of the living
you will feel free
i said i do not think you know who in the hell you are talking to
as a very young boy i
had the ghosts of child soldiers visit me in the night
and tell me you are never too young to die
what about the German's ear
Fyodor guffawed he said that silly bastard
had the jitters that is why i told you to stay still
i said alright i will do as you ask Fyodor
but from one blade man to another you should know
when i get invited under the big top i
also have a mind to thrill the crowd
i left i was humming hammering spikes
Frederick called from inside the other tent
he said is that you
i said who
he said him
i said i do not know if i am he but i am me
he chuckled in there i went to his door
i said well it appears we are neighbors
he said yes come in i have good news
i peeled the flap and ducked inside he was reading a book
about metalworking perhaps it was his father's
he said ever since we played music i have been dreaming
of the parade and how i never want to wear that wig again i
had been dreaming of setting fire to Alf's caravan i know it

is wrong he had the heart to hire me when not too many
circuses will take on Negroes even as clean-up boys but i
decided that still does not give him the right to degrade me
and pay me less than my counterpart i went to his caravan
while you were talking with Fyodor i told him i
was hoping for a quarter raise in fairness
and that i did not wish to clown especially with that wig i
mentioned how you and i had got a bit of
attention with the two of us plus the mule
imagine if some performers joined in he
said he was forward-thinking on the question of race
why else would he hire a Jew and a Negro
to be his clean-up boys he
conceded my wage was an oversight he
had been meaning to give me a quarter raise he
told me i would not have to clown as long as i
could find something else constructive to do
the menagerie always needs an extra hand he
said we will be taking an off-season break of
12 weeks instead of ten once we reach Los Angeles i
said that is fine by me i will have extra time in Washington DC
i said Frederick that is the best news i have heard today
good on you for plucking up your courage i
know you have much riding on this job
Frederick said yes and the best part he said our circus
may not be in the best shape financially so he said to my parade
idea why not give it a try and he said i may lead it
i said whoa congratulations may i be a part of it
Frederick said of course i was going to ask you
to be up front with me playing your guitar i
will get going on that mouth harp i
will also ask Wu the Chinese violinist i
know of a wicker wheelchair we can borrow from Vernon
the skin and bones man he will not want to come on the parade i
am afraid life gets very dangerous for him outside the caravan and the
sideshow tent worse than death haunting his steps is the threat of broken
bones Vernon travels with Seth the world's tallest man they are friends i
can ask Seth to push Wu in Vernon's wheelchair
i said i saw a clown on a penny-farthing bicycle he had a monkey on him

he would be a good one to ask too
Frederick said that is Alexandre i will definitely bark up his tree
Frederick was very much coming alive
i was feeling glad for my new friend
after all i
have seen the front legs of an old war horse shatter i
have seen my uncles weeping at the gravesite of an infant i
have seen a sunny day darkened with the ashes of 65 buffalo i
have seen a man kneeling on the railroad track with a stack of
poems before him he had been writing them in secret since
he was a boy his name was Joshua Fly it was the night
of his 90th birthday i told him to get off the tracks
but he just laughed and lit the poems afire
right before the thundering train rolled him i
read some that fluttered in the sky he was a pretty good poet i
have entertained the notion that the fruit prohibited in the garden
was set out by a false god the snake was the hero to wake them up i
was blinking in the front row a thousand were cheering under the big top
Fyodor had thrown six knives into the wood cutout of an Indian chief
two right inside the eyes one in his heart one at each of his ankles
and one piercing the chief's manhood
Fyodor took a bow he had ostrich feathers all over his coat
Alf limping around in his clawhammer tuxedo and black top hat with
his booming voice said and now he will choose the bravest among you
for a feat so daring it spits in the face of death
the William Tell
gasps of terror swirled around the spectators
the two young Gypsy aerialists Rosa and Lola removed the Indian cutout
they carried in the wooden board with the bullseye on it
one of them had a shiny red apple
Fyodor went around the crowd pointing with his knife
like he was deliberating his choice
folks ducked behind one another some laughing thrilled
some genuinely afraid
Nadezhda looked on from above in the trapeze bird's nest
with the father of the girls who were assisting below under the glow
of the electric lights Fyodor's blade signaled to me i had just shoveled
a huge mouthful of popcorn on purpose to manufacture myself as
the surprised rube i swished my head around with chipmunk cheeks

the crowd roared
they love when the arrow of fire strikes the unsuspecting fool
Alf dragged himself over he said yes you young man step right up
you have been chosen he appears very brave doesn't he folks
there was laughing with the applause i fiddled with my fiddler's cap
and made like i tripped over the barrier spilling myself into the ring
my antics provoked a wave of merriment around the throng
Alf put his arm around me and said loudly what is your name son
i said in a squeaky voice my name is Lucky
Alf acted like a hurricane breeze had knocked him backward
he said your name is Lucky
i said yes sir Lucky Peppercorn
that got one last good chuckle out of the crowd
Alf said well let us see how lucky you are tonight
the girls came up and directed me to the bullseye i eyed
Guinevere off to the side inside the performer's tunnel lurking in her
green robe the girls took my hat they nailed the apple over me they
knotted the black bandana around my eyes they
tied me with rope to the bullseye board and spun it like a wheel
the crowd counted out one two three four
they counted Fyodor's paces until he was 25 away from me i
will be damned with that blindfold and the snare drumroll the spinning i
did see my life as a boat full of forgotten stories sailing off into a dream i
did see the final door of liberty with for once no bondage behind it i
did see swimming salty gulf waters with the coast out of reach i
did hear a homesick song from my grave but
not to bring bad luck upon myself especially with my stage moniker i
did what Fyodor had asked i dreamed the Statue of Liberty
with a sweat-beaded upper lip she was singing
i learned that the
pledge of allegiance
is a suicide pact
if there ever was one
the crowd fell silent
the hum of the knife slit the air like a silver bullet
thwack
it punched to the left of my shoulder the crowd shrieking
i heard Alf say not that one
thwack

another one punched to the right of my other shoulder
the crowd beside themselves i heard Alf say
nope not that one either now Fyodor you have only got one knife left
the snare drum roll recommenced Fyodor milked the moment
thwack
that knife slammed into the apple an inch above my skull
the congregated souls erupted in my blindness
Alf walked up stopped the wheel and removed my blindfold
he said you sure are Lucky tonight
the crowd guffawed
Alf said how about a hand for this young man
the girls untied me
but one of the knives had pinned my sleeve to the board
the crowd was knee-slapping at that
but i actually did not think it was too goddamn funny
that striped marinière was my favorite garment
Guinevere with a sultry stride showed up right on cue
she spoke loud with a good stage voice
let me help you with that young man
she pulled the knife from the board and threw a sassy eyeball
to Fyodor as his blade rolled off her hand onto the earth
the crowd said *oooooouu*
we could all see Fyodor looked steamed i
stepped forth with the apple still pinned behind me i
unleashed shouting that startled the crowd into silence
who among you wishes me to bathe in my ignorance 'til i am dead
Guinevere feigned surprise
Fyodor and Alf wore aghast masks of mortified fascination i
pointed to the apple i
yelled i say who among you claim this fruit is forbidden
i unsheathed my blade i menaced the crowd they had their
saucer-wide eyes locked upon me i prowled low like a troll i
swung around back to the board and with a decisive strike of my knife
as if delivering the coup de grâce to the neck of my enemy i
split the apple one half flew off into Guinevere's two hands
the other into my free mitt Fyodor's blade remained on the board i
could not have choreographed it any better
there was a flashbulb burst and she shed her robe to sharp shrieks
all over they saw the boa constrictor slithering around her naked body

i peeled my shirt off i had not planned to drop trou
but with her exposed the air crackling with temptation and excitement
i thought well let us not half-ass it now we are putting on a show
i threw my pants around my ankles buck naked like her
i said to the gobsmacked quiet crowd you find us indecent
apparently there is none among you who has read the Bible
a swell of laughter rose from the crowd
like a relief valve had been twisted
Guinevere offered her apple half to me
i ate
i offered to her
she ate we bowed
the snake tranquil she had it well-trained she was a master of her craft
baffled Fyodor and Alf who had never seen the likes of it bowed
the ensuing volcano of applause made the William Tell reaction feel like a
shadow of gratitude i scooped my clothes and hat she her robe
we streaked giddily through the tunnel
Alf and Fyodor on our trail we flew outside the big top
into the brisk evening a handful of folks were
scattered around the lantern-lit grounds
a few fires already going yonder i
got dressed saying you blew them away Guinevere
she put on her robe saying are you kidding
you were Shakespearean in your fury and madness
Fyodor bolted to us i gripped the handle of my blade
he was breathing heavy after sprinting
he said to me you will come to my caravan at midnight
or i will find you wherever
you may lay your head tonight and i will cut your throat
do you understand
i said yes sir
in his eyes i detected no bluff
he said to Guinevere now you come here
he dipped her in his arms even with the snake
he kissed her with their tongues slithering under the glinting moon
her robe slipped open
he said i have never wanted you more i am the snake in your garden
let the Lord watch and despair as i
eat your fruit and swallow the holy juices

Guinevere with his ass in her clutches
rammed his crotch to her vagina they writhed
she said my cup runneth over for you
paradise shall be flooded tonight
they laughed like growling dogs
kissing passionately as they drifted away
Alf trotted up to me and said where are they going
i said well Alf from what i heard i would bet you a shiny double eagle
they are headed to fuck each other silly
Alf licked his lips lost in thought
i said alright then and started to slink off
but Alf said not another damn step get back here
what in the hell did you think you were pulling out there tonight
i said Alf the crowd got a kick out of it
Alf said and you are damn lucky Lucky
otherwise i would be fixing to boot your ass right out of my circus
public nudity does not offend me i
do not run a Sunday School circus like Ringling i
would rather go bankrupt
but what bothers me is you upstaging Fyodor one of my biggest stars
as a general rule i do not like improvisation one bit
and have you considered
maybe your little Gypsy sweetheart
did not get a kick out of you baring your pecker
for all the world to see
i choked a gulp of uneasy air
the high of performance had dwarfed even that goof dust i
had once sniffed
but i could feel the ecstatic energy rush out of my body
like my soul flying away i
had got so wrapped up with dazzling the crowd i
had lost sight that the whole reason i
had even devised such a stunt was to impress Nadezhda
the thought that i had gone too far and put her off sank me
i was like a doomed dying city its last light flickering
or like a hobo so drunk i pissed in my own wine
or like a warrior who had fought a war on a false rumor
Alf said so for your official punishment you will not be back under
that big top as a performer or spectator any time soon

during the show you will shovel elephant shit horse shit and tonight
you will shovel Babou's shit have you seen her yet
i said no i have not i saw her tent with the sign i know she is a tiger
Alf's eyes grew grave he said there is a reason she cannot be
in the menagerie with the other animals
oh i tell you young Sloman she is a killer i
have never seen anything like it in man or beast i
have seen her slash
Alf drew his arm back mimicking a tiger's striking claws
he said with a fistful of knives through the strongest of men
like they were warm butter i
have personally seen her kill three men in total
not to mention she shredded 15 baby hippopotami in Baltimore
they had just arrived to port i
had not had them for more than a day when her killer instinct took over i
will give you a word of advice that may save your sorry life
do not look into her eyes
i was staring into Alf's
he said the three men i have seen killed by her they all had stared into
her eyes she does not like that one bit it stirs the bloodlust in her soul
the crimson of man and beast she drinks it warm i
give you this key to her cage you shovel her shit and you get out
if she shows her face you avert your eyes and pray to sweet baby Jesus
i said i will do nothing of the sort Alf you know i am Hebrew
Alf said well then call upon sweet baby Moses in the bulrushes
for i will ask Meriwether Cloud the Chickasaw man
who trains her and if he tells me of old shit in her cage
you will be off this circus and banished from the grounds
Fat Ali will not be selling you a ticket i
will run you off with my cobra dagger
good luck Sloman if your flesh still lingers upon your bones
return that key to me when you are done
Alf limped back inside the big top i trudged to Babou's tent i
examined the key the Locksmith on my mind i
heard cheering from inside the big top Nadezhda was probably
flying through the air defying death i intended to do the same on earth
the tent's entry was tied open i slipped in
it was quite the expansive cage
bigger than some ships i have dreamed sinking

there were stand-up boards inside with two-foot-wide holes near the bottom
there were wooden ramps and walls
there were a few battered baseballs must have been toys
there were bales of hay stacked like towers
it appeared all arranged like a tiger maze
she was plain to see dozing in the back corner
orange black stripes it was my first time seeing one in real life
there was the shovel outside her cage i
was moving with the stealth of a ghost i
did not want to become one yet i
spotted turds of hers along with the skeleton of a wild boar
only its snout and hooves remained i
was hoping she had been well-fed recently i
put the key inside the padlock biting my lip i
twisted with the deft delicate hand of a master spy
the shackle shot up i
kept my eyes upon her she did not move i
tiptoed to the shovel and carried it in i set some dung outside
the cage i scooped another pile and one more i was closing in on my
mission there was one last area of droppings about ten feet from her i
crept to them i nudged them onto the shovel with my boot i did not
even risk the scraping noises of scooping but she must have detected
faint vibrations in the ground from my nearby movements she rose with
her back to me i was not expecting the Lord to lock her jaw
like the lions with Daniel
after all Daniel was blameless and i
had once beat the sneering crippled boy whose arm
had been chewed off in the threshing machine now it
was my turn to lose a limb or two i could feel the teeth i stepped
backward my rampaging heart throbbed into my dirt-covered fingertips
one of those Statue of Liberty sweat mustaches above my lip
Babou rocked forward stretching so magnificently
splendorous beauty washed over me like a baptism
it may have been the calming whisper of Hashem if
he would not rescue me at least he had let me behold the majesty
of the tiger who would take my life
perhaps that was my reward for when i got guilt gnawed after i
thrashed the one-armed boy i
took to the road and did not speak for 30 days i was a silent monk i

gathered walnuts from the orchard i
presented them to him on one knee
he said aw get up and crack some of these walnuts with me
Babou turned to me but before i could meet her eyes i
had squeezed mine shut i
was tightrope walking in reverse she growled i could feel the red in
my waking mind her slashing claws of death she was gaining on me i
would not make it through the cage door i hid behind one of the boards
she came closer i saw a blur of orange and black stripes i dove behind
the bales of hay she was sniffing vigorously she was onto my scent
chasing me all over this obstacle course she had mapped out every inch i
knew i would not last there i drew my knife i carved some hay off
the bale i heard her prowling behind one of the wooden boards i
tucked my blade away i chucked the hay her way
she pawed at it thank you sweet baby Moses i
had scored a diversion for my exodus
but my boot rolled over one of her baseballs
my feet flew in the air i
landed hard and knocked the wind out
my hat had flown off i thought i might have broke my ass i
coughed and strained to pull my body up
that is when i felt the presence i glimpsed the colors of her arrival i
shut my eyes her breath gave heat like the words of glowing embers i
had seen in the book of the dead
her giant paw stepped upon my arm
my bags were light for a journey across the bridge so soon
it would have to be her i was already mourning her loss i
would have to get lucky through her ribs and pierce the heart
or she would have a middling wound to remember me by
if she remembered me at all
lying on the ground with my eyes shut i unsheathed my blade i
held it tight she was practically standing on top of me
growling low like a deep grumble the prelude to a vicious attack i
do not believe in taking life without looking the other in the eyes i
was ready to be one of the few who had ever up close with no cage
gazed into her soul i was preparing to commune with the dead
when i opened my eyes i saw she had none
they had been stitched shut
she lowered her head to mine and nuzzled i pet her neck i

caressed her back with my knuckles holding the knife
she rubbed her face into my mine forcefully
she was trying to itch her empty eye sockets on my chin she chuffed
she seemed to really like that i set my blade on the ground to pet
her better i twirled my fingers in her whiskers she was friendly
and funny too practically ramming her forehead against mine
to get me to scratch her ears
her wild playfulness had me laughing
when she sauntered off it did become plenty clear that
Alf had set me up for a zinger
Babou's walk was unusual i
could see looking closer at her gate that she was blind
but she found her way through every obstacle
that explained the sign outside announcing her magic whiskers
i gathered her turds and tossed them behind the tent
i locked the cage saying good night Babou i wish i had a vast patch
of land where you could roam free but i will see to it Alf is taking care
of you i will visit again you have made a new friend tonight
she sat near the bars looking regal sniffing the evening air
like a royal bidding me adieu
i left to get popcorn at the food tent they
had four pushcarts and a ten-foot-long counter there was
the flame-haired Irishman about 30 years of age wiping them
down i sat at the end of one of the picnic tables with my popcorn
he lit a cig with a deep exhale
he said can you believe what this world is coming to
we have either to choose prison exile or death
all other roads are cowardice
i slowed my chewing he took another drag
he said and i am the biggest fucking coward of them all
i said say where are you from
he said most recently i
have spent five years at a mill in Pawtucket Rhode Island
but i was not made to wither at machines i
had to shove along i was born and raised in Dublin
the flood of folks rolled out of the big top i told the Irishman
well i have a mule to feed
a key to return
and a Russian to fight i

Reagan M. Sova

will see you down the road and in the meantime
we will store all our anger and hope
the foundation of courage i believe
we will draw upon it one day
good evening to you
he stomped his cig saying same to you boyo

פֿינפֿט

i waited outside the silver trailer
Alf walked up with a Texas-mile-wide grin
he said did you meet Babou
i said i sure did and with you painting a villain
out of her she is damn lucky to be alive
Alf doubled over laughing heartily i
returned him the key
he said that sweet snoring angel would not harm the devil i
hope you dispatched her excrement plenty far i
do not need my men slipping on tiger shit
i said tell them they would do well to look out for baseballs
now what time is it
Alf eyed his silver pocket watch and said quarter to midnight
he called after me as i walked away
i hope you learned the lesson of the day it is my show
but i knew the lesson learning was not done yet
i stood before Fyodor's caravan
there was a chair out front with a garland of
roses around the top the stems intertwined i
said i am here Fyodor what is it you have to say
i drew my blade as he stepped outside the door
the crowd was gone from the grounds the last few campfires
glowed in the moonlight he was holding a bucket
wearing only his pants two of his knives holstered
on each side he said do you know where Guinevere is
i said no
he said she is sleeping peacefully in my bed
we have done such things tonight

you may never be able to comprehend i
would bet you heaven will feel like hell to me after
the great morsels of life i have devoured with that woman
i said well good for you Fyodor now are we going to fight
he said you young American men with your fighting if i
wanted to kill you by now my knife would be buried in your heart
do you not remember i make my living throwing knives
at remarkable distances with deadly accuracy
that did seem a true point i sheathed mine
he said come and sit
i eyed the chair of roses
he again said come
i walked to the chair with some reluctance and had a seat
he struck a match and lit a cigarette
he said try it it is hashish
i smoked a bit he
said you did not even cough i knew you were a man
standing behind me he took my hat
he said lean back your head
i did
the roses jabbed my cranium like a crown of thorns i
dreamed a childhood memory of my mother at dusk
showing me night-blooming flowers in the garden
with my eyes closed Fyodor sharpened his knife with a stone i
saw him as an ancient swordsman before the battle i
saw the family of smoking wolf dogs standing vigil over my grave i
saw the unicorn from the Bible looking like Sweet Kiss i
said are you going to cut my throat
he chuckled and scraped the blade across my forehead
moving back into my scalp he did it again he dipped the knife
into the bucket the water must have had mint soaking in it he
said what you did tonight created a debt you stole my thunder
you know when a man steals from you you must make him pay i
do not accept money it means nothing to me i take only blood
he dragged his blade slow above my ears
my black raven feathers fell to the earth he was shaving me bald
he said but tonight is the first time in my life i have allowed
a debt to be paid with human hair do you know why
i said i do not Fyodor might you tell me

he said because i have once thrown a knife into the chest
of one of the tsar's soldiers as i was falling from my horse i
have once smashed the head of a lame dog with a sledgehammer i
have once killed a chicken in the mind of a man
and poured the blood over his mother's doorstep i
see you grasp that the circus is a place where mortals
feel other mortals dance with death and desire
and the clowns laugh at man's sad stupid vanity in the face of death
Fyodor quaked with dark laughter he
said i shave your head so that you can repay me with the sight of life
growing defiantly each day the color black you have stolen
from death that is a debt you will repay in time
i burst out laughing
Fyodor jumped back with his knife
startled by the madman with half his hair gone
i said my whole life every breath was stolen i
will never pay that debt i
will leave my treasures upon the earth
death will find me to be a disappointing meal as i
laugh like thunder next to the mountain
even the virgin with the eye patch and the mule will be laughing
we will laugh our guts out
that is how strange and good my death will be
as we laugh as hard as we weep for the death of death
our sacred enemy our brother we mourn the day
the earth will float along silent another cold empty rock
do you ever feel that sadness Fyodor
he did not speak but by the time he had finished shaving my head
he was weeping
i stole away in my tent leaning out of
the opening to catch the right angle of moonlight on the page
dear Nadezhda
i wrote until the morning light
sitting outside the door of my tent i caught Seth
the giant
heading up from the river toward camp
i said say Seth can you do me a favor and deliver this letter
to the Gypsy aerialist with the eyes of two different colors
towering above he said you must have mistaken me

for the world's tallest mailman
we chuckled he said why have you shaved your head
i said i had to settle a debt
Seth said you have not slept have you
i said sleep is but one of the enemies i have vanquished
do you ever do battle in the night sometimes
Seth said yes i fight deadly duels against almighty sadness
very often he is David and i am Goliath he strikes me
between the eyes with his sling one of these nights i
fear he will come with his sword to sever my neck
bury my body
and walk off with the head
i said what gives him his power
Seth said my body
my prayers to stop it growing have gone ignored i
do not like to see children flee from me screaming that does not
get easier with time i might have liked to take a wife
but it is getting dark in the day for that
i said what about a shield do you have one
Seth said my friend Vernon he is skin and bones
his body has betrayed him worse than mine
at least i get to rescue cats from trees those have been some
of the greatest moments of my life
Vernon's gums are crawling from his teeth
he is vanishing day by day but he can still be funny sometimes
he has a spark
Seth flashed the smile of a doomed wounded man as he tucked
the letter in his breast pocket
saying welcome to the circus

זעקסט

i slogged my way through the following few days
we packed up the circus with our blood sweat and muscle
traveling the road to our next destination Albuquerque we
made camp and trekked all the next day and made camp again
Frederick Leonardo and i headed out around dinnertime
looking for a border settlement
we stumbled upon two hunters in the woods i
asked them where we could find some victuals
one said the son of a bitch is back
he aimed his rifle tracking a sprinting pheasant
he swung toward the bird taking flight and shot his hunting partner
the man collapsed to his knees clutching his neck wound
Frederick and i yelped in shock
he fell over choking in his blood
within seconds his hands and arms were painted red up to his elbows
the other hunter went to him
and by the time we had rushed over the man was dead
the living hunter beat the earth with his bloody fist
he ripped his shirt crying i am a fucking dead man he was powerful he
dined with President Roosevelt just last week he was set to be the first
governor of New Mexico once this territory gets its statehood it will
happen sooner than you realize oh God what have i done i
train his horses i shovel shit they will kill me
please will you help me bring him to town i
will face what i have done like a man i will wear the noose
i said i am sorry for the loss of your friend and for your predicament
you see how death sometimes strikes lightning quick we will get the body if
you get his arms we can lay him across my mule

Wildcat Dreams in the Death Light

Frederick stopped me with a hand on my shoulder
he whispered i do not like this one bit
when we get to town you may see his story change
we do not know this man
i said you think he may pin it on us
Frederick said with a paint job like mine you cannot be too careful i
have seen north south east and west they load the dice when you are
a Negro coming to town
it does not matter how you throw them you will roll snake eyes
i said that is a good point Frederick i think i know what he needs to hear
Frederick said what
i said i will tell him to flee to Mexico
what do you think about that
Frederick said that is good yes you tell him
i walked with Leonardo to the man lying in the tall grass weeping
i said sir listen to me
he quieted
i asked did you kill him on purpose
he shouted are you insane i am no killer why would i wait around
to shoot a man in the neck when there are witnesses present
why would i drag the body back to town
i said do you have a wife and family
he said no
i said good you are not a killer you are unattached you are a man
who needs to give up the gun
mount the fastest horse you know
and ride deep into Mexico
forget your name and learn Spanish
the word for water is *agua*
if anyone asks of your past tell them you are a pilgrim
who has come to dance with Quetzalcoatl the feathered serpent god
you never saw two young men walking to town
but you may keep nestled in your memory the storm of death i brought
if you mention us i will unleash
the whole fucking flood now fare thee well
he said what if someone sees me and asks of the blood on my hands
behind me and the mule Frederick said tell them it is goose blood
we walked on with Leonardo but the man had us whipping around when
he screamed with the pistol at his chin i am giving up the gun

may God have mercy on my soul
he pulled the trigger his brain blasted sky-high like a geyser
Frederick vomited
i patted his back and helped him up
i said get on him there you go
he rode Leonardo back to camp near the road with me walking
alongside
i said do you have the stomach for waffles
he said i would be much obliged
i paid the Irishman to knock us off a couple i
built a fire Frederick shivered in the grass as the batter sizzled in
the Irishman's griddle he said have you read *The Bread Book*
i said no i have not yet what is your name by the way
he said my name is Tomás i can lend it to you boys
he said to Frederick can you read
Frederick snapped at him yes i can read Tomás
i sat on the ground next to Frederick by the fire
i said we are literate men
Tomás said ok i meant no offense you know better than me
how the doors of many a schoolhouse are shut to the Negro
Frederick said that is true but we find our way
Tomás said aye have you read Frederick Douglass
Frederick said yes matter of fact i was named for him
Tomás said i can lend you one
of his if you like i have a pamphlet written by
Eugene V. Debs called The Negro in the Class Struggle
it is one both of you may find interesting i
have also got Walt Whitman the poet and Leo Tolstoy
Tomás got us some books from his caravan
we thanked him for lending them
he said think nothing of it i
am always glad to do my part corrupting the youth
sorry i meant literate men
we three had a good chuckle i believe it was cleansing
for Frederick and me after what we had seen
we sat under the moonlight by our tents the night was cool
he said those were the second and third men i
have seen turn from living to dead before my eyes
the first was my father when the tools fell on him

with all that has been going on sometimes i wonder why they pray
where his mercy went i could not tell you
i said yes i have seen a few cross the bridge myself i
have seen a hobo upon the steps of the library in Battle Creek
he asked me is it your birthday and as a matter of fact it was i
said to him yes sir i turned six today how did you know
well before he could answer his eyes rolled back into his head i
thought for a moment he would be speaking in tongues
but he slumped over
they loaded him onto the undertaker's wagon i
said to the policeman where will you take him
the policeman said we are taking him to the circus he will have
the jolliest time of his life
but i knew that that was a lie i wanted to make come true i
followed the wagon to the cemetery i
juggled walnuts over his grave i
did a cartwheel over the disturbed earth i
did not have a big top but i cupped my hands
speaking into his dirt mound
sir i hope you have enjoyed the circus of death fare thee well
i had already seen the train with my family in it burn up i
knew then it was not a one-off death is haunting my steps i
have learned of the old country blood accusations
and leaving in the night i
have met many travelers with no homes outlaws on the run i
have learned a bit of your people and the men who seek
to dominate you from cradle to grave
Frederick said yes i have known many days i thought would be my last i
have known a man who was lynched for simply passing through i
have heard of some cowboys with their horses
dragging Negroes by the neck
across miles of dirt my people have been dragged across oceans
the weight of our burden
the bullwhip pain
the rivers of blood
the pastures of tears could sink mankind
but that is not all our story we rise
unfathomably and fall in love every day i
am not blind even if the poor white man is i

have seen him suck shit and eat dirt and pound his body to hell
to make profit other people keep
my father once told me of a white man from North Carolina
who was stabbed and whipped with a chain 'til he died
he was a senator
not to mention my mother once saw
a white woman die choking on a toothpick i
have talked to war veterans of all colors i
have heard them speak of their fallen brothers and weep i
have dreamed the falcon who always returns i
know through time for all men the whole world is a circus of death i
will ride the black stallion with my eyes closed i
will meet death with the secret blade of my stolen ancestors
i said yes though we have traveled different terrain
it is my good fortune to have met you upon the path i
hope to walk with you the day i complete my mission i
aim to honor Frank the spirit rider and my Aunt J i
will make for them a ceremony of light
a procession that stops seven times the Hebrew way
and in the seven pauses
our remembrances will be so strong and strange and good that each
will feel like a dagger into the eye of death he will weep and despair
Frederick said i do not know if you have heard how some Negroes
in New Orleans play music in their funeral processions if
you would like musical accompaniment in your procession
you at least will have one mouth harp i
will walk with you and stop seven times
i said i feel like we have known each other for years
Frederick said it is the same with me
perhaps it is kindness trust
and the manifest presence of death that has deepened our bond
if he has taken all your family i will defy death and be your brother i
have the rag in my pocket i know you have the blade i have one as well
i made a small slit in my left forearm and he did his on the right he
tied them together with the bandana
we lay side by side upon the earth we would later nourish
the light of the stars and the moon made the
long journey into the eyes of the blood brothers
i rose from my bedroll in the morning to find

next to my bald head the wax-sealed letter
dear Sloman
it sounds like you have had yourself some first day at
the circus i saw you riding your mule you did not
see me but i was wondering why you were baldheaded
in answer to your question i have never been bald not
even when i was a baby i crawled out they told me
with a swirling head of dark hair
to your other question
i have handled a sword one time in Boston two and a half
years ago there was a man in our circus who has since
lit out for work elsewhere he did juggle swords
he was kind and taught me to read he
let my brother and me chop some watermelons i
tossed some pieces and my brother swung the sword
he tried but i am glad
he is a razorback and not a warrior or a baseball player
ever since you tricked him he
has been saving for a violin maybe one day you two will make
music together after i turn 14 my mother said that is when
we may speak to you i am surprised you have taken to the road
even knowing you may not speak to me for so long i
trust you will find the keys you need
for the ceremony for your kin
in my dreams i have seen the dead rider
there was a woman on the horse with him
when he crossed the bridge a victory bird flew from her chest
i followed it into the sky
it had become a falcon of the bridge
for the past two nights after i have done my part
and the show clears out i put on my thickest sweater it was my
grandmother's though she once traded it for a plate of beans
my father walked for two days in winter with an injured lung
to the village of Уржум where he collapsed
and woke at the card table with a family of Mongolian migrants
he lost his head before he won it back and the sweater also
my mother said you played a trick on her cards i
know you bet horses but do you play cards i
wear that sweater by the fire and dream you are next to me

like when we were holding hands and flying
with the eagles at the picnic i think about it
i thank you for asking but i was not mad at you for
getting naked in front of them i understand performance
that is my life and i will stay a performer until i die
yours truly
N
i folded the letter and shut my eyes in my tent
i heard the morning motion the packing
but i had to linger i had to bask
a man could live a long time on a letter like that

זיבעט

we rambled to Albuquerque
unfortunately our performers gave Frederick the brush-off
but i walked with him with my guitar
and Leonardo did not mind being in the parade
we had another small one in Silver City and we clowned
around with whisky in Tombstone but it was not until
we arrived in Bisbee that Seth saw Frederick
around the fire Seth said i just got a new cane i would like
to try plus a new cape and top hat i feel like going out
if your offer still stands i will walk in your parade tonight
Seth was an eye-popper especially with his long lacquered
hickory stick in one hand and an explorer's torch in the other
his dapper cape and the top hat surely
nudged him above nine foot we
had a couple dozen youngsters and a few friendly dogs
trailing us singing along with some simple songs i played
i was having lunch the next day in our dusty desert camp with
Frederick Seth and Vernon when Fyodor told me Alf wanted to
see me i finished my rice and beans and found the fat brown cow
outside the silver caravan i knocked upon the door
Alf opened and said good afternoon
i said good afternoon Alf
he smiled staying mum playing coy trying to get me to sweat
but i stared him down ready to ride the game into the night
he cracked not a minute later he said you see this brown cow
i said well of course i do Alf she is standing right there
Alf waited like he was studying me before he handed me
what appeared to be a bone saw he said i would like you to

dismember this cow and feed her to Babou
i shielded the sunshine with my hand i eyed the saw and the
cow blinking with her long lashes one of the sweetest things
upon four legs i had seen along with Leonardo and Babou i
looked back to Alf i said you know Alf i have hunted and fished
in my day but i have never sneaked up on a sweet ol' creature like
this and took her life away
Alf said i did not take you for a fella who starves blind tigers to death
Babou has not eaten in three days i was damn lucky even to find the
ranch nearby to purchase such a fat beast i was ready to sacrifice a horse
sensing my reluctance Alf said if you want you can just push her
in the cage and let Babou feast but between you and me
that would be a terrifying and painful way to go for this lovely heifer
the kind thing to do would be to cut her throat i
do also have a stick of dynamite you could use to blow her head off
in the blink of an eye
i examined my options scratching my chin i said i will cut the throat Alf
Alf smacked his hands together gleefully
he said good deal Babou has just been moved from her wagon
into her cage in the tent all the tents are now up here you take this
Alf stuffed the dynamite stick in my back pocket he
said case you change your mind all you have to do is reach behind you
Alf disappeared into his caravan
i led the cow by the rope to Babou's tent
when i ducked inside Babou unleashed a cry that was not roaring
it was a wounded sound
with her sweet eye holes shut she sniffed the air inside her cage
she moaned and i kissed the cow on the top of the head
i said would you like to hear a song
i tied her to Babou's empty wagon outside the tent i
hurried back with my guitar in the blazing sun
workmen performers and animals rushing around i
crossed the Negro dwarf riding the white horse
galloping past he said outta my way peckerwood
i sang to the heifer in the shade of the tent
over Babou's anguished lamenting coming from inside
it's cold
our home
a giant flood of people forced to roam

pilgrims on their knees
crawling not to freeze
the orphan fire's mine
one day the sun will shine
you know it's cold
our home
a price tag on the river and it's sold
he left with money fast
but i had my rifle
i shot him in the throat
on his motorcycle
yeah it's cold
our home
gamblers with the black dice we rolled
snake eyes in the ground
all my stories found
on a ship of pages
sailing with the sages yeah
it's cold our home
i strummed the final note and began to cry
an Indian voice said that cow really liked that song
i looked behind me it was Meriwether Cloud Babou's trainer
he said i think your music might soothe her for a peaceful passage
i wiped my tears with my marinière
there was still a tiny hole in the sleeve from Fyodor's knife
i said i did not mean for you to find me weeping
he said it is honorable to shed tears for innocent cows
and the death of the human race i
weep when i sing ancient hymns to newborn wolf cubs
they hear them when they die i
have wept smoking vision pipes with storytellers
who leave death with scars he reveals after sundown
now let us bring this heifer into the tent and nourish our sister Babou
i led the cow inside with Meriwether
he said let us lay her down so she does not tumble over undignified
we bent her knees and brought her to the dusty desert floor on her
side Meriwether said what would you like me to do
would you like me to do it
the cow was blinking at me she seemed confused or like she

was about to try to get up Babou grumbled so hard i
thought she would retch i set my guitar upon the ground i
said i would like you to sing the soothing ancient hymn the
wolf cubs hear this heifer has the bravery of any fanged
beast who has howled at the moon i
will be in your debt please let us hear it
Meriwether stepped back with sad wild eyes he sang in Chickasaw i
fell to my knees and drew my knife speaking tenderly into her ear i
said you shall not die nameless
yours is Scarlett the color of life and death now fare thee well
i slit her neck forcefully with an aching heart full of loss
like for an enchanting song you know you will never hear again
the blood sprayed a river running into the dust as if
it had been foretold by a holy soothsayer
Babou wailed she was not one to starve quietly Meriwether kneeled as
he crooned he placed his open palm upon the struggling cow's ribs i
held her tight lying next to her with my scarlet hands petting her chin
and shoulder i had let the blade fall into the river
her movements calmed to peaceful stillness
she crossed i
sawed the leg off Babou snatched it through the bars
we dragged the whole body inside while she was
feasting her salvation trembling in ecstasy
they say hunger is the best chef
i said shall we leave her
Meriwether said no she will cry it makes her sad to eat alone
we watched the big cat get her fill for a moment
Meriwether said i will walk in the parade with Frederick
we can sing to honor this fine beast
who has revived our beloved Babou
i said may she come as well
Meriwether said yes
i told Frederick the good news we walked our best parade yet with a
hymn for Scarlett who grazes the pastures of the dead unknown poets
Frederick had been playing dominoes with the clowns on the road
to Tucson and for winning on a bet Alexandre and his penny-farthing
and the juggling monkey named RT joined the burgeoning procession
the parade success showed in the circus attendance
Alf even raised ticket prices for the second and third nights

all two thousand places sold out for
each night they all said that that had never happened
the last night in Tucson i
fell asleep with my tent door open to get the cool desert breeze i
dreamed Babou as a tiger cub she had eyes she prowled
the jungle with her kin and feasted on boars and brown cows
she grew bigger nourished by death the way of the wild in my dream she
grew so big her eyes ballooned with her they popped out of her head
but she kept roaming the jungle weeping blood from her empty sockets
she became us all walking through town in the parade
our torches the burning orange stripes
except the parade did not consume the dead it fueled death
in the form of a dark pink sunset cloud swirling above our heads
it bloomed commensurate to the size of the parade
the swirling cloud made a strange rattling sound
Frederick up front with me like he was panicked
said do not move a muscle
do you hear me Sloman not a muscle
i awoke to the snake eyes three feet from mine
forked tongue flickering
Frederick with a long broom saying not one muscle
he gently raked the rattlesnake
outside the tent walking slowly backward
when i inhaled my giant breath of life i
heard the knife strike and a screeching hiss i
peered out to find the snake pinned to the desert floor
by Fyodor's blade
he severed the head with a single machete chop
and told Frederick stand back
he said i have seen
a lone snakehead bite several minutes after he was decapitated
it is the same with a guillotined head
they blink and look you in the eye i have
even seen one spit now who among you has tasted rattlesnake soup
Frederick said not me and i will not be trying any today no thank you
all i have on my mind is to quit the Arizona Territory i
hear Los Angeles is a Garden of Eden what do you say Sloman
i said Frederick i hope you are dead wrong i have seen plenty of
snakes for the time being

Frederick and Fyodor guffawed i
packed up with the dynamite in my knapsack
full of gratitude i let Frederick ride Leonardo
as much as he wanted on the road he
said this is a good old boy
Leonardo bucked his head back joyful with praise
we gave him a rest from our weight when
we occupied the spot atop Babou's caged wagon i
did some writing up there over the course of four days
past the sandstone bluffs the wild cacti
through the desolate desert landscape once blanketed by lava
i began the letter *dear Nadezhda*
after 20 days we reached Los Angeles on December 15th
my hair had plenty returned i
got Frederick a snakeskin belt and a bottle of wine for Christmas
before he struck across country for Washington DC the card said
to my brother Frederick on Christmas
you are sleep
you are water
you are the rude beauty of fire
you are smoke
you are a warm wide smile
you are the screaming fast rock that strikes the soft throat of death
i believe you are the good falcon i
have seen you swoop down to save a fool's life i
will never forget you are a champion
bon voyage
Sloman
Frederick got me a guitar capo i hummingbird strummed with it
i sang out loud while he went fire-breathing on the mouth harp
we had a wild good time on our final parade of the year
Fyodor playing his khromka accordion
Wu the Chinese emperor's great granddaughter on violin
Seth holding the torch pushing her in Vernon's wheelchair
Guinevere with her best-behaved snake
Alexandre and RT up high on the big wheel
Meriwether and Babou strolling
all of Los Angeles knew we had gotten to town
the circus did five nights in the city

Alf let me back inside the big top during the last show
Nadezhda and her kin were joined by some Mexican aerialists
they performed a few Hanukkah miracles
Nadezhda flipped and dangled upside down by her knees
and swung to the other trapeze she
caught her uncle Merripen at the end of his double flip i
was wise not to take goof dust before that show or it might have
been my last night on earth a man can only handle so much i
was told by Guinevere after the show to go see
Scotch Castle tied outside the big top i found him in the dark
there was the letter dangling from his harness i
untied the string off him the letter had my name on it
dear Sloman
if you are reading this on the last night of
our show in Los Angeles then it is the final night of
Hanukkah i wish you a lovely and miraculous holiday i
will be heading north with my kin we will be spending
the off-season near San Francisco i like the air there i
dream up there about a man with a busted leg by a river
he said he jumped i
dream up there about walnut cake i
dream up there about a big welcome home party for a man
as if he had been raised from the dead i
heard you playing that song to the cow i liked it i
am glad to hear Frederick saved your life and has been
a brother to you i myself have never been snakebitten
but my brother has
the serpent had been hiding under his legs in the canoe
he also has been attacked by wild boars in the forest
he has been trampled by buffalo
one time he had his nose bloodied by four British sailors i
was headbutted on my backside by a billy goat i
did not see it coming they said he looked like pure evil i
told them he could be the devil he could be the lord i
laugh at them all except the Holy Ghost i do not fool with him i
am excited our circus is growing i know next season
we will have more musicians
a woman shot from a cannon
a hot air balloon

a grizzly bear who dances with eagles i
will not be sad to pass the off-season quickly i
thank you for telling me about Tu BiShvat
i do not think it odd you disappear into the forest
every year for it in fact i would like to try it myself
my favorite holiday is Halloween i dress up
and trick even the spirit riders
you will not have a way to reach me this off-season
but that is ok
we will see if fate intends our futures entwined i
have my calendar marked i
know of the Monterey Cypress tree in San Francisco
where the painters gather round i will find my way there
on Tu BiShvat i will think of you
fare thee well until we meet again
yours truly
N
i put the letter under my pillow and slept over it
every night at an LA boardinghouse three dollars a month

אַכט

i disappeared into the forest with my guitar on Tu BiShvat i
returned to the ocean and found a gunnysack washed ashore
it looked like it might have been full of potatoes i
peered inside it was dead puppies i
tied Leonardo to the post by the jetty i
kissed his forehead i
gathered some rocks and placed them in the sack i
swam out past the buoys i
swam with the sea lions i
swam with the orphan dolphin i
treaded deep swaying waters with the sack i
sang the song of the brave smoking wolf dogs i
sang the song of the thirst for life slaked with a brimming cup of
    poison i
sang the song of holy fig trees guarded by warrior monks i
sang the song of giant dancing vines and angel fish i
named the puppies Daniel Henri Julia Connor Arthur and Zenobia i
dropped them to the ocean floor and swam back to shore i
was grateful for golden California sunshine still a couple hours left
to dry me on the beach there a young hobo did approach me i
did not feel much like talking but it seemed he did he
told me about pitching two seasons for the Chicago Orphans he
told me about the more he worked the more money he lost he
told me about traveling with the man who shot the king of Italy he
told me about traveling with the man who shot the president of
    America he
told me about the newborn baby dipped in gold he
told me about the powder-blue tailcoat tuxedo he

told me about fucking an Eskimo in the woods outside Vancouver he
told me about Harry Houdini stealing his ideas i
eyed the ocean and pictured the puppies with a special key
unlocking the chains of death an underwater escape trick
he offered me his wine i said thank you i do not mind if i do
i drank a fair gulp and handed the jug he
said no friend you keep it wow that is a fine-looking mule
i said that is my brother Leonardo he has carried me across America
he said wow that is a fine-looking guitar
i said yes the bride of the dead Gypsy has bequeathed it to me
say i do not feel well
i stood but fell backward upon the sand the sun blurred hazy i
said did you slip sleeping potion in this wine when i was not looking
he loomed over me his dead eyes smoldered with nothingness
mine rolled back into my head like my throat had been slit i
lost consciousness reaching for my blade i
fell into dreamless sleep i
blinked awake in the dark of night i
saw the embers of the fire i
saw my soul walking away from my body in my clothes
the striped marinière the black cap the guitar on his back
even the boots i
flipped over in nothing but my drawers
and crawled like a snake on the belly i
needed my soul back but after two crawls
across the sand my light flickered out again i
was sure that with my spirit traveling on
the Gypsy's mountain prophecy had been vanished by
the cold finger of death but he delayed
as the gulls the ocean waves and the sun returned triumphant i
woke next to a suit the color of the sky
it was the powder-blue tailcoat tuxedo
my knife it was gone
he had taken my guitar i looked to the blackened extinguished
beach fire there were seagulls picking at the scattered bones
and Leonardo's severed head i
crawled to it shaking with tears and a string of saliva
from my quivering mouth softly saying no no no
i touched the part where i had kissed him the day before i

touched his ears i
held his head and wept forcefully i
told him he was true and brave i
told him i would carry memories of him across the bridge i
told him i hoped i would again walk alongside him i
told him i did not mean for it to be the sweet kiss of death i
told him his memory would be a blessing always i
told him i would think of him on my wedding day i
told him he would be honored in the ceremony
of light alongside Frank and Aunt J for it was Frank's victory
that had cemented my bond with the precious beast
oh i wailed for him on my side
death had bushwhacked me hard with that one i
staggered to my feet to gather his remains i took up his head with them
what beautiful buzzing had been silenced in his brain i
thought he might like to rest with the young dogs i
collected more rocks from the jetty and put them in his mouth i
swam with him past the buoys i
pressed his forehead to mine i
treaded water rising and falling i sang to him i
laid him in an ocean grave i
marched barefoot in the blue tuxedo to the boardinghouse
the old Mexican with flowers in her hair at the lobby desk chuckled
she said that is one dandy suit
i was swept on past by the spirit winds of revenge up to my room
peeling 20 dollars from my roll 130 left i was lucky
not to have more than a couple bucks on me at the beach but i
was not going to be jumping up and shouting hallelujah about it
i walked out the door and back through the lobby
the flower-haired woman said is that dynamite in your hand
i bought a lighter i
scoured the city barefoot
i saw construction everywhere i
interrogated shipbuilders
i learned the city's population had doubled in the past six years i
shouted at buggy drivers
i barely tasted food i wolfed it in two seconds i
prayed to the sly hunting foxes
i saw the synagogue but did not go inside i

knew the rabbi would only attempt to dissuade me of revenge
i slept in the alley clutching dynamite i
dreamed violence not even a wild animal would do
after two weeks my rage had been fading to despair
when i was seven years of age three of my classmates told me my name
was Death they locked me in the coffin and buried it i was screaming
in there all night 'til morning i can say with honesty
Los Angeles was worse i was weeping
on my knees on the sidewalk of the bustling business district
when a woman stood over me and said you scum sucker
right down in the gutter where i knew you would be
she kicked me the hell over as i was lifting my head
i was surprised she did not bust her leg on me
she thundered now give me my five dollars you chalky thief
or i will beat your ass worse than the Galveston Giant
i was crumpled in a ball on my side i uncovered my startled face
to lay eyes upon the heaviest set Negro prostitute i could have imagined
she dropped her jaw and said oh my God i thought you were Coleman he
is the only man i know who wears a suit like that and with your black hair i
thought dead certain you was him oh my Lord
the woman helped me to my feet brushing me off as rubberneckers
slowly passed she said please excuse me i did not mean to harm you
i said good God woman you almost booted my ass back to Battle Creek
wait a minute you know the man who owns this suit
she examined me up and down
she said that sure does look like Coleman's suit
i said is he an ex-ball player
she said oh yeah he is always bragging about almost throwing a no no
against the Boston Beaneaters he is stuck in his glory days i
have fucked a few sad bastards in my day but he is one sorry blowhard
he even brags about running with the assassins
i excitedly said that is him do you know where he is i am looking for him
the woman cocked her brow and said if i knew where he was i would
have gone to him and collected my money is he your friend
i said hell no i am fixing to kill him he murdered my mule
the woman crossed her arms and said well if you kill him i will never get
my five dollars how about if you pay his debt i will tell you what i know
i said lady you already kicked me hard and now you are shaking me down
she said you are damn right white boy

i said i am not white i am Hebrew
she said well it do not matter to me
i forked over the five she counted them one by one and stuffed the bills
between her breasts she told me of the Calle de los Indios flophouse
where he had been laying his deranged head each night i went there i
found the grizzled old lord of the manor at the desk in his office i
knocked outside the door getting his attention
i said yes i am looking for an ex-ball player named Coleman i
believe he used to stay here
without looking up from the newspaper the man said
i do not give out information about lodgers
i said why but good sir he is my friend i may have a dollar for you
he was not too goddamn friendly clenching his teeth at me
lifting his head and raising his voice saying look kid
this is a flophouse we put up all manner of
cheats runaways outlaws and scoundrels if
word gets out we are loose-lipped about people's affairs
do you think they will want to stay here
i rushed him and lit the stick of dynamite
he said what in the hell
i grabbed a fistful of his greasy blonde hair i
nearly tugged it from his scalp i bugged my eyes i
shouted into his contorted face i am not playing old man
this is live dynamite
death is my twin brother i
will paint these fucking walls with our guts
now where is Coleman
the man stammered choking on his fat tongue i i i i Hornbuckle
i heard he was striking out to the valley with Roscoe Hornbuckle
silver prospector in Angelino Heights keeps silver in his peg leg
Coleman spoke of stealing it that is all i know i swear
i bit the sparking fuse burning my lips i spit it in the garbage can
next to his desk i got lucky that Hornbuckle was a man of
some influence in the Angelino Heights several knew his home
i arrived to glimpse the vision of myself from a distance i
was loading the wagon in the street but it was not me
it was Coleman in my clothes even with my guitar on his back
i blew in like a gentle breeze through the trees outside the cold
Victorian mansion blocking the sun i flicked the lighter once right

behind him if it had caught he would have had a live stick of dynamite
inside his pants but the sound caused him to spin around
he dropped the basket of almonds when he saw me he
lifted his arms like i had a gun he said wait please have mercy
i said you slipped me the poison wine
you killed my brother
you stole my belongings
you got my skull kicked in by a Negro prostitute
you have cast a dark cloud of death upon me since you arrived
i flicked the lighter's tiny flame and held it near the remaining fuse i
said throw my knife on the ground or i light this and whip it at your feet
you can try to run i will send you crawling to hell without legs
the blade with the handle of the spirit rider clanged upon the dusty road
next to my bare feet
he said there now withdraw that lighter from the fuse i see it is short
i said sorry Coleman but your cursed fate was sealed upon your first
bite of mule meat
i brought the flame ever-closer to the dynamite
ready to kill a man
Coleman with his hands out shouted wait do not light that stick
if you think nothing of me think of this fine guitar on my back i
know it is a special guitar
a limited edition of one
i have felt its call
i saw the dead Gypsy strumming it in my dreams
i beg your forgiveness i am sorry i ate your mule
i was starving and he fed me for days
have you not ever had to kill something to stay alive
we are living in a world that feasts upon peaceful creatures i
could have left you dead and naked in the night but i let you live i
could have yanked the gold tooth from your head i left you all intact i
only ask of you the same consideration
Coleman's words did bring me to a bovine memory of Scarlett
and the synagogue of mercy whose door i did not cross
i said for the sweet spirit of Leonardo the mule and Scarlett the cow i
will let you live though next time rob a restaurant if you see one near
do not kill a man's brother
i flipped the lighter lid closed and recovered my knife off the ground
i said so great is my mercy i will not even ask of you the five dollars i

have paid to the prostitute on your behalf
now set the guitar down and let us trade clothes again before i
change course and bury this blade into your chest
the sandpaper voice hollered yonder from the mansion footsteps
Coleman you promised me no headaches yet there appears to be
a young man threatening you with a stick of dynamite
Coleman yelled back but sir i do not know this boy he is raving mad
i said he is lying he means to steal the silver from your peg leg
he will put you into a deep sleep with his wine and rob you
he has done it to me
Hornbuckle got going red-faced smacking his tongue outside his lips
he said i should have trusted my gut i knew you were riffraff
now both of you get out of my sight before i draw my Peacemaker
go find a sunny valley where you can kill yourselves
i looked back at Coleman and with his face scrunched
like he might cry he said see what you have done
he bolted down the street with my clothes and guitar i
commenced pursuit i
yelled this is your doing Coleman now return my things
your blood is not worthy to stain my blade
Coleman led me on a footrace through the city
its backyards markets henhouses outhouses whorehouses
slaughterhouses bathhouses adobe houses he threw a
large tropical bird flapping at me in a baker's living room
he tripped over the migrant family napping in the stables
i swiped my blade a step away as he wobbled but he
regained his balance we galloped the thirsty dusty field
we dashed past a dozen dead peacocks
i hurdled over the long-forgotten movie star on his knees vomiting
    in the alley i
plowed over the fang-tooth politician bribing voters with bean baskets
the beans went flying
Coleman had us weaving through the dustiest noisiest part of Los Angeles
we dodged wagons and horse dung chicken cages
children selling newspapers with cigarettes dangling
fruit vendors shouting Spanish incantations
he zipped into the train station the men with navy blue coats and
whistles could not stop us i slid off the platform to the tracks below he
had caught a lightning bolt of good luck an ace off the bottom of

the deck there was a train that had just departed he chased it down i
was so close to him within striking distance if i had had a sword or even
a machete all i had was the knife the spirits of worthy beasts and riders
living on the edge in his sprint his fingertips caught the black ladder of
the caboose i saw my boots bouncing on the track before he pulled all
his body weight up the train accelerated slightly leaving me a foot behind
two feet my feet hurt
another train on the track next to us roared in the opposite direction its
thunder knocked me tumbling into the thicket but i popped back up
and lit the dynamite i hurled it at Coleman on the caboose
the stick exploded with a cloud of debris
i waited but past the dirt in the air blowing away
there was Coleman with my guitar frontwards
strumming it on the caboose he was laughing
i did not even have a ten count to catch my breath
those railroad men came yelling i flew through the city again
back to the boardinghouse on my mattress of defeat
every youth is a king who meets the guillotine of time i
dreamed Leonardo in the house of mirrors i
dreamed death strumming my lost guitar and laughing i
dreamed the governor's gun kicked so hard his pants fell around his ankles i
dreamed the Locksmith had nothing to say i
dreamed cutting the nobleman's throat i
dreamed Alf's brain turned into a pile of snakes i
dreamed the falcon with the ace of spades in its beak i
dreamed the pyramid the pharaoh built for himself it was a coffin i
dreamed my death by the mountain i
wandered the city like a phantom i returned to the boardinghouse
the Mexican woman behind the counter said oh my Lord it is you i
have only just thrown your backpack and sleeping bag into the trash pit
i said lady why in the hell would you do that
she said because it was reported in the newspaper that you are dead
look there is even your picture
she held up the paper for my viewing and true as ocean waves there i was
standing next to Guinevere it was the night i had gone wild in the circus
the newspaper headline quickened my pulse
CIRCUS BOY DIES ON TRACKS
the article below said
known only to his fellow circus performers as Sloman

the boy was killed in a railroad incident on Monday
he was believed to be 13 years of age
the station agent on duty Weston Sexton reported seeing the youth
pursued by another young man in a powder-blue tailcoat tuxedo
Sloman boarded the caboose of the Fresno-bound train without
a ticket he was attempting to cross from one car to another when
the train decreased speed suddenly according to the conductor
there was a wild mule on the track
the lurching motion caused the coupler joining the rolling stock to
pinch Sloman's leg which was severed the fatal blow was struck when
he fell from the train and smashed his face on a rock
Col Alf Jackson the proprietor of the circus was aboard
the train by happenstance en route to Bakersfield for business
he identified the boy as one of his workers who
had been a member of the circus advertising brigade
and had once performed under the big top
Col Jackson did not know the boy's origins
nor the location of his next of kin
i looked up thunderstruck to the Mexican woman
i said so Coleman is dead
she said who
i said he was the man i had sworn to kill but i
showed him mercy it appears i was not his only enemy
death did pursue him on those tracks
his memory will not be a blessing to me
but i hope it is to someone
now where is that trash pit if you would be so kind
she showed me to it around back i
retrieved my effects and dusted them off
inside my bag all my money was still there
i said ma'am you are some honest woman
she said not always however i do not trifle the belongings of the dead
i said well if you accept money from the living i
am still traveling that side of the bridge as far as i know
here is a dollar if i may offer it to you for your help
she said oh my thank you i will treat my growing son to a fine dinner
i caught a two-wheel hansom cab back to the warehouse
that was Alf's circus headquarters i told the driver
if you stop whipping this horse i have a tip for you

inside they were all training for the imminent season only days away
i did not see Nadezhda among the familiar faces
the Ukrainian strong woman Olena
rode four horses standing on their backs
Rosa and Lola the Gypsy daughters
Fyodor in the distance
and a few new performers all prepared their acts
there were two men with penny-farthing bicycles
twisting along the loop de loop the dip of death
a man and woman on unicycles each juggling lit torches
there was an old man instructing the bear and the eagles
the young woman painting the cannon black
Alf's voice behind me said i have not seen a clawhammer tuxedo
that fine since
i turned to him and stopped him cold like a blade in the gut
his top hat trembled upon his head
he said oh my good Lord Sloman is that you
i said yes i read in the paper you had identified me but
that was a young man who had killed my mule and stole my clothes
Alf's hand rose to his mouth so much was his astonishment
he said i do not believe this i feel as if
there is a ghost standing in my midst i
have just paid a visit to the Gypsies to deliver the news of
your death personally i know Nadezhda was fond of you
i said with luck she still is
Alf said i would bet so listen to this i told her the news this morning
they had completed their journey from the north not two days ago
well she was pretty broke up as i had expected but she said
i foolishly thought if he kept my mother's terms he would die
the good death by the mountain i would like to see him
i told her sweetheart his face was awfully mutilated i
only recognized him by his belongings would you like them
she said yes please i brought them to her and do you know
what was the first thing she said when she examined them
i said what Alf
Alf said she said where is his knife
i told her they did not find it he took quite a tumble
it probably has been lost along the track
she held up your striped shirt

she said i know he plays the dead man's guitar
it was my father's i will wash the blood from this dead man's shirt
he will wear it again
i thought to myself let the girl mourn in her strange way
but here you are before me i do not believe it
you know the Jews gave the other fellow a suit and a box
they buried him this morning
we had planned to have a ceremony for you tonight
your friend Frederick said knowing you
you would probably prefer it at dusk
i could not help grinning i said that goes to show
he is no longer just my friend
he is my brother
if you do not mind Alf i say we keep the evening scheduled as is
i will trick death once again as i did when i was born
14 years ago on this very day
can you tell me is my guitar still in one piece
Alf said matter of fact yes it is
i was stunned to find it intact
shall i also invite the new Negro razorbacks and the rag band
i said hell yes Alf invite them all please
i had never seen so many surprised faces
behind the warehouse about 50 of us
i drank wine on my birthday i
kissed zebras i
kissed Babou i
kissed my arms and legs i
joyfully played the dead Gypsy's guitar
it did not even have a scratch on it
i wore the clothes of the dead
the pants my grandfather was wearing across the bridge
the boots had belonged to my uncle
they had survived the London to New York City
voyage though he did not
there are so many spirit riders upon my knife edge
Leonardo is one i
sing for them i
stand upon tables and rave about them i
sing stories i

sang with Frederick while he poured the rum he had been saving for
    a special occasion i
sang while leaping over the fire i
sang to Fyodor when he was seeing how long he could do
    a headstand i
sang to all the spirits of the animals Babou had eaten i
sang to her eyeballs wherever they were i
sang to her whiskers i
sang to Nadezhda eyeing me in the distance she
wrote to me in the rain she
wrote to me in the aftermath of the Great San Francisco Earthquake
    of 1906 she
wrote to me of haunted voices in the rubble she
wrote to me aboard the train to Sacramento she
wrote to me of her appreciation for Walt Whitman she
wrote to me in ink invisible to the eye unless exposed to heat she
wrote to me of dancing in the orchard she
wrote to me of her aerial routines each one tempting death more than
    the last she
wrote to me of the human pyramid with her Gypsy kin and the
    Manxwoman Mary she
wrote to me how they shot Mary from the cannon she
wrote to me of five thousand women in Oakland demanding the vote she
wrote to me of getting cussed out by the Negro dwarf Titus for
simply petting his horse he had already once called me peckerwood she
wrote to me wishing i had not pulled Titus backward by the straps of
his overalls while he was eating dinner in front of everyone they
    laughed at him
she wrote to me of Titus weeping as he beat the buffalo drum with
    the bear bone
that was his act he made people think he was a Gabonese savage
but he was a former cobbler's assistant from Louisville Kentucky i
wrote to her that Titus and i had drunk the special rum and made amends
i wrote that Titus was an orphan like me
except his parents left him at the orphanage when they saw his
legs bow he was a young child they never did return for him
he told me aw it actually does not bother me
in all likelihood they were not my real parents anyway i
have it on pretty good authority my father was a friar

who was handing out magnolias to the wounded of
the Sheepeater Indian War of 1879 that is how he met
my mother the only Negro nurse in Idaho at that time
i wrote Nadezhda about the handful of orphans i met
the circus must attract them
even circus animals are orphan animals
Alf acquired them young with no parents in sight
Nadezhda wrote to me of the shocking death
of her cousin Rosa attempting the salto mortale
the Leap of Death
i witnessed the river funeral from a distance
their loud bitter wailing cut like time
they said she had loved Joan of Arc
they said she had loved the color red
the pyre burned at dusk
Nadezhda did not write to me for several weeks she
wrote to me that she did not fear fire she
wrote to me of her mother's heat wave illness in Pittsburgh
and the curative water from Jerusalem she bought
she said she knew it was regular American water
however her mother did recover so who knows i
replied with care and at times told of my rambling
among the troupe
one year passed
as i wrote to her about how i
had played my guitar up front in Frederick's parade i
had shoveled mountains of animal shit i too
had seen the Manxwoman Mary shot from the cannon i
had heard the ragtime band outside the sideshow i
had swum the dead sea waters of Salt Lake City i
had waded neck-deep in the river with my knife in my teeth i
had sliced thrashing catfish dead in the brain in my hands for dinner i
had slept many nights in my uncle's work boots i
had dreamed the gunnysack of puppies on the ocean road with Leonardo i
had eaten many dinners in the company of Babou i
had seen the Yale baseball team all fucking each other in the meadow i
had seen people pay a quarter to go up in the hot air balloon i
had seen the balloon man sniffing goof dust when he took me up
he even offered me some but i had quit by then i could not believe

his name was Prince Triangle
he wore a wooden belt he himself had carved i
had seen children working in a factory rolling cigarettes i
had seen the circus snowball in the August heat adding a ring
sometimes by train sometimes horse-drawn we traveled America
i had gone west coast to east and back again twice
on a long dusty road to the moment in Syracuse she
appeared in the night mist sitting sideways upon Scotch Castle
in the dress of emerald that matched her left eye
Seth strolled alongside with his cane he helped her down
by his sturdy forearm Ahimoth's violin song playing we
all clapped the couple dozen gathered
Seth stooped to hug her he said happy birthday
you were mesmerizing tonight as always
she said thank you Seth you are a gentleman
he tied the horse to the ground stake
my wine-soaked heart pounding i stood by the campfire
and she did not go to them she came to me
i said it has been a long time but you have never left my dreams
she whispered it is the same for me let us wake in each other's arms
we embraced
she went to her mother
Ahimoth finished his song
Alf's unmistakable top hat materialized through the fog he
stirred inside the cauldron of stew over the fire he
examined the food upon the table in front of their caravan
he checked under the caravan and eyed the trash pile
people paid him no mind as he sniffed the jug of wine
i said ok Alf what are you looking for
Ahimoth said he always does this whenever we celebrate
it is as if he suspects our Gypsy ways
the mother tossed her son a hard glance
she said i have told you it does no harm to let him look
i said good God Alf what is next
you will wish to check under my hat for horns of Moses
Alf said you ridiculous boys are lucky i
am hard to offend i
keep my eye on everything
he took Nadezhda's hand kissing it before announcing

happy birthday to the jewel in my circus crown
a few scattered tin cups were hoisted with mumbling
Nadezhda squirming with her arm held said thank you Alf
what else could she
i said well Alf i think it is time for you to hit the road
we will let you know if the cake was any good
Frederick and Vernon averted their grinning faces
Alf threw me the side eye
but he did straighten his vest and slink off
Ahimoth said i did not appreciate when you stole my father's guitar
but you know how to make a friend out of me
now how about one of your strange songs
i took up the guitar i picked it i tuned it i
said to her would you like to hear one
Nadezhda said yes please
i strummed wildly playing one of my funny songs
oh it was a sultry Monday night
i was a hunk of drunk meat making witty remarks
oh i had the words of poets sleeping on my tongue
oh i was a Florida farm hand
i was a rude beauty
oh at the muleskinner's ball
aboard that steamship Princess Hannah Van Buren
oh i saw fast talkers
i saw wheat raisers
Texas cattle grazers
i saw pipeliners
and i saw
i let the note hang
circus boss Alf Jackson
they laughed and whooped
oh he had sacks and sacks of gold
attached to his belt
oh they were dragging
they were heavy from his true blue wise workers toiling with no raises
more laughing and mug hoisting
and the captain of the boat
he took one look at me
he fell backwards with a lantern

oh he caught that boat afire
oh i did tell you i was a rude beauty
i whipped into a mad solo with their merriment
oh now the boat's sinking
and we are treading water
the whole crew
the whole country treading water
oh except Alf Jackson
oh Alf would not let go
of his sacks of gold
and he sank right to the bottom
all the way down
oh in less than an hour
i was back on dry land
in dry clothes with my hair combed
sunbathing atop the Gypsy's caravan
gobbling road
dreaming the aerialist dreaming me
oh i do believe i did mention
i was a rude beauty
they did clap guffawing and her grin may have been widest
i got her the walnut cake rolled up on itself the
shape was a spiral like the cycle of life death and rebirth
she had mentioned such a cake at our picnic
and a present i also found her was
the Deathbed Edition of Walt Whitman's *Leaves of Grass*
the others danced with Ahimoth's violin and Frederick's mouth harp
Nadezhda and i took a breather on the table bench with
Seth who was not able to dance nor was his traveling companion
Vernon who was by the fire in his wheelchair
heating a tin cup held with a rag
i had seen him the day before on his hands
and knees vomiting behind his caravan
Seth the collossal caretaker tending him said can you bring a ginger ale
Nadezhda addressing Seth and Vernon said what do you men think
of this music
Seth said i like it
Vernon said yes it is gay
Nadezhda said i am glad i like it also

she leaned to me with her hand on my knee she
said thank you for my book she picked it up off the table
i said you are most welcome i hope you find beauty
and encouragement on the page
she cracked it open eyeing the holy words in the firelight
she gasped and said look
she pointed to the date listed on the biography page
she glanced at me astonished like i had done a magic trick
like i had created a goose out of thin air
she said did you know you were born the day Walt Whitman died
is that why words for your songs flow so freely from you
i said well i could not say i am no poet and i only feel
like a musician when i have the right guitar in my hands
Vernon piped up he said i am a poet
his voice drew the attention of Seth Nadezhda and myself
when Vernon talked it sounded like
he had been whacked in the throat with a metal bar
like grumbling sandpaper he typically grunted his words
he said most every time i cannot get to my journal they
write themselves in my head and sear the brain but i like them
Nadezhda said well you never told me Vernon we would
like to hear one if you would do us the honor
i said i sure would like to hear one
Seth said me too i love your poems
Vernon's smile lit so wide you could see the gums crawling
away from his teeth his spittle glinted in the firelight
flames licking the black cauldron suspended in the middle
Vernon sipped his hot buttermilk
he said i can i wrote one today in fact
i was listening intently
he said this one is called Chicago
he recited it very slowly
the most beautiful thing
i have ever seen
is rain rolling off a black casket
the poem struck me with the force of a lashing storm
and gathered some water in my eye i had to blink off
judging by their faces i was not alone but i was
returned to the moment by Professor Walnut

Nadezhda's cat hopping in my lap he sure was a circus cat
with a dirty head he battled all the big top rats i
scratched behind his ears and said whoa Vernon
you made a big claim but now i know you are not just a poet
you are a damn good one
he smiled like it was soon to be all that remained of him
like the Cheshire cat he had been vanishing
each day his weight dipping
his grin stretched across his whole face
wonderful and terrifying
Seth said that might be my favorite one yet
Nadezhda said to Vernon that was so lovely you made my night
in the field after the party standing close to Nadezhda
i said Ahimoth was right
i stole your father's guitar
i stole the rich man's potpie
i stole my life
i stole the thief's shot at the silver in Hornbuckle's peg leg
i stole hidden words in a country full of things i could not see
if you speak them i will steal a moonlight kiss
i dipped her as if we were ballroom dancing
Nadezhda said what strange wild times you must have in your head
i said they were hidden yet somehow you knew them
our kiss was so bright several stars retired in shame
our kiss stopped all the clocks within a ten-mile radius
i set my navy overcoat on the dewy ground we laid upon it
she said i fear for Vernon he is not well
i said yes they say life and death each deal us a hand but
i see some who get jaguar claws across the face
i see some dealt hands of no hands they have hooks instead
do you think i am crazy if i hear the voices of the dead
she said i reckon you are crazy but not because of that
there are many regular people who wish upon shooting stars
but shooting stars are dead by the time their light reaches you
i said i ask because Vernon's poem tonight was like a gift from
someone who has already crossed the bridge i
hope he will be free of pain there
Nadezhda said yes i hope he is feeling well when he visits me
in my dreams that is where the dead have spoken to me

that is where i knew you were the one for me i
told you i had dreamed of a man who was welcomed home
as if he had been raised from the dead
well the night before you returned to us
in Los Angeles i dreamed i
was in the grand library of Paris with a winter storm raging outside
a man came in holding a cat the snow whipping behind him
he set the cat down and closed the door and when he stepped
into the light i saw your face you held me and kissed me like this
she pulled my shirt and kissed me so that the moon had a red hue
they had said it was a blood moon but i knew it was blushing
she said and after we kissed that is when i asked you your name
and you said it is Death
but that cannot be true
i have been wondering what is your first name
i said well it is true in the places where French is spoken
my name means death
your dream did not lie
i am Mort

נײַנט

we traveled on 13 months
and the morning did come
when Seth's tears flowed in East Nashville he limped on his cane
i did not even have to ask it was written upon his face i did anyway
has he crossed i said
Seth said yes in the night my only friend is dead i am going to tell Alf
i said i am sorry Seth his memory will be a very special blessing
i hugged him
he patted my shoulder and as he departed wiping his eyes
he slipped on zebra shit
i tried to catch him he was way too big though
i fell with the grieving giant we both laid on our backs in the grass
i said have you broken anything
Seth said i believe all my bones are intact
i said let us look at this gray sky for a moment and think of something funny and good he did
within a minute our tears were diluted we were laughing in the rain
Alf announced we would pause until midday and we would bury him in the evening on the road to Bowling Green his home rolled on wheels
his family was Seth he gave me cash to buy the casket
and the graveyard plot
so i struck out on another
holy quest for the dead before i had finished the other
but there came a shout hey where are you going
Frederick had run me down at the edge of camp
with his floppy pointed ruffle-brimmed hat and the rain running off it
he could have been a young Negro wizard i
said i am going to find the black casket for Vernon

he said do you think you can just carry it over your head c'mon now
he borrowed a pull wagon from one of the menagerie razorbacks
we trudged the mud wood amidst
the devil weeping in the grotto
the falcons in 50-foot free fall
the Indian arrowhead we dug up out of the ground
the moated medieval chateau
the snap and the screaming of the young woman
like she was being tortured
Frederick and i glanced at one another with trouble eyes we
picked up the pace in the direction of the cries they were harrowing
my heart was galloping
Frederick spied the young woman
crawling the floor of the wood in her dress
he pointed and shouted there she is
we left the wagon and rushed to her
her white gloves were dripping red blood slathered down her leg
she had stepped into a rusty metal game trap her screams were the
piercing kind Frederick and i set to pulling it apart she got her leg out
when we let go that thing spring-snapped like an angry gator i
was lucky to retain all my digits Frederick too
she had two puncture wounds to the calf
one in the shin
maybe a broken shin bone
i shed my shirt and tied it to stem the blood flowing
Frederick was placing a stick in her mouth to bite on like
they do for women giving birth or men in the world of pain
he tenderly said we are going to hoist you onto our wagon
we have got to get you to the doctor your leg may need stitching
we will see to it that you get fine and dandy again ok
as we lifted i noticed her Negro features though she had light skin i
did hope we would quickly find ourselves a reasonable doctor i
asked a withered innkeeper inside the first of the city buildings
i said where is the nearest doctor we are in need
he said from behind his desk who is we and where is your shirt
i said my brother and i have found a young woman on the road with
an injured leg my shirt went to bind her wounds now tell me sir
he named streets i said i do not know many streets in this city
can you point the way

he said very well and trembled outside with his hunchback
the woman on the wagon was sleeping with her mouth open
he looked her over and said good God is she dead
Frederick said i reckon not she still has a heartbeat
but she needs a doctor
can you tell us where the nearest one might be sir
the old-timer said is she your kin
Frederick said no sir we found her in the woods
the old-timer said i am sorry i do not know of a doctor for her
i said now how is that possible how long have you lived here
he spoke pointed he said long enough to know i could tell you of
the hospital nearby but you would be wasting time you should tend
to this woman yourselves pour whisky on her wounds bind them proper i
see this young woman is of Negro stock
the hospital does not treat Negroes
there is only one that does and it is not open at this time of the year
Frederick looked upward seething
even the sky was confederate gray
i said well frankly sir that is bullshit
the old man said i do not make the rules you asked i answered
he sold me the whisky and the bedsheet i cut with my knife
she stirred awake and i yelled loudly lady this might sting
she screamed her eyes rolled back into the head again
with Frederick holding her shoulders
i told him we have to get her to the Gypsy she knows healing remedies
we wheeled this young woman back to Nadezhda's caravan
with Ahimoth and the mother out front
they jumped out of their chairs
i said she has been wounded in a game trap
the mother examined her and listened to her chest
she inspected the blood-soaked linen and sniffed it
she said you boys have done good
the young woman moaned writhing
she balled her gloved fists and clenched her teeth when
the mother touched her leg
she spoke to her son in the Gypsy tongue
Ahimoth dashed inside the caravan
he returned with a tiny brown bottle the laudanum the
young woman was crying in Latin and screaming about Ezekiel

and all the crazy boys who have ever been lost in cornfields
she calmed with the tincture and closed her eyes
a small crowd had gathered with the commotion
Alexandre and RT
Fyodor in a damn trifold hat
Guinevere at his side in silk
Seth on his cane
Olena the strongwoman tightrope walker
Nadezhda and her mother removed the young woman's right-hand glove
there was a sharp gasp all around
the young woman had a hole through her hand
the mother pulled the left glove to reveal
this young woman sure did have the stigmata
if she would have cupped her hands to receive peas i
reckon several would have fallen through
questions flew at Frederick and me from
every direction we said what we knew
Nadezhda's mother said the woman needs rest
and to have her wounds cleaned and dressed again after lunch
Frederick said he would stay with the woman
and feed her some soup when she came awake
i said that is good i will go back out for the black casket
and graveyard plot Seth said thank you
we moved the woman to the blanket on the ground by the Gypsy's fire
i slathered the black paint upon the coffin in the city
i paid the undertaker and the gravediggers
i hauled the pine box
the paint and blood had dried upon the wagon by the time i got back
the young woman was sitting up
talking with her back against the caravan wheel
there was an empty soup bowl at her side she was looking like she belonged
among the living again but she did stop with wide fearful eyes on me as i
walked to them Seth making some regular chair look dollhouse size
Nadezhda and Frederick in their company too
i said miss i see your startled expression
but i should let you know we
have recently lost a good friend
this will be his coffin i
do not believe you will be crossing that bridge any time soon

even if you are limping awhile
Frederick said to the woman this is my brother Sloman
he is a alright fella
he has had wild times woven into his name
he stole the dead Gypsy's guitar and plays it pretty ok i
would say if he says your time of dying is far off
then that is a good sign for you he knows death
like a blood enemy he told me his very birth had tricked
the trickster i almost did not believe him
'til i read in the *Los Angeles Times* that he had died i
was sure he was a true goner before his time but he
came straggling back like a old barn cat talking about the good death
awaiting him and the ceremony of light for his kin the spirit riders
i said that is the fairest portrait of myself i reckon i will get so i will let
the paint dry and say pleased to meet you how do you do
the young woman cleared her throat like it was hard for her to talk
she said still sore but much better i
thank you for prying that trap off my leg
i said what is your name where are you from
she said my name is Violet i
hail from New Orleans by way of Savannah Georgia
that was where i was before i took to the road i
am trying to get to Chicago i
have kin there
i did want to ask about the stigmata
but i was sure that would come up in time
Seth said Violet would you like to come to Vernon's funeral he was
my best friend
Violet said well if he was a friend of yours i
would be honored to come hear of his life
next to her Frederick said i can help find you some clothes and crutches
Nadezhda was preparing torches
i said well that is good we will make for him a ceremony of light
Seth was one of those holding a torch the fading sun in his full eyes
he addressed the crowd of 50 in the cemetery at dusk i
held a torch next to Nadezhda my guitar at my back my hat in my hand
Frederick had rustled up Violet some crutches
she seemed at ease with him
i bet she could sense my brother was a gentleman

Vernon in the black casket looked like he was dreaming fireworks i
could not believe it but i did glimpse the Locksmith ducking behind
one of the tombstones
i drifted over a couple steps to see her better but she had vanished
Seth said my best friend Vernon had a soul screaming in him he
had eyes like island lighthouses he
loved poems like the ancients did it makes me hope
friends centuries from now will love each other like we did
he is the only one i know of who could have faced what he did
and resisted the abyss of despair and rage
he was there to remind them of death yet
all he did was lift my spirits and return to me my time of living
i yelled mine too Seth
some other sideshow folks called amen
Wu the Chinese daughter and the Negro woman Bessie of 110
years of age said here here
Seth said Vernon and i once saw
an old one-armed hobo lying in the ditch in Los Angeles
and it got to him so that he made me turn
the caravan around to go check on him
the hobo woke and eyed me at the reins and Vernon peering out
the door he said well aren't you two a pair of odd ducks
i had a mind to let him tumble back into the ditch bed but
Vernon said yes sir but we bleed and choke on smoke like any other
the man said beg your pardon i have not had a meal in so long i
have become a stranger to myself i never knew myself
to be such a grouch
Seth's lips quivered way up high before he beat back his tears
he said so Vernon says we were just about to get
supper going let us tie our horse make a fire and fix you a plate
the hobo said you will be fixing something for a broken soul i
thank you sincerely
we did eat our salty hot beans with a thimble of honey
the hobo produced a revolver and shot himself in the chest
he fell off the seat onto his knees saying i was a painter i
have always wanted to go like Vincent Van Gogh
Vernon lit his pipe and offered it to the trembling hobo
who took it and said the kindness will last forever
with smoke coming out of his mouth

he handed it back got up and walked off into the night
Seth eyed Vernon in the box and said
my sweet fellow prisoner you made the jailbreak
i love you forever Vernon
Frederick and i each handed our torches off
to the women at our sides the silence was our cue
we played our instruments as the sky burst
they closed the casket and lowered him in
rain skated off the coffin
i saw that poem beautiful as he spoke it
i said fare thee well with the rose i
visited him every time i passed through Nashville
he has rolled into my dreams
as the tortured monk who would not yield
Bessie welcomed Violet to travel in her caravan
in every city Alf brought in more sellers' booths
they were hawking electric belts to shock the fat off you
gun powder
gold dust
goof dust
dusty guns
butter buns
wine that makes you recall past lives
scented candles to calm even the most rambunctious of hogs i
did not like the sound of their desperate noisy voices barking lies i
know by their grumbling the razorbacks did not like it
they had to set up and take down the booths
more work extra hours
the extra pay however gone with the wind i
myself did not have time to pester Alf for a raise i
was slitting the throat of a fattened deer for Babou i
was loading llamas in Lawrence Kansas
shoveling peacock shit goat shit bear shit i
got my head shaved again by Fyodor
Nadezhda did not look up from her wash bucket
outside her caravan when she said i do not like you so bald
i said well i do not like leaning back
in the chair for a stranger with a blade i
have never been to the barber in my life i would not go if

i had Rip Van Winkle hair growing past my knees
she eyed me
i said aw alright i will give it a try
days disappeared while i played guitar in the cities i
wanted to know if my new songs were any good
hell yes they were the cup of coins proved it i
was also scouring for the good picnic spots
with a full head of black hair back again i
planned us a double date one afternoon
Nadezhda and i shared the blanket
by the river in southern Illinois with Frederick and Violet
i asked her how her leg was healing after almost
two months since we had found her howling she
said fine Bessie recited scripture prayers and poured honey
on my wounds for a week it worked plus Frederick has been
looking after me keeping my spirits up
without him i doubt i would be limping this good
i said well Frederick once saved my life from a rattlesnake
ready to plunge its fangs into me he is honest and true
definitely someone you want in your corner
i winked at my brother who blushed shaking his shy grin
i cut the melon after a moment
i said speaking of scripture snakes praying and spirits
i hope you will forgive me for asking
but how did you get those holes in your hands
was it a religious injury
Violet said well i suppose you could say that
i was in a convent in Georgia but
i could no longer abide the severe laws of life so i fled but
his wrath will find you i myself got caught in the middle
of a bank robbery not a week later
the outlaw told them to open the safe or he would shoot me
in the face i had happened just to be standing next to him
the banker said we do not have a safe
i was praying my Latin prayers when the man
aimed the gun between my eyes and pulled the trigger
with my hands held out the bullet pierced them both
and redirected flying past my head into the wall i
fell like dead and did not move 'til the outlaw announced that

he felt stupid robbing a bank and that he had lost the will to live
right then and there he blew his brains out
Nadezhda Frederick and me of course had our jaws open
i had never heard a tale quite like that
i said do you still believe in God
she held up her gloved hands
and said well i mean how could i not i
pray to God and Jesus and Mary every night i
pray for the soul of the outlaw who shot me i
pray for the soul of my father they used as the canary in the coal mine i
pray for the queen of the centaurs i
pray myself to the edge of madness i
pray for the wild hog who bolted with the knife sticking in his back i
pray for the hobo coughing with dust bowl pneumonia i
pray for the world of shack houses where i grew up i
pray for Saint Francis of Assisi
and the wild wolves sniffing my tracks
in the dirt i
was with the Franciscan sisters
i said i actually had a man in my life named Francis
he was called Frank and now he rides with the dead
you must get along well with Bessie being she knows
the Hebrew and Christian scriptures cover to cover
Violet said yes she has shown me hospitality
though we do not discuss much i
have seen her in the sideshow speaking the Bible by heart
but when she is off the clock she keeps speaking the holy word
aside from good morning and good night that is honestly it
Frederick said yes she has been a mystery to me i
once found her eating popcorn at the table
i asked her if she had any stories to tell
she said no
i asked her have you seen anything remarkable
she said yes
i asked her like what
she said like everything even a fly is remarkable if you look at it closely
i said well that is true
and after some silence i asked her what work she had known in her life
she said before or after the break

i knew she was referencing the abolition of slavery
the old-timers in my youth spoke of the break followed by
another stretch of hard time at hand i
said to Bessie before or after i am just interested to hear of your travels
and what has been memorable to you in your time
she folded the empty paper popcorn sack
when she finished chewing she said i have been a spy
and she walked off
Violet and Nadezhda lifted their eyes in surprise
i said to Frederick damn
Nadezhda said you know once when we were children
my brother asked her how she had managed to live so long
she quoted Psalms 37 and dumped a cup of buttermilk over his head
all dripping he said why in the hell did you do that lady
she said to help you remember Psalms 37 i bet you will now
we all at the picnic chuckled at this
ten days later in Chicago we were having the last supper Violet
was about to leave us and bunk with her relatives for a while
Frederick and i had carried one of the picnic tables into the field
near the circus grounds we had caught fish in Lake Michigan
we had cleaned the shovels and shovel-fried them
we had bought some vegetables and crumb cake
we had even found rolled candles of beeswax
the four of us were having a few laughs with hobo honey wine
trying not to think of it like goodbye
the circus did come through Chicago at least once a year
though i know when you have a sweetheart
once a year feels like once every ten thousand years
we could see in the distance the crowd streaming through the
board fence our parade had half of Pilsen dancing along with us
and it was the last of the five-night stand
Nadezhda was already dressed in her leotard underneath her shawl
there were some preachers passing out pamphlets by the gate
some peddlers and panhandlers and a man shouting on a soapbox
so loud we could hear him from where we were sitting
he said tonight i am speaking to you as a member
of the mightiest movement in the history of mankind
the socialist movement
it is high time we workers topple the stupid greedy ruling class

the profit-seeking exploiter cannot see an inch in front of his nose
together we can fight back and unite for industrial democracy
join the Industrial Workers of the World
and cast your ballot in November for the Socialist Party ticket
look for my name Eugene V. Debs along with Ben Hanford
i said to Frederick whoa
to the ladies i said Frederick and i have read his essays
and what he wrote made good sense to me
Frederick said let us go say hello to him
we said a kind word to the man and shook his hand he
was breathing fire on the soapbox but he was a friendly fella
when we spoke he told the ladies they would have the vote
in four years' time he had been fighting for it he asked me
point blank now where do you stand in the struggle for free
and humanizing institutions we will need strong young builders
like you and your comrades for the world that is to come
i said Mr. Debs i have seen the smoking child laborers with
hard faces of woe you have a vow from me i will do my part
he squeezed my shoulder with a broad smile
saying young man i take you at your word i trust i
will see you on the road bound for glory
i eyed in the distance the dark outline like the silhouette of death
at our table i said it looks like someone is fixing to finish our dinner
we should get back a pleasure and an honor to meet you Mr. Debs
we walked back i said hello friend can we help you
the figure in the black cloak turned her face to the candlelight
it was Bessie
my friends appeared as surprised as me they said good evening Bessie
i said Bessie ma'am would you like some crumb cake
we were just about to have some
Bessie spoke like an old bullfrog she said i would indeed
Frederick wiped the knife clean and said i will serve it
he cut and Violet said how are you tonight Bessie
she did not answer
louder Violet said how are you tonight ma'am
Bessie said what
Violet almost yelled how are you doing this evening
Bessie said this breeze feels nice
i raised my voice and said sure does

we all enjoyed our slices of cake in contented silence with
the dimming horizon the candles lighting our faces
Nadezhda checked her pocket watch on the table
and i said how are you doing on time
she said i have 30 minutes
Bessie said what
Nadezhda replied loudly i was just saying i have to go
in 30 minutes i soon have to prepare to perform
Bessie said pardon
Nadezhda shouted i have to leave in 30 minutes
Bessie stood drawing all our eyes
she said i have to leave soon too so i will tell you my story
is buried in the word of God i
have been lashed for whistling i
have been lashed in the peach orchard with my dress peeled to my waist i
have been eating out of the hog trough i
have been sleeping on the floor the first 50 years of my life i
have been the white man's wallpaper unnoticed in the background i
have been listening to their plans i
have been spying for the union i
have been remembering everything and telling them i
have been watching their rifles surround them i
have been walking through the field of blood i
have been weeping over the dead battle horses i
have been singing to the horses who came back riderless i
have been eyeing those Yankees leave with all the good horses and not
    a word of thanks i
have been traveling through dust i
have been living in silence in a hole in the ground i
have been making love in a river shanty i
have been giving birth to children so beautiful it was almost painful i
have been dwelling in the light of my five generations we will shine on
fare thee well for now i go to take my rest
Bessie departed our table but Frederick took up one of the candles
i did the same so did the women we were four lights
following her like a slow train
we walked all the way to her caravan
before she shut the door she eyed us
with a warmth i had never seen glow in her she said thank you children

and when she closed the door Violet and Nadezhda were weeping
later that night word traveled to all workers and performers to gather
in the big top for an announcement from Alf
we huddled into the big top after the crowd had emptied
we had 30 performers 15 sideshow folks five menagerie animal keepers
30 razorbacks eight in the rag band and ten others either like
Tomás making the food or like Nadezhda's mother reading cards
or like me and Frederick doing advertising brigade shoveling shit
playing songs
Alf had some grin on him with his top hat growing taller by the day
he said i would like to make a grand announcement
i was thinking grand announcement well
this is not what i had expected
Alf said i would like you to join me on the adventure of a lifetime in
England Belgium France Switzerland Luxembourg Germany Monaco
Italy Spain Portugal and Morocco where we will be performing
for a bevy of kings queens emperors diplomats generals admirals
vice admirals counts viscounts
dukes archdukes grand dukes high dukes put your dukes up
earls vice earls viceroys barons baronesses knights rooks duchesses
doctors artists actors musicians merchants and industrialists
in the course of the next two weeks i
will need you to sign the contract if
you will be embarking upon this trip of a lifetime
our timetable is such that
we will conclude the current season in two months in Los Angeles
we will take our off-season break
but when we reconvene in February
we will perform our way across the country
to New York City where we will cast off and bring America to the world
i found Nadezhda in the buzzing circus crowd when Alf had finished
each of her eyes sparkled brighter than ever
we went out i made the late night fire we sat around just us two
i said you really want to travel across the ocean
have you not heard how deep it is
she said i have done it once when i was a very little girl i
fly through the air i dance with death why would i fear water
i stirred the fire and said well you make a good point
the finger of death stretches across dry land as well as the sea i

Wildcat Dreams in the Death Light

have seen my Aunt J on the boat lean back in ecstasy i
have seen her lean forward looking down in the water
she could have been looking for her husband in the deep grave
she could have been eyeing herself in reflection her head
drooped over the starboard edge like she was about to be guillotined
when Frank and the jockeys came aboard i
did understand why seafaring vessels have women's names
every pregnant woman carries life and death inside the womb i
know you have dreamed yourself as a ship at one time
if i sail with you i sail with hope

צענט

i met Frederick at the breakfast table early the next day
not even many others stirring yet
i said i did not see you after Alf's announcement did you hear
Frederick said yes i slipped out to be with Violet on her last night
i could tell he was down about it i
had a mind to get him looking ahead
i said will you be traveling across the ocean this spring
he said i am afraid i will not i
have made a big decision i would like to tell you without delay
i stopped cold with a cheekful of Cream of Wheat
he said i do not think my heart can take being parted from this woman i
am going to stay here in Chicago i
might even start going to church if need be i
have some money to put myself up for a while i
have seen worse things than some ratty flophouse i
will dance and play harmonica in the street or work in a mill
or i know some metalworking perhaps i will take up my father's trade
i swallowed my food and inhaled a deep breath i
was more steady on the exhale i eyed him again
i said i understand a thousand percent i would do the same
even if i am across the ocean we will be brothers
Frederick said that is true Sloman i appreciate you saying that i
will host you anytime you are in Chicago
i said i will surely pass through then
what did Violet say when you told her
he said well i am still working up to it
i said whoa
he said yes after we parted i was thinking up a storm all night i

have only slept one hour
light was just returning to the sky when i dozed a moment
Frederick stood with his bowl
he said i intend to tell her now i will also see if Bessie wakes up
Frederick returned not more than ten minutes later breathing
like he had been running
i was splashing my face outside my tent with a jug of water
he said in Bessie's caravan the bedding is gone from where she slept
no trace of Violet no blanket on the ground
no Bible not even salt and pepper on the table it is
as if they have vanished
Frederick and i knocked on the door of Alf's big silver caravan
he opened and striking us with the force of a magic trick
out walked Violet in a pair of peacock-blue gloves
she touched one to Frederick's arm
she said i have some big news
Frederick's posture was bolt upright he said what
she said come with me unless you have business with Alf
Frederick said no i was just heading back to camp i will walk you
they strode along
Alf said to me ok what is it i have a busy morning contracts to prepare
i said we had come here to tell you Violet and Bessie had vanished
but now the only mystery that remains is where is Bessie
Alf was combing his greasy graying mustache
he said well she said she is certain death is riding to meet her soon she
paid one of the Negro razorbacks with my blessing they left at first light
they are on the train heading down to Charleston South Carolina where i
am guessing she will meet the mother of sleep in the company of her kin
i said i am glad to hear that
Alf said will you be coming to Europe
i said i reckon so
once you have Nadezhda's signature you shall have mine i
thank you for the invitation
i tipped my hat and walked on
the big news was that Bessie had gifted her caravan to Violet and
Violet had persuaded Alf to give her Bessie's spot in the sideshow
praying in Latin and unveiling the stigmata holes in her hands
i got more gung ho about Europe with Nadezhda
my brother and my friend Violet along for the voyage

i turned 17 years of age on a giant old cattle barge
crossing the Atlantic but there was no birthday party for me
i was near dead on the bottom bunk with the bucket
i must have caught an ocean fever i
was laid up seasick for four days
my brother above me said this is from Nadezhda
he slipped the card in my pocket and poured water down my gullet
he said hang in there get some rest
i awoke in the early morning to a woman's pleasant voice
saying you must not fail this one spirit rider
otherwise you fail them all
the dizzy sloshing nausea tossed me with the waves i lifted my eye with
Herculean strength all i got was to open it a thin slit sure enough i
saw the Locksmith bare-chested as ever with the sunbeam on her
i fell into a dream of eternal night
there were men hawking goods on the moon
there were peasants and nakedly vicious overlords
there were goddesses moaning and guzzling fox blood
there were Maine lobstermen jumping off bridges
there were automobiles at the bottom of the ocean
there were camels beheaded by fiery swords
there were no fathers to kill no mothers to fuck
a world without oracles
i stirred awake in my sweat i
staggered to the head i
must have lost weight in there i
crawled back and woke again in the night i
flicked the lighter Frederick was sleeping i
did not want to wake him nor the two razorbacks
one named Benson had shown me his pistol and said if you
have any problems let me know
but you never know how some people will disguise a threat
i sparked the flame once again i eyed the card from Nadezhda
there was a picture of an archangel with a sword striking a demon
it said *Arcángel Miguel* on top below it said *curación*
why she was having him slip Mexican cards in my pocket
while i had death hovering over me i did not know
in my overcoat i
trudged to the middle of the deck and lay down watching stars

my lungs had never tasted air so brisk i
saw RT the monkey slide by drinking a flask i lifted my head
and said hey you RT get back here
but i lay back down spent and immobile
a young bearded mariner stood over me he
spoke British he said you look green mate
i said i reckon so
he vanished but soon returned with a glass bottle
and some cut up pieces of ginger
he said sit up drink this suck these
i did and the cool water rushed inside my body i
had never felt such nourishment from water
i said thank you friend it has not been smooth sailing for me
he said your first time across the ocean
i said yes i have been on the move for years across land
but the sea is some rough road i have never known
he said aye she is
the motion the mysteries her shroud of fog
even when i am on land i feel her swaying waves
i said have you ever seen any unnatural aquatic animals
he said no but i have seen many strange things i
was once upon a ship and saw a black dog running
around the deck i asked but they all said what black dog
an hour later the ship was sinking i
have also seen the most majestic island off the coast of Brazil
but when we began to explore we discovered
it was teeming with golden vipers
and to be honest with you
the reason i found you just now is that i
needed a quick stroll around the ship to clear me mind
he hesitated i said why what happened
he said well a moment ago i was sure i glimpsed my
older brother in a rowboat out of the corner of my eye
it was only a tiny reef upon closer look but the vision shook me
i said how did he cross that bridge
the mariner eyed me surprised
i said i know death like a dark laugh
echoing through the hills
the mariner said my brother was a doctor

who went to aid in the Boer War he caught a fever
i said i am very sorry what was his name
he said Michael
i said may his memory be a blessing
he said aye
he said i should go i am the iceberg lookout
i said oh by all means then i
do not want to distract you of all people i
thank you sir for this life preserver
i held up the water bottle
he said fare thee well and went way up to the tip of the bow
i stumbled back to my bunk and slumbered again i
woke to the ship's horn announcing our approach to the port of
Liverpool my fellow workers were chuckling when i
fell to my knees and kissed the earth i was not joking though
we unloaded and made camp outside Liverpool that evening
poor Babou as grumbly as ever
showing her years
i stopped by the butcher and fetched her a smoked goat leg
on my own dime she and i were both finding our bearings
the next morning i pawed for the card in my pocket
in my cold tent i eyed it again i
had lunch at the Gypsies' table
Nadezhda across from me we spoke of the voyage
i asked her about the card
she said it is Saint Michael the card is for healing
the Mexican aerialist gave it to me when your death
had been reported i thought you could use it
i told her of the iceberg lookout
the Boer War doctor
the Locksmith
the magic nightmare
the monkey guzzling liquor on the deck
she said surely you are tall-tale peacocking
i said not even a little i have never done that
we were smiling bright
i had a mind to find a ring and ask her to marry me
i kept an eye out for the right shops when we paraded
but i was not surprised i unearthed the one a month later in Paris

the city where Nadezhda had some fond memories
even if i was baffled by what they fed their horses and dogs
every city has its share of shit on the road and sidewalks
but in Paris it flowed knee-deep i
did also see a disheveled prostitute limping with a dagger
and a blind man weeping on a park bench with an owl
and a painter raving and burning his own paintings in the street
and a toothless beggar gnawing a hardened baguette with bloody gums
but as is the Parisian way i was slowly seduced i
found a fine shop in Montmartre where
the shopkeeper was a grand dame of the Belle Époque
there were rams and gazelles mounted to the wall
she said i have never seen a person wear his guitar
on his back with twine
i said i will play you a song like you have never heard
if you knock a few francs off this ring
she laughed delightfully sharp
she said you have a deal monsieur let us hear it
i strummed and i sang
we lay down on that good green ground
with pregnant dreams of birth
stirring up trouble stirring up souls
building a house of earth
i got as much a kick out of her as she did out of me
i had heard many Americans all my life tell me
how foreign i was in the face in my food
even down to my striped shirt but that French lady
said your speaking your singing your habits i do not believe
i have ever encountered anyone more American
i said madame i do not know if i should take that as
a compliment or an insult but i am taking it
she laughed again and said this is exactly what i mean
i left with the ring and though my money supply
had been halved it was worth every franc i
had traded for at the bank
all i had left to find was the right moment i
did my circus work then got the exploring itch i
was a flâneur with a compass a knife and a guitar i
played my songs when i found a good situation i

went down to the Bois de Vincennes
they had some kind of exhibition
of all the colonized lands of France
they had booths
they had artifacts garments and food
they even had three tribesmen on display
one with a bone through his nose i
looked them over but i saw their chains i
did not like them in bondage i
had bought a load of exotic fruit i had in the gunnysack i
cut the tribesmen some pineapple mangoes bananas i
ate with them i did not know a single word of their tongue
nor did they know mine
but we communicated by smiling and lifting the fruit until
some military man came hollering at me i did not know the
French tongue except one word i yelled my name back at him
Mort i pointed at him Mort i said Mort i choked myself i
thankfully disturbed him enough
he walked away shaking his head
i had feared he would whip the tribesmen on my account
i got back to camp with the fruit an hour before supper
Frederick Violet and Nadezhda all got the saucer eyes
i said how about we wolf this fruit it will not be riper than now
Nadezhda said we were just about to get ourselves ready
Violet said you men start cutting we will join you very soon
they left to the caravans yonder
Frederick and i cut the fruit up i had never seen so much
pineapple mango banana all mixed up in a stew cauldron
i said to Frederick well i suppose we get started with a little
he said you know maybe we should i have heard you can
lose some flavor leaving it out
i said plus the flies gather
we ate the fruit off of knifepoint piece by piece
five minutes passed then ten i called out with my mouth full
ladies i do not know what is keeping you but you should return soon
i was laughing Frederick knee-slapping he said c'mon back ladies
we cannot slow down with this fruit
oh my Lord we laughed ourselves silly we paused to save the rest
for the ladies but surely another ten minutes had passed with no sign

of them i stabbed another mango piece i said i will have just one more
Frederick said ok i will also
as we chewed i said but you took a banana
he said i suppose i did
i skewered a banana piece and said there now we are even
he said although now you have had a mango and a banana piece
and i have just had banana
i said well go on then
he took his
i said well actually we have each had a mango and a banana piece
that makes no sense not to complete the trinity
Frederick said i do not sit on second if there is a triple to be had
we speared some pineapple pieces
i said although if we are talking baseball we should end on a home run
Frederick said you mean like one final wild card stab for as many
pieces as you can get
i said now how did you read my mind
we laughed and in total over the span of some 40 minutes we
had eaten most all that fruit
we had some dolled-up hopping mad women on our hands
i said well i figured you two were gone so long you must not
have wanted that fruit
Nadezhda crossed her arms she said i most certainly did want
some i was looking forward to it in fact
Violet said i see their ears are changing they are growing pig ears
Frederick said you cannot leave a giant bowl of fruit in front of
a man and not expect him to eat of it did you not learn the lesson
of the Garden of Eden
i had to steady myself from tumbling over in mirth
Frederick turned and covered his mouth to conceal his
i called out to them as they left aw c'mon we will find more fruit
we had to test this batch to make sure it was not poisonous
we are your royal tasters
oh Lord we had a good laugh in our mischief even near night's end
by the fire i started chuckling repeating his words
the lesson of the Garden of Eden
Frederick grinning
he said now we need to find our way out of the doghouse
the next morning we struck out early and found the patisserie

with the pain au chocolat they must have baked in heaven plus we
got some orange juice several bananas we waited outside their
caravans Nadezhda poked her head out the window
she said i cannot tell you how good that smells
it is like my childhood beckoning me back
i said i was hoping you would like it we have got plenty
for you your mother Ahimoth Violet Frederick and me
Frederick rapped Violet's abode
Nadezhda said i am coming be sure you do not
eat the whole breakfast before i have stepped out of the door
well we did have one of the most lovely reconciliation meals
ever to be had among members of a traveling circus
Ahimoth with his hair rustling in the wind said
i am gunpowder drying by the fire
i run schemes for life
i may soon meet my wife
we all chuckled i basked in the harmoniousness of the moment
which is why Frederick and i were so stunned in our river bath
the next day after we had rolled northeast to Compiègne i
was lathered in soap Frederick was underwater doing a handstand
only his feet showing
the bushes moving in the corner of my eye drew my glance
our hanging clothes had vanished i saw the profile
of young women dashing off obscured by forest foliage
but i knew it was them
Frederick said what in the hell are we going to do now
i said when we see people we will have to run
we traipsed through the wood easily enough but at the edge of
the trees there was a grand city hall even the smaller cities had them
and worse there was a picnic with 200 people in fine suits of clothes
Frederick said well these folks are about to see
a buck-ass naked Negro in full sprint
i said i say we go together i will race you to camp
we flew across the grounds and through the town square
people did stare but the worst they hit us with was
some ladies saying mon Dieu
after all who had never seen a swinging tallywhacker at least once
we were not flaunting our crown jewels
just galloping posthaste for the sprawling circus kingdom

parked for a five-day stand i could not believe we were
not pursued we were laughing in our tents having evaded all
danger if there ever was any
they had left our clothes folded nice in our respective tents
we dressed
we passed the sideshow folks Guinevere must have seen us
she wolf whistled Seth laughed
we saw the ladies outside their caravans
braiding each other's hair all innocent
Nadezhda said you men must have been banished from the Garden
were you ashamed of your nakedness
they were laughing
i said just because you ladies wanted an eyeful
we were all four laughing and teasing
in the evening at the fire Frederick said i love being here
you can find fun mischief when the specter of hanging is gone

עלפֿט

the next day Nadezhda and i followed the river into the deep wood
where we saw the nine wild dogs
the eldest had a long white Methuselah beard
we saw the hunchback pilgrim with the scepter and the scroll
we saw the two-caravan Gypsy camp with the fine little boat
they must have been breeding Shetland ponies
like the wild dogs there were nine
Nadezhda spoke the Gypsy tongue to one of the men
at the camp i said what did you say to him
she said i asked if we could borrow the boat but he said no
he said he cannot be sure if we will return it
the man was young with a black-brimmed hat and a cigar
he spoke smoke
Nadezhda said he says he will lend us the boat if
you let him keep your guitar for collateral
all the Gypsies eyed me
five youngsters four women and two other men around their fire
i touched the warm wood and the strings on my back
i said please tell him i have already come to some trouble
keeping hold of this guitar i no longer let it out of my sight
they chattered Nadezhda said he says he wants to know
how you got a Gypsy's guitar when you are not one
i said ask him how he knows it is a Gypsy's guitar
she asked him she said he says he just knows
i said you can tell him the truth i stole it
she relayed this and the two other men stood up
she said we should go
we turned to leave but he hollered

we kept going but he pursued menacingly with the two others
i said to Nadezhda i may have to draw my knife
i unsheathed it and exploded
like i was in a dog war settled by barking
with my blade tip aimed downward for stabbing i
pointed in his face yelling get the fuck back to your camp
or we will be sailing that boat on the river of your blood
he too drew his knife as did the two others
the color had drained from Nadezhda's face
in desperation she said something to the men
one of the others spoke back
she began to cry
i said what did he tell you
she said he says you do not deserve that guitar and that he will think
of your bones buried here when he is strumming it and laughing
her tears wounded me more than any blade could i
sheathed mine into the scabbard
i said tell him i will play a song for that
woman yonder and if she decides i do not deserve this guitar i
will surrender it to them
however if she finds my song true and worthy
he will give us the boat
Nadezhda told him and he spoke back
she said he says which woman
i said the woman in the black cloak with the eye patch
she interpreted for me in the Gypsy tongue
they burst out laughing and holstered their knives
the man with the cigar spoke for a bit until the woman
with the eye patch growled some hostile words our way
Nadezhda said he says you have a deal he says
that guitar is as good as mine my sister you picked is the most
miserable woman to have ever walked the face of the earth
she lives in the darkness of a sandstorm so thick
that birds fall dead from the sky
when she was a crawling baby her first words were
bury me standing up i have been on my knees all my life
i have even heard her cussing about a rainbow
she once stabbed me for insulting her in a dream
she complains she will never find a husband

but she will never find a husband because she complains
he says you can try your hand young man but she
hates flowers she hates sunsets she
hates the annual roundup of sheep she
hates her twin sister who died in our mother's arms
the world to her is nothing
but treachery brutality frustration and strife
we all walked over to the fire with their whole clan of a dozen
i said Nadezhda could you please interpret to this woman i
would like to say to her miss i have a story to sing you
it was handed down to me by my Aunt J just before she
killed herself it rings true to me all i ask is that you tell me if
you think the song is true and if so might then you find me
worthy to play this guitar it did belong to a Gypsy who i am told
could do anything and after he died i stole it but i got the blessing
of his widow and i believe as a Hebrew i am kin to the Gypsy
Nadezhda relayed my words to the woman with her brother pacing
outside the gathering he smoked quietly he knew if he told her
what to do it would surely backfire and sway her in my favor
he knocked upon the door to one of the caravans
and an old blind man who had hooks for hands came out to join us
i waited to begin while he ambled toward the table
the woman with the eye patch got up and led him to her seat
i asked Nadezhda to interpret the words as i sang
i saw a man
meet his end one time
from a pack of bears
they were giving chase
the man ran up a tree
cussing gracefully
he was dangling there
i was young and scared
and i threw a rock
the bears did not leave
they just laughed at me
and resumed the hunt
suspended in air
like a living ghost
fighting gravity

and the frothing bears
and their claws of death
and the beehive dangling
between the man's two arms
and the swarm did sting
one thousand times
a bear slashed his leg
i still feel the red
in my racing mind
but before he fell
his mouth opened wide
to catch them honey drops
dripping from the hive
he smiled at me
and fell to the bears
and now i know
when them bears give chase
and them bees do sting
when there's no holding on
i know what to do
i know how to go

her stunned silent stillness reminded me
of the monk i had seen icicle-gored
a person frozen upon the bridge
with one eye upon life the other fixed upon death
she spoke standing
with her kin and Nadezhda listening intently
Nadezhda interpreted saying even after all my eye has seen
the businessman sinking in quicksand
the two wild horses fighting to the death
the graves of my mother and twin
the youth gang blinding my father with an ice pick
the authorities burning my painting
the absurd misfortunes one after the other i
still believe in the honey even if it is
one drop among an ocean of sorrow even if it is
solidarity among siblings in a hopeless war
the song is true you are worthy of that guitar
the brother's cigar had fallen from his slack mouth

he remained statue-still keeping his dignity in defeat
i rowed Nadezhda back to the circus camp in our new boat
i was awakened in my tent in the dead of night
it was Nadezhda in a silk robe she had sneaked out
the moon was like a shipwrecked mariner's dream of water
she lay atop me we held each other
she grazed her lashes upon my cheek
she made love to me and left without ever having spoken a word
the following night on the eve of our departure from Compiègne
i held her hand on a lantern walk around the town
she said will you take me back to that Gypsy camp i
have spoken with my mother i aim to bring the father and the brother
to meet my kin i have been thinking of that woman respectfully giving
her seat to the blind father she judged your song true with her spirit of
perseverance in the merciless face of the world
i said i would be glad to see you there safely we can depart at first light
and hopefully reach them before they ramble
i rowed in the early morning with both oars on the river
i said if you would like to offer them back this boat at any point
during the negotiations it is yours
she kissed me and helped me row
and the brother kindly helped on the way back
he and his father had a sit-down with the Gypsies of our circus
there was the wedding two days later in St. Quentin
the bride's name was Mónika
the Gypsies rubbed spices all over Ahimoth i eyed
him in joy like a vision of my future i
played music with Fyodor and Frederick
Alf tried to recruit the hook-handed father into the sideshow
but the father said they would be traveling on
only Mónika would be joining the circus she would be
cooking cleaning cutting hair sketching painting
her kin got their boat back and some money
they gave up one of their caravans to the bride and groom
their party lived into the night i
was leaping over the fire dancing i
was doing simple coin magic for Gypsy children i
was telling secrets through an old whispering stick i
was kissing Nadezhda behind Babou's tent i

was imbibing French wine i
was startled like finding ghosts of my life among the sideshow folks
at their table when i saw the tribesmen from the Bois de Vincennes
i found Alf and said what in the hell are those tribesmen doing here i
saw them in chains did you buy them
he struck a proud posture his top hat nearly floating over his head
like an angel's halo
he said they deserved a better life away from their military
stewards who dress fine but can behave as nasty and brutish as any savage
with us those tribesmen can earn their way and delight the crowds
they will not be subjected to corporal punishment as they had been
i said do you speak to them
how do you know you have not kidnapped them
Alf eyed me with a hard look
he said they are the same as you if they wish to leave
they are free to go i am no slaver
except when i crack the whip on my clean-up boys
he swatted my ass and laughed
i jumped forward saying goddammit Alf
i also did not like it when in Belgium
Alf hired Laura the fat lady and said he would pay her by the pound
she devoured her dinner with a terrible passion she ate whole pies
like every bite she was whipping a horse in a dead sprint to the cliff edge
i could feel some deep sadness had befallen her to get her started
Alf did not lie though when he spoke of performances for nobility
i spied the lords dukes duchesses kings and wealthy industrialists
i learned when they are not drinking blood they are breathing smoke
in Monaco we even set up the whole circus to perform for one person
the Javanese princess of priestly Hindu birth she wore
a bejeweled headdress in the shape of a swan
she graced the grounds afterward with her bodyguards
Alf tagging along the rag band was playing their gay song i
held open the entry to Babou's tent
she strolled inside and kneeled to get a view of Babou
lounging in the rear of the cage
she must have noticed the guitar on my back
she said come play me a song boy
Alf glared at me bulging his eyes
but i looked around i said your highness with respect

you have mistaken me for a boy when i am actually a young man
the princess rose with an impish grin she said is that so
i said yes your highness in fact one other valuable circus tip i
can impart to you is that circuses are magical places
so pretty much they run on the magic word
she stepped closer seemingly thrilled by my insolence
Alf clawed his own face ready to lose his damn mind
she said and what is the magic word young man
i said please
she burst out laughing she said you have outdone all the clowns
young man let us see if you can also surpass the band as one man
i started strumming i said we will see i sang
i am the singer the spies love to hate
they saw me cutting the nobleman's throat
i dream of hogs riding on a ship
my mother hid a blade in her wheelchair
i saw the future slide into the house of mirrors
i was close behind
losing toes
clawing my way up the mountain
to the multitude
a union plan
the curse thinking we could not break it we could
i struck the lightning with a lifetime of fire
i wrote the thunder with the hot glowing words
none of the nightmare kings could touch me
with all the gold i had smuggled from my youth
and the graveyards of rage on the brink of rebellion
i saw the future slide into the house of mirrors
i was close behind
losing toes
clawing my way up the mountain
to the multitude
a union plan
the curse thinking we could not break it we could
when i finished my song Babou had arrived to the bars
the princess was beaming
with an announcement like she was speaking to an imaginary friend
she softly said i came for thrills and i got them

it got me thinking it must be lonely being a royal
everyone around you is hiding themselves with a mask
i could tell Alf had had a royal payday by his cigar that night
outside the food tent he smacked my back so hard i
dropped my waffle he said Lucky Peppercorn you sure are lucky
you almost met death a second time
he was acting aggressive in that hidden way bosses use
when there is a threat behind their smile i
said jeezus Alf you just startled the shit out of me
he laughed and walked on like
he was in a peachy mood saying you are damn
lucky she liked you you have no idea the money
you were playing with i
would have buried you deep

צוועלפֿט

we traveled to Italy where
Alf said he paid the value of a gold brick to acquire Jaymus
the crippled Maltese man who was blind deaf and bald
i did not know how he had lost his arms and legs
Alf advertised that they had been eaten off by cannibals
Jaymus had stubs at his thighs and shoulders
the toothless mute caretaker who traveled with him
in the small blue caravan
spent his free time squeezing apples so hard they would pop
he sucked the pieces
Jaymus often screamed like his brain had become glass and shattered
like he was suffocating inside his own body
he sounded like a creature even death had abandoned i
did have a few quicksand nightmares when he came aboard i
asked my friends around the fire if i was the only one uneasy with the idea
that we might be traveling with captives
how could we know what Jaymus was thinking
he could not even make hand signals
Frederick said Alf has done kind things for me i
will never forget but he has been testing me this past year
fake tribesmen is one thing but when he acquired the real ones i
did not like that either Jaymus bless his soul gives me the willies
the fact he may be kidnapped makes it worse
Violet said i do not know if we can ever know if
Jaymus prefers to be here
but i am glad he has a guardian i
have learned the sideshow cuts like a sword
it is good for some strange folks who might otherwise go homeless i

myself do not mind it is easy work compared to milking cows and if
the Lord can speak through me in a strange place even better but i
know some of them are not a part of the show for the fun of it i
have been praying for a world where everybody has a home
i wrestled in my mind after hearing Violet's words
i did not know if i was angry with Alf or the world i
did not feel the mood was right to drop to one knee
to ask Nadezhda the big question until some months later
when we drank tea in the tent of some Berber nomads
Frederick and i played music with them they drummed
Nadezhda and i rode their camels on our last full day
before boarding the ship to return to America
it had been eight months in Europe and one in Morocco
i said to myself if i do not take ill on the vessel i
will propose in the presence of the sea
well Alf had met with an animal dealer
a German Baron at the last minute
he bought a Noah's ark-sized assortment of baby animals off the Baron
he was galloping with his limp actually helping the razorbacks load them
through the gangway into the belly of the ship
he was barking frantic orders rushing around finding fault with everyone
i trotted with the snarling baby hyena in my arms i placed it in the cage
when i peered outside the ship and down the gangway
one young camel slipped and fell onto the stone dock below
he came close to landing in the water which would have been better
but on the stone he busted both his front legs the bones stuck out i
dashed down with the razorback who had been wrangling him
the camel howled his poor lungs out
the old sun-fried razorback had his eyes
filling as he yelled oh sweet jeezus God no
i said let us help him across
i kneeled to the beast singing Meriwether's ancient hymn
i leaned his head over the edge of the dock with my knife
ready to open his throat into the salty sea
but with two shoves Alf pushed him into the shallow water
the young camel splashed below and burned
two more terrible yowls into our souls before he sunk for good
i rose to my feet gripping my knife i shouted
Alf you no-respect-having motherfucker

that was a living creature who deserved to cross in peace
with the blade and the hymn
Alf drew his cobra dagger with murderous eyes
he slashed my arm
my shoulder bloomed red
he said sheath that knife
but i had a mind to do no such thing with my wound
and the haunting broken camel in my ears
i said i was not threatening to harm you Alf
but you have made the last and gravest mistake of your life
you might as well be begging at the feet of the Angel of Death
Alf prowled around me he said say what you will i only hope
for your sake you know when you strike at a king you must kill him
he swiped again i
dodged and grabbed his arm i stabbed his finger enough
for him to let go of the dagger it clanged the dock
one of the dozen onlooking razorbacks jumped between us
it was actually somewhat heroic
Newt had joined our circus at the start of the trip
he always wore a black British bowler hat
he said what's the big idea kid
put that knife away before someone gets hurt
i said who in the hell do you think you are Alf's bodyguard
some of the men chuckled Newt said i just do not think you
should be threatening the one man responsible for bringing us
all over to Europe and giving us jobs
i said did you not see the bastard drown that camel in disrespect
and then slice my arm
speaking to Alf i said if you had not rushed these animals
that camel would not have slipped
one courageous razorback among the 11 spoke up
an old fella named Marvin
he said the boy is right Alf
Marvin was a gray-haired Negro so the balls that took
to raise his voice i
did not even begrudge him calling me boy
Alf spoke with a dash of surprising humility
he said none of us can change what just happened
but let us all proceed with a bit more care yes

he picked up his dagger and tucked it away
the men grumbling some yeses and returning to work
i sheathed my blade and wetted my fingers with shoulder blood
Marvin tossed me his back pocket rag
he said put pressure on it
you may need needle and thread if it does not stop
i tipped my hat as i passed he whispered
i think ol' Newt has his billycock head mixed up
this trip this circus could not run without our labor
i said i say amen to that Marvin
Nadezhda stitched my cut
i got sick on the way home i was glad it was a sturdy vessel i
was not the captain but i was so weak i would have been
going down with the ship if it sunk
i likely would have been dead without Nadezhda's card
when we were two hours from Boston harbor Frederick
roused me from my bunk he really had to shout and shake me
he said there is bad news brewing on the deck
i soldiered up there to find Nadezhda weeping
in her favorite sweater she wrapped her arms around me
she said my mother is very ill she has a fever
i said we better get her this card you gave me
i produced the image of the archangel with his sword
Nadezhda said i worry it may be too late
i said well then let us make haste
we departed for their family quarters with a swift step i
halted with a burp nearly barfing once more i held it
outside the door i asked Nadezhda may i have a moment
with your mother i will not be long
i could tell this had surprised her but she granted my request
Ahimoth and Mónika were keeping vigil over the mother's bed i
said i do beg your pardon may i have a moment to speak to this
woman she has told me the pillars of a good man when i had no
other guidance she has told me of my death by the mountain
Ahimoth eyed his bride they exited i kneeled at the mother's
bedside i said ma'am it is me Sloman i have brought for you
a card Nadezhda once gave me when i was ill i
hope it will see you restored as it did me
it has even guarded me the past couple days

the mother opened her eyes in a wet pale fever
like a woman giving birth in a creek
with the pain of knowing she will soon die
she turned her head to me and whispered thin-lipped i
carried a hog's tooth in my pocket for good luck i
lost it the day the soldiers pulled all his teeth from him i
hummed incantations over him as he went from living to dead i
loved him so much the sight of him laughing could make me weep i
made love to the swordsman forgive me life is long i
have played tennis by the sea i
have given birth to three children two of them living i
have taught my son and daughter skill and survival i
hope you sharpen your blade with a stone i
will tell you look out for masked robbers i
once stabbed one through the eye i
met an owl in the woods who was my shadow self i
fed flesh to flies and buzzards i
honestly wept when i heard you had died in Los Angeles
what is your first memory
i said it is my father painting blood
above the door with a shank bone
the Angel of Death visited me in my dream that night anyway he
said i have never played by the rules you fool
he pulled me out of bed clawing my arms he
pulled me across the dewy field the moon was gliding he
pulled me to the river and meant to drown me i
slashed his throat with my hidden tree knife
his blood was black like the ink of a fountain pen i
woke in my bed with scratches and cold wet grass on my feet
the mother said what do you hope will be your last
i said in the death you have foretold i
hope to cross the bridge upon a memory
of looking into your daughter's eyes just after we have
been married i will be covered in spices the Gypsy way i
will stomp the wrapped glass the Hebrew way
when it shatters is the moment i die
the mother offered a dim smile with her eyes closed
tears sliding from the corners she said i am glad i got to see
that before i go though i am wary of a hasty marriage i

would like you to wait three years
if you have upheld the pillars
and you still wish to spend your stolen life with my daughter
you have my blessing to ask her hand
you tell her i said this and if she believes you she will say yes
i said thank you ma'am i am slipping this card under your pillow
your kin will return to you fare thee well
i was on my bunk when there was a knock at the door
Nadezhda with her eyes bloodshot said my mother has died
i embraced her saying i am so sorry
may her memory be a blessing to you always
she said as is our Gypsy way we do not lay a hand upon the dead
would you and your brother move my mother
upon a wagon with her possessions i know i ask a great favor
i said for my part i would be honored i bet you Frederick will help
i found Frederick on the deck
he said that is tough news she was not so old
yes i would be honored to give a hand however if you said she died
in a fever i think we should wear gloves and face coverings
i said you know what i think that would be wise
we arrived in bandanas like bandits sent by death
Nadezhda was outside the room weeping in a red cloak
with her uncle Merripen and the lone daughter Lola
Ahimoth and Mónika also mourned
Frederick and i wrapped her in her sheet i
eyed her cold blue face and remembered finding Aunt J
i remembered several moments like
almost giving up my pursuit of Nadezhda
'til i saw the mother walking and gave it a try
the mother's shock when i returned with the stolen guitar
her kindness bequeathing it to me
we brought up a wagon at the Port of Boston
and rolled her down the gangway to the caravan
already unloaded from the ship we gathered her belongings
Ahimoth harnessed the horse
he said would you drive her to our camp
we will make one on the outskirts of the city
the whole circus dispersed for the off-season
Frederick and Violet joined me upon the wagon

Seth Fyodor Guinevere and Wu also followed the Gypsies
we made camp but i slept near the body set apart
a good distance from the others that is the Gypsy custom
in the morning i played my guitar with Frederick and his mouth harp
Fyodor and his khromka
Wu on violin
with Seth pushing her wooden wheelchair much like our parades
except i could barely hear the music
the Gypsies wailed their mourning with screams they did not hold back
when we reached the shallow rushing river Ahimoth and Merripen
led the horse and the wagon into the water we watched upon the banks
Merripen drew the horse ashore and Ahimoth spoke words of the Gypsy
tongue he set the wagon afire with the body
and all her earthly things
blazing like Nadezhda's ferocious crying in my arms i
dammed my tears i wanted to be a steady pillar she could lean on
even though the fire's heat landed like i had lost another mother
i made them all shovel-fried omelets for lunch it was a cold day
Nadezhda spoke to me but it was more like she was talking to the wind
she said i liked the way you all played music i wish i could have used
my talents to honor her too
she rubbed her plugged nose she said although it is hard to trapeze
in an outdoor procession
i listened to her say that
i dreamed her say that
i dreamed her swinging on uneven bars
a moving structure afire on the sides
yes the Locksmith in a fox mask had lit them
i dreamed my sacred duty that
could be registered by them across the bridge
i dreamed America was a giant fucking beehive
i dreamed America was a giant fucking a beehive
when i awoke every city i saw was crawling with automobiles
last time i was in Los Angeles there was only ten cars there
when i next returned there must have been ten thousand

דרײַצנט

starting that spring i did not wear socks for six months
i saw seven soldiers' skulls in the swamp outside Toledo
i made a habit of slaughtering Babou's animals in the moonlight
i ate chilled melon by the fire after a long circus day in August
i petted Professor Walnut and cleaned the cobwebs from his whiskers
i saw a billboard in Texas that said *more authentic than the original*
two whole seasons passed like the dead flash of a shooting star
during my 20th birthday party in Cincinnati i
invited Jaymus and his caretaker they did not come
i knocked upon the door of their little caravan with a plate of
cake Nadezhda had suggested we say hello and bring them some
she was with me as was Frederick Violet Seth Fyodor and Guinevere
there were strange gurgling sounds like someone had had their
throat slit i said hello i am coming inside
i dropped the cake when i found the caretaker's neck a fountain of
blood i yanked the curtains off the window and pressed them to the wound
he had sliced himself ear to ear i yelped help help
i let go pressure when he lamely tried to slash my arm with his knife
that is when i knew he really wanted to die
Frederick and Fyodor rushed inside as his eyes fell blank
and rolled back into the head Jaymus was lying in bed all still
Fyodor yelled Jaymus
Frederick said he is deaf remember
Fyodor stepped to him and shook him
he lifted his blanket
and said my God he has been strangled with twine
Fyodor wound it around his hand and passed it to me like
a strange gift i was too dazed to question i pocketed it

in the tiny caravan with five people two of them dead
i could almost hear the dirt landing upon the roof i
was in the coffin being buried alive again i knew it i had
wanted to at least place a couple coins over Jaymus' eyes
but that caravan vomited me like Jonah and the whale i
stumbled outside bent over shaking
the women pierced my ears shrieking
i did look like a bucket of blood had been splashed upon me i
pointed breathing panicked with my other hand on my thigh i
yelled please go ladies you do not want to see this
Frederick exited behind me he went to them
he said he is alright there has been a tragedy
Alf without warning
burned their caravan deep in the night
and in the morning cinders the scandal festered
we had had the funeral planned i
confronted Alf near his caravan i
said that is the second time you have denied the dead their due i
have not forgotten about that camel
he grabbed two fistfuls of my shirt there was a demon swirling in him
he said you ungrateful bastard you
are damn lucky i do not blindfold you
drug you with potion
and give you incurable leprosy i
know the dark arts that would have you praying at my feet i
am the lord of death i have fought wars that would make you
shit yourself i just now remembered when i slashed your arm if i feel
you are questioning me again i will bury you alive so deep in the dirt i
will demand of your darling the salto mortale i
can make that happen i have done it once i
suggest you keep your mouth shut and live the good life i gave you
before you wake up one day to find it has been engulfed in flames
he shoved me i
frankly did wish to draw my knife but his threatening
Nadezhda pummeled my brain off balance
i had been under the impression Rosa's death was a grave accident
but Alf made it sound like he had had a hand in it
i told Nadezhda at the table before dinner that night
she said i know

i said you do
she said yes this matter has been festering between Lola
and my uncle Merripen for seven years
they have been estranged since Rosa died
Lola blames Alf
he had been pushing us to master the salto mortale
but my uncle Merripen believes no one is at fault
he said we aerialists ride the knife edge of life and death
i said what do you think
Nadezhda like she was a bit agitated said i mourn her
i did not press her but i kept my eyes wide i
burst awake sweat-covered dreaming of a top hat
and Jaymus screaming with the face of a camel i
did not hardly speak for two months until the tragedy in Boston
the windy city of death
it is actually windier than Chicago
plus their roads do not make sense
we had constructed the circus next to the ocean on a gusty October day
the wind whipping i
was not going to speak to Alf but i told some razorbacks unrolling
canvas now this is madness
even the big top will be blown away
the gruff old-timer Tex with his corncob pipe
said our orders are to build it Alf told us if
this circus stopped for every small storm we would go bust
i said now c'mon Tex that is some bullshit you know Alf is rich i
have a woman performing in here
those men ignored me i said to Nadezhda in her caravan you
do not have to perform if you do not want to
she said if the show is happening i am performing i
will go down with the ship this is my life
i tamped down the frustration rising in me i
said very well you know i do not quell your talents
i left while i had upheld my pillars
hoping he would cancel but everything had been set up i
could not believe they were going whole hog
Prince Triangle took a young twin sister up in his
balloon and they caught the tempest gust from hell
the portion of the basket the rope was tied to busted off completely

and fell to the earth while the balloon and basket floated over the ocean
they vanished into the gray clouds i helplessly watched them with the
crowd of a thousand all having swallowed dragonflies Frederick next
to me pointed discreetly to the water he said oh my Lord
that is the other twin poor soul
she was weeping on the shore on her knees the cold salty waters licking her
legs like death's wet forked tongue it salivates greedily every moment
the authorities covered her in a blanket i assume they took her home
the Revenue Cutter Service and the Navy said they would keep an eye
peeled but they never found them after four days i
stole away with Babou and mourned privately for the two torn twins
the one who vanished in the balloon was named Flossie
the Massachusetts State Police arrested Alf in Salem he raved all
the way to the patrol wagon yelling the witch hunts never ceased i
am innocent as baby Jesus you will see
with uncertainty in the air filling all our lungs
the show persisted that evening with Fyodor stepping in as ringmaster
at that point he was accurately throwing knives while standing on his head
Tomás rushed around the grounds having ventured from his food tent
after the show let out i finished my shoveling and feeding i
did a bit of strumming with the ten-man rag band
behind the sideshow singing by lantern light
Tomás said listen up
Alf's arrest is the first step on the long path of
justice he is not fit to buy our labor no man is
now is the time we make our destiny i
have been a coward my whole life
but tonight we spread the word
tell them all to come to Gallows Hill
at midnight we will take our fate into our own hands
i said Tomás you do not have to ask me twice
with Alf's crooked decisions
we have been living in the circus of death i
am with you we need to fight back
the chubby Negro trumpeter Able tooted his horn at Tomás
he said why should i after you denied me a hot dog last night
Tomás said Able i told you Seth came and ate 17 right
before you showed up i was fresh out
Able said alright well next time just save me one off to the side

Tomás said aw you know i do not do requests if i do one i
will have the whole show expecting me to be their butler
Able said fine have it your way he loosed a thunderous fart
all the band cracked up i had to chuckle
it was so loud and well-timed
Tomás even smirked though he said great fart Able i bet
your mother would be proud of what a gentleman you are
Able's grin vanished he said who in the hell do you think
you are mentioning my mother
Tomás said relax i was joking look believe me when i say
we have got bigger hot dogs to grill tonight i will see
you all at Gallows Hill at midnight do not be late
Tomás bolted with his mission i slung my guitar around my
back the banjo man Curtis in his wicker wheelchair said where are you
headed Sloman i was just getting warmed up to your strange songs
a couple others concurred the tall skinny bass player Darth
said play us one more we will be your backing band anytime you ask
i said well i should give Tomás a hand spreading the word who
knows how long Alf may be in the lockup we should get organized
Curtis said now why are you going to stick your neck out with those
radicals you know Alf has money and fancy lawyers he could be rolling
up here any minute i have heard of him cutting a throat a time or two we
are music men i do not see why we need to go get ourselves in trouble
with him he hired us for a fair wage when all the other circuses would
pay us peanuts most the time they only take Negroes in the sideshow
i pondered Curtis' words in an evening daydream
that finished with Alf's imminent arrival
the dagger slitting my neck
my body carried into the ocean with Triangle
Flossie
the gunnysack puppies and my mule i
envisioned him demanding Nadezhda attempt the salto mortale
Curtis said i mean you can go if you want to but i will make you a deal i
have a glowing silver horse
the color of the moon she
has eyes of crystal she
has once sneezed gold dust she
has stomped a cobra slithering on its way to kill me in my sleep she
has brought peace to two warring Mongolian villages she

has walked inside the Chicago nickelodeon all by herself and watched
   a movie
if you play us a few more i will let you ride her to Gallows Hill i
will be there right behind you holding the rope she pulls me
this is my chariot he smacked his wheelchair i
do not see myself going along with some revolution but i
will at least come hear what Tomás and them have to say
i said well
they all eyed me like to say aw c'mon
i said that does sound like one hell of an entrance
they laughed with merriment Darth said there he is hot damn
we played a few more
i rode atop the glinting horse
Curtis rolling behind picking his banjo with the others playing their
tune the gathered circus workers eyed me with smiles some of them
reached to pet her i hopped down and patted her face
i said you have got one fine beast on your hands Curtis
he said much obliged i get a kick out of your songs i
know the others do too
i tipped my hat and went to my woman and friends they
were not hard to find only about a quarter of the show had shown
60 people mostly razorback men a couple dozen with torches lighting
the night Frederick said we were wondering where you were
i said i have been trying to coax the band into coming
it was half the truth
i said are more on their way
Violet eyed her watch she said i doubt so
it is midnight now
Tomás
Marvin
and the Manxwoman Mary
all stepped to the front with wooden boxes to stand upon
torches in hand they stood up high
Tomás in the middle shouted fiery like
Eugene V. Debs but speaking the Irish way
how many of you are satisfied with your wage
there was some grumbling among the crowd
he said how many of you are satisfied with
the measures taken to keep you safe on the job

there were more dissatisfied rumblings
how many of you know Alf Jackson the profiteer of our labor
who is now sitting in a jail cell
has been charged with negligent homicide
gasps and murmurs ran around those gathered
Tomás continued Alf Jackson's unscrupulous greed
and poor management has led to the death of an innocent girl
a twin who perished undoubtedly in horrible terror with one
of our dear fellow workers Prince Triangle
Alf has further exploited one severely crippled midget
who had no capacity to consent to travel with this circus
and ladies and gentlemen i say with great shame
you and i played a part in Jaymus' tragic murder
you and i have stood idly by as Alf has made unconscionable decisions
that by the sweat of our labor we have earned the right to take
the crowd liked that i joined in with a hardy here here
Tomás said Alf's circus has grown bigger and his profits have
doubled in the past five years but have you seen your wages double
or even increase by a nickel a day
our angry cheering grew louder a dozen more workers had arrived
with thundering words Tomás said if anything Alf's arrest
and our fine functioning this evening has proven what i
and you know in your hearts to be true
the boss needs us we do not need him
Tomás garnered himself some roaring applause with this i
was clapping with Nadezhda and Violet i pumped my fist Frederick
shouted into my ear you know he is damn right about that actually
we quieted a bit Tomás said therefore fellow workers i
believe now is the time for us to cast off the profiteer's yoke
and seize the equipment which by right ought to be ours
for the first time we have the chance to control our destiny
and receive the fruits of our labor i
say tomorrow at daybreak we vote to unionize with
the Wobblies of the Industrial Workers of the World
the enthusiasm in their applause indicated we would have a vote
lastly Tomás said and unlike the other unions
the IWW is one big union for all workers
it does not matter your trade
your color

your sex
if you have a peg leg
an old bed
or a gold tooth in your ugly head
he got the crowd laughing with that line
he said that is why i am proud to stand alongside Marvin and Mary
they would like to share a few words with you as to why they feel the IWW
will help steer our mighty ship of wonder to the living waters
the crowd of mixed races far-flung national origins and disparate
customs cheered this note of big-tent respect and equality
Marvin yelled i wholeheartedly support the unionization of
this circus with the IWW i have been a worker a long time on farms
cable tool rigs
ships
trains
every time i have seen that the working class
and the employing class have nothing in common
that is why he may put you in harm's way
even to your death
if it keeps his pockets fat
a few in the crowd rumbled yeah yes that is right
Marvin said and i will give the devil his due i
will say good on Alf for hiring men of all races
however he knows we Negroes have nowhere else to go
that is the reason his profits have been going up and up
but i myself have not seen a wage increase in five years
Frederick blurted seven for me i yelled same
we were not the only ones a few more lifted their voices
Marvin said but the thing profiteers like Alf fear most
is what you see happening before you this evening
a Negro
an Irishman
and a Manxwoman
joining together that is the way it should be because
let me tell you fellow workers our differences
do not matter in the face of our common class struggle
he got a few amens
let me tell you Marvin said
with the IWW an injury to one is an injury to all

that got some more here heres
and let me tell you one last thing when we
but before Marvin could finish his sentence
there came an interrupting shout from the rear of the crowd
we all twisted our heads like owls to get a look at him he
shouted Marvin since you speak of solidarity between the races
perhaps it would interest you to know how the man beside you
calls you a fool nigger behind your back
the murmured words of trouble bounced around
Tomás stepped down from his box into the crowd
he pointed to the back and yelled
who in the hell is speaking that goddamn lie show your face
i glanced at Frederick who eyed me with complete surprise
the fella hollering from the rear said the man you all denigrate this evening
Alf Jackson is the reason we are one of the only integrated circuses
in the whole United States he has always been a forward-thinking man
he has always paid a fair wage
Nadezhda said lift me up
i wrapped my arms around her thighs and hoisted her to see
when she landed back to earth she
said it is that one razorback with the round black hat
i said to my friends oh i know him his name is Newt
Frederick said i know Newt too he is an ass kisser
Newt was ranting he said if you want to ask for a raise
even if you want a union that is fine
but you cannot trust a man who once said to me
hey why is Alf bringing on all these lazy niggers
Frederick cupped his hands and shouted we do not believe you
Tomás was fighting his way through the incensed crowd they
were whipped up into all sorts of passions accusing arguing
Able the trumpeter blocked Tomás' path with a pair of wide white eyes
and a finger in the Irishman's face he said now i know why it seems like
it would kill you to do me a favor
Tomás' blood must have been thumping
he said you are still raving about your lost hot dog
get the fuck out of my way Able
when he tried to slide past
Able said do not touch me you mick bastard i will lay you out
Darth stepped in front of Tomás on purpose

that did ignite some shoving among Tomás and the band
i did not even see who started punching
but i did see Titus down below uppercut a white razorback in the nuts
a brawl had broken out in the crowd
Nadezhda and Violet got scared
Frederick yelled to me over the tumult
we should get these ladies the hell out of here
i said to the women get low stay behind us
i told Nadezhda to grab the back of my shirt
we weaved through the pushing and shouting i
saw one black man and a white man choking each other i
saw Fyodor fighting Juan Carlos the bare-chested Mexican hunchback
he was a new sideshow fella Fyodor bit his nipple off and spit it out he
had blood in his mouth in the torchlight he looked like Count Dracula
Juan Carlos' chest was a face with one eye weeping blood i
even saw RT the monkey with a nosebleed like he had been coldcocked
we were coming to the clear i turned back to the sad sight of
everybody screaming in each other's faces
some folks playing peacemaker getting pulled into brawls
i bumped right in to a tall sturdy man i
lifted my eyes to see if he would forgive it or if he
had a desire to join the spirits on the stone-sharpened edge of my blade
but before my eyes had risen to his face i saw the silver
cobra dagger handle i
would have recognized it in a deep maritime sickness
he also had a pistol he fired three bullets into heaven
he skirted past me and my friends to the startled crowd
like the ghost of himself had returned to crack the spirit bullwhip
and extract their souls' gold
Alf's top hat sat above all others wading into the scared silence
he said who is the fool who has smashed my circus into anarchy
he eyeballed each worker as he slowly made his way past them
most recoiled cowering shamefacedly like beaten dogs
Alf growled louder who here has assembled these good people
to incite hatred and violence
in my circus when we have been functioning harmoniously
for eight years
aside from the tragic accident
for which the Commonwealth of Massachusetts

has recently determined i am not liable
who then who among you
after some delay the Manxwoman Mary replied it was me Alf
your greed and poor management has led to the deaths of four people
many animals have perished unnecessarily too
you are exploiting our labor to become rich while we are
performing dangerous stunts for crumbs with no injury insurance
Alf sneered back well i am glad someone finally had the balls to answer me
he got a few laughs with that he was a showman after all
he said if you do not like your arrangement with my circus i
invite you to quit and work for one of my competitors
and if you do not find their conditions satisfactory you are free
to start your own damn circus this is how America works
Tomás showed himself and eyed Alf severely
he said Alf you know this game is rigged
any one of us could work a lifetime barely surviving
yet your wealthy grandfather
received government contracts to make weapons for the marines
all because his uncle was the president i
have done my homework on you Alf
Marvin found his footing adding with a shout
we are still living under feudalism except this time
it is not land it is capital
Alf roared back can you name me one other circus paying
white man's wages to Negroes and Irishmen yet some thanks i get
if any one of you would like to leave
you are free to run along and make revolution
but for all those of you who wish to stay
you will receive an extra dime per hour
and a fine Christmas goose i
will assume all of you have assembled here for curiosity
but if you remain harboring insurrectionary notions
drummed up by these fool anarchists
in all likelihood paid provocateurs sent by the Ringling Brothers i
will find you out
you will receive the treatment i have given all my enemies
they do not go peacefully
we leave for Portland in the morning
Alf tucked his gun to depart but he doubled back pointing his dagger

he said except of course for Mary Marvin and Tomás
so great is my benevolence i will allow you two hours to flee
if i see any one of your ugly faces after that i
will smash your feet with the sledgehammer of justice i
will box your faces bloody i have arms like jackhammers
people will think a buffalo kicked your skull i
will bathe in your blood in a President Taft-sized bathtub i
will see to it all your family members die blinded and alone
God giving his son Jesus was a small offering
compared to what i have sacrificed for this circus i
have plunged my thumbs into the eye sockets
of outlaw militiamen who were demanding illegal tolls i
have fought the long rainy Indian Wars with arrows humming past i
have survived all the predawn ambushes i
have cut the throats of clowns and kings no one can stop me i
will dream the animal beauty of this circus with blood in my eyes
as death takes me
this is the last time i extend my grace to any one of you
we are already in a war with Charles Edward Ringling
we should not be fighting each other we
load up and head to the station at dawn
Newt wiped a tear from his eye and clapped spurring a smattering of
small applause Alf sheathed his dagger and the crowd dispersed with
a whimper i was hounded by the demon of sleeplessness that night
in my mind's eye i spied
the dead twin strolling swaying ocean vines with my mule
Jaymus choking as the caretaker's twine constricted his throat
Rosa pushed off the plank of a ghost ship
Laura eating herself into the jaws of death
the camel who deserved to cross with the light of a peaceful hymn
our ever-expanding circus the spark ignited by Frederick's parade
death feasting on oozing piles of raw horse meat
the perverse consequences of all good intentions fueling the bad
the more he worked the poorer he got
the bigger the parade the more money in Alf's pocket
the more i loved Babou the more animals i killed for her
the Aztec god who gains power from sacrificing his brothers
my own ego and cowardice playing with the band
making grand entrances on moon mares while Tomás Marvin Mary

scrambled to gather every one of us i should have done more i
woke with the words roaring through my mind like a fireball
Nadezhda's mother on her deathbed
look out for masked men
i knew then Newt was wearing a mask i
needed to look underneath i
peered outside my tent to the night stars of possibility i
was still young i
saw the world's tallest man sleepwalking through camp i
whispered Seth but he did not slow down his steps spoke of a mission i
got dressed with mine in mind i would honor Frank and Aunt J Leonardo
with the ceremony of light and in the meantime the great tree knife at
    my side
plus the small wax candle i would haunt my wrongs with the ghost
    of right
outside my tent i stood gathering my courage in case i had to kill a man i
saw my breath like smoke i
saw six prostitutes in the moonlight on a two-mule-drawn wagon with
an elderly dwarf standing holding the reins i let them pass like a ship
in the dark i eyed Nadezhda's caravan in the distance
i considered circus unionization to be within the remit
of my promised pillars Nadezhda and the other aerialists
had been performing without a net for too long
when trouble comes knocking i do not mope around i
sharpen my blade i sheathed it i
prowled the razorback's section i peered inside
two dozen tents of dozing men with my candle until i found Newt
sleeping open-mouthed with a long-tailed nightcap down over his eyes i
slipped soundlessly through the flap door i
had debated with my temptation to kick him in the ribs
and demand his backstory but i
eyed the zipper satchel padlocked beside him i
set the candle on the tent floor in a moment of hesitation before
i said to myself what the hell you must find facts i
retrieved the sack ever so slowly i
sliced through it like an enemy's belly i
emptied it like the silent piñata i
examined the contents
the rabbit foot

the straight razor
the pocket King James Bible
the brass knuckles i pocketed
the photo locket of the child in the sailor suit
the big black wallet and that was all of it
i shook the satchel to be sure i
sheathed my blade and lifted the wallet
holding the candle close eyeing him
he stirred to his other side i set the wallet on the ground and gripped
the tree knife handle my heart thumped wild while he smacked
his lips back to still sleep i
opened the wallet there were four crisp tens inside though
most notably a solid silver badge engraved with a star and the words
Pinkerton National Detective Agency
i pocketed that as well i
saw the pistol glinting by his head i
reached slowly for the handle he snorted sending lightning
through me i
dropped the candle he
thrashed in the dark i
pulled my blade and
seized the gun he
did not move i
took my leave
the first hint of light glowing in the dark sky
i was a one-man stampede to the camp area of
Marvin Tomás Mary they had vanished in the night i
returned to where i had been laying my head i
said Frederick wake up i have some big news

פֿערצנט

Frederick moaned from inside his tent
i said c'mon i stole Newt's gun he is a paid spy
his besmirchment of Tomás is a union-busting lie
my brother soon appeared fastening his suspenders
he said what did you find
by where our fire had been i showed him
the badge wallet knuckles and gun i
had already unloaded it Frederick hammered the barrel crooked with three
strikes it would never fire again he tossed it in the trash
i said i will alert the camp they have been lied into hatred there is only
one enemy our class enemy i will present my findings at Gallows Hill
now that Mary Marvin and Tomás have fled
Frederick said i will speak alongside you i
think after that brawl our brotherhood can set the example
we can show them how your paint job should not matter
especially in the task of running the boss out of town
i said i know your horseback spirit could out-gallop death but if
there is failure on the horizon again i do not want it to touch you i know
Alf will be circus dynamite ready to explode after i reveal this news
Frederick said well if you truly know me you know i
am a man of action i could not look myself in the mirror if
i did not ride out to meet you and our fellow workers
the more i ponder this situation the more i see for me
it is not personal against Alf
he has done me some kindnesses along the way hiring me for
one hiring Violet for two but along with not raising our wage
while he stacks his money with big help from our parade he
has made some calls that should have been ours i

am ready to make history by bringing democracy to the circus let us
wake our women i would bet my pinky on the chopping block they
will mount the charge with us
Frederick sheathed his blade and buttoned his coat i
knew it was a done deal we shook hands gripping each other's forearms
like how kings shake hands to check for daggers
we roused our women respectively Nadezhda had worry in her heart at
the door of her caravan she said i do not want you stirring trouble with
Alf again you saw how he banished Tomás Mary Marvin he said next time
it will be a killing i have lost so much in my life i
have already received news of your death once i
cannot stand to imagine you truly crossing before you reach the mountain
i said if i uphold my pillars you will not find me sorrowful in death
every moment i see your face and touch your skin it is like honey
from the beehive the bears can slash me to pieces i will keep drinking i
will taste the honey on the other side of the bridge
Alf has a role where all he can do is exploit
maybe he did not want to ask Rosa to attempt that move
but profiteers only have two ideas in their heads
two words in their vocabularies
more and war
i know you are fearless but i have just one question after Rosa
Jaymus
the mute caretaker
Prince Triangle
and the twin Flossie i
pose it to you sincerely who will be the next to die
Nadezhda sat on the caravan step and covered her face
she said my mother never stood up to Alf when he
went suspecting our Gypsy ways i
knew he should not have been urging us to attempt the salto mortale
but you are wrong about one thing i
am not fearless i fear Alf will plunge his dagger into your chest i
fear i will lose my circus life there is nothing else for me to do i
would love to tell you i bake cakes i
shoot guns i
study boulders i
collect ribbons i
play baseball i

dream unicorns i
drink buttermilk but
i do none of those things i
am simply a performer that is all i do i
dreamed last night of a wounded wildcat dying in the fog i
have been seeing carrion vultures out of the corner of my eye i
fear you will fight Alf to the death and even if you win it will be
the gallows for you the ballrooms of the rich and powerful
only hold 400 or so but they stick together with rituals
and blood pacts that would cause the devil to claw his own eyes out
they will avenge their own so if you challenge him
win
lose
or draw you are already dead
i lifted her chin so she understood me eye to eye i
said you mean either way i am already death you know my name
in this life the shadow of death has claimed all
we must steal back our time and labor
it should have been ours nothing is given in this life not even a reason
why we have been born now we have the boss employing spies
might he have them kill us in our sleep i
fight for you and our fellow workers
we will not fail again
Nadezhda said let me see your blade a moment
i said will you give it back
she sniffed and said yes
i surrendered it to her she closed the door of her caravan i
waited a couple minutes contemplating how things might go
i said so what are you doing in there my dear i must leave soon
there came no answer my dark mind leapt to her blood running
out the wound of my blade with some worry i said Nadezhda
she did not respond i said you are frightening me woman i
must enter i threw open the door she was there in the kitchen
blowing on the knife with smoldering eyes they made me fearful
she extended me the handle she said take care with this blade
it has been soaked in poison i know when you strike at a king
you must kill him
i tried to speak i wanted to tell her i had heard that before
but the dragonfly of death fluttered in my throat

she said but you should avoid a fight if at all you can i
saw you at your best with the Gypsies of France i
will be praying for such an outcome
i accepted my knife back and sheathed it
i said will you help us gather our fellow workers to Gallows Hill i
have my pillars to uphold but you are the circus pillar
they marvel at your grace they will listen to you
she said yes you have my trust
she spoke of her love with a kiss
i made haste around the camp clandestinely gathering our forces
Newt had vanished like a hired man who believes in nothing
Frederick Violet and Nadezhda persuaded many with the explosive
news of the Pinkerton spy sowing hate there was crackling outrage
in the misty morning i arrived to Gallows Hill where i saw
a small encampment two caravans and a tent Tomás Marvin Mary i
ran to them they had not yet risen i showed them my findings their
dead faces leapt up like Lazeruses and more poured in the razorback
men they soon matched the number of the previous evening but then
came the sideshow through the salty ocean fog with Nadezhda on that
Clydesdale Seth walking her on his cane as he had at her 14th birthday
party she was on that day in that field a woman approaching 20 years
with her green scarf and red-lipped mouth i nearly lost my damn mind
she sure did top my moon pony entrance it was not even close i
was hoping that would calm us all with the fight the night before
the wheels needed greasing
Frederick and i were shaking everybody's hands
like we were hobos running for mayor
i told Fyodor if he apologized to Juan Carlos i
would let him shave my head and treat them both to a dinner
of biscuits and gravy he did they made up
Tomás said young men time is of the essence
Frederick and i ran up front underneath the leaning tree they
had used to hang those convicted of witchcraft
there was the multitude of 150 the razorbacks
the menagerie crew of a dozen women and men
almost all the performers they were buzzing i
left my guitar in my tent i knew we did not have time
for even one song i launched right into it
ladies and gentlemen fellow workers we were assembled

at this very spot last night
when a man named Newt Crowfoot hurled an incendiary accusation
at my friend Tomás well i had the words of the dead ringing in my head i
knew Newt had been wearing a mask
this is what i found among his effects
i thrust the badge yelling the Pinkerton National Detective Agency
these foul-brained goons have workers' blood on their hands
Alf hired them to spy on you
but i smelled their eggs hatch a new generation of snakes
they could not trick the trickster i
will tell you i have sliced my arm and tied the bandana
for the greatest honor of my life
please hear a word from my blood brother
the grand marshal of our parade
Frederick
he said i will be brief i just wanted to give you what i know
to be the truth of our age
that the owners of our society fear solidarity among the races
more than they fear fire engulfing them
for it is the same either way they know they are finished i
stand in peace and solidarity with my Hebrew brother i
stand in peace and solidarity with my Irish brother i
stand in peace and solidarity with all my Negro brothers and sisters i
stand in peace and solidarity with all my white brothers and sisters i
stand in peace and solidarity with my Gypsy brothers and sisters i
stand in peace and solidarity with my brothers and sisters
of all colors from all lands i
will face down the grave and immediate threats with you all i
will be casting my vote for our unionization with the iww
today is the day we reclaim our labor and lives thank you all
Frederick could juice up his charisma like electricity so strong it
could have killed an elephant the crowd cheered in relief i
think some of them were ashamed of their fighting
they could see Newt's lies and their folly in the light of day
Tomás had his ballots and his box ready from the night before
they started the vote
passing the papers around and lining up to stuff them in
Alf sauntered up calmly except he had white powder all over his

face he was holding up a severed goat head he silenced everyone
in the whole field under a sky the gray of a 300-year-old tombstone
Alf was prowling around with his dagger in his other hand he
said i have made the sacrifice like i always do all is atoned let us forget
this nonsense before i have to fire every last one of you and start fresh i
will do it i will spill your guts upon the earth if i must
Marvin said you are too late Alf the workers have spoken
the final few were filing in one after the other
with their ballots ignoring Alf's menacing presence the best they could
the last to vote was Able the trumpeter he dropped his ballot in
and said to Tomás i did not mean to be a pain in your ass i
should not have suspected you saying those terrible things i
know you are not like that
Tomás tipped his cap
he said i appreciate you saying that Able
all in all i am glad to be on this circus with you
it will be even better in our hands
Alf hovering around the field said ok
i understand you care about more than wages
is that so
no one spoke
Alf spiked the goat head upon the field
he shouted is that so somebody answer me goddammit
there came several saying yes
Alexandre
Titus
Erskine the man with the horseshoes dangling off his tits
Alf said then we will make a charter i will consider your input i
will take out insurance policies for all of you even the aerialists you
have no idea how expensive you high fliers run i will guarantee right now
a 50-dollar bonus for every employee of this circus i know it has been a
tough year that is what has brought upon this union outburst but i ask you
to consider circus business is hard and dangerous you will find accidents
in each and every one of the outfits that travel this great land of ours
i was collecting pencils from folks when Lola the Gypsy daughter
came screaming into Alf's face like a shewolf demon with ten thousand
years of rage tucked in her breast she yelled you selfish
stupid murderer he made my sister attempt the Leap of Death
Alf said i never made anyone do anything Rosa chose that herself

Lola said some choice at 15 when the boss demands you master
the most difficult and deadly of moves within three months
and you
she pointed to her father Merripen
the crowd parted like her finger any moment could have
sprouted into a sword she said you stupid coward
you encouraged us to satisfy Alf's insane whims
you did not even demand a thing after she died
you are like having rotted teeth when
the only meal is stones
all of you you forgot about her but i do not forget
Lola came very close to Alf
she said you will see her when you die in flames
if you do not leave forever
this circus will be nothing
it will be ashes it will be
the smoke choking your lungs
Alf tucked his dagger and drew his pistol he shot Lola in the chest
she collapsed on her knees clutching her wound i could not breathe in the
silence it was like the dream i had had of the dead man hitching my mule
Lola coughed choking she was laughing she said to Alf i will go to my
sister and kin you will die as nameless as piss in the ocean
she tumbled onto the field with blood bubbling from her mouth down
her cheeks into her black hair her father Merripen fought his way to her
Alf shouted so anarchist chuckleheads and mistaken Gypsy daughters
they will be the ones to rob me of all i have built
and to think i had lost sleep over the Ringling Brothers now i
will guarantee each and every one of you a union
a whopping hundred-dollar bonus
and a promise of no further retribution if
you stop this madness once and for all
you can see like the Lord i
have a strong capacity for vengeance as well as mercy
but right now you all have one last tiny window for mercy
take it
Merripen sprung up shouting you will die bathed in flames
your fortune flowing with blood will burn my spirit is a hunter
he was restrained by several in the crowd
Alf said even mercy for you Merripen

as the Gypsy father fell to his knees and tore his clothes weeping
Marvin standing by my side said you think you have scared us Alf
but now you have just hardened our hearts
Lola was right we did forsake Rosa to my great shame
we should have been demanding changes before she died certainly after
but now
with all your spying you still do not see that labor built your circus
we carried it across this country the ocean the desert now i
have a feeling we will be taking over this circus we have built
pending the votes collected in that box so you have two choices
one is you can put that gun down this instant and let the Lord find you
for the sisters' revenge i will see
to your escape with all your wealth myself
or your second choice is if you do anything
besides drop that gun and vanish
from our midst i cannot stop the mob justice coming to you
in fact i will be leading the charge
Alf shot Marvin through the eye
the mist of his blood speckled my cheek i
cried shaking i kneeled to him
he definitely had crossed the bridge in the snap of death's fingers
Alf waved his pistol toward the crowd who yelled
some ducked behind others
some stood their ground hollering back with
all the defiance of a sea captain hurling his rage at the storm
some inched closer to Alf like prowling cheetahs
Fyodor had his knife ready to throw
Alf cried do it Fyodor there will be at least
four more dead i will be aiming between Guinevere's pretty eyes
i was in the huddle of Tomás Frederick and Mary around Marvin i
was trembling with anger so strong it tasted like blood in my mouth i
knew Alf would be taking another life sure as the poison upon my
    knife i
eyed them i said do you all trust me i have a plan to kill him
they gave me intense glances with no objection i
drew my blade i held it Statue of Liberty high i yelled wait
all of you
let my voice be heard for two seconds before any more killing i
have a proposal to make

you will want to hear this especially you Alf i
know you want nothing more than
your circus of death back in your hands i
may know a way
i had chopped the fuse burning to the circus dynamite if
only for a moment with the exception of some grumbling
and an angry voice calling it is not his circus anymore
i had all eyes on me i yelled to Alf so they all could hear
no matter the vote tally in that box you will be our boss again
we will never again mutiny your vessel if
you empty your gun slice my palm and i will cut yours
we will shake hands as blood brothers in forgiveness and mercy
we will make your circus the grandest the world has ever known
John Ringling will fold his tent and go insane
your cousin Andrew Jackson IV will cry and moan for a month
the crowd was really bucking and yowling in their displeasure
Frederick stepped forth from the huddle around Marvin
he said this is a good deal actually there
has been too much death dealt out for one day that is for sure
the furious workers' anger was giving way to the shock of betrayal
Alf hesitated with his pistol like he was ready to put it away if
they would go along with me
there came a yelling overtop all of it
the voice said i agree they should slit their hands i
am kin to Lola and Rosa i can forgive Alf i say
we all forge a new path sealed in the spirit
of blood brotherhood let us let life flourish in this circus again
there were sharp fevered murmurs as they all searched
for Nadezhda atop that horse looking like the secret queen of death
a teardrop down her dark cheek
she announced yes i vote for reconciliation
the workers rumbled stunned i hollered this is what we shall do
our shed blood ends the bloodshed
i offered my palm to Alf i
said empty your gun
open my hand
choose life
get your circus back there has been enough death in this field
Alf licked his lips and eyed the crowd barely kept at bay by

Frederick Tomás and Mary trying to stay their vengeance
for a moment more
he flipped open the cylinder of his revolver
his four remaining bullets thudded
the dewy earth
he produced the silver cobra dagger and gripped my fingers
he gritted his teeth with steam rising off of him we eyed each other
like Viking warriors along the pale blue river he slit my hand deep
and offered his i
had never killed a man
i pictured him as a baby on a picnic blanket with his mother
i was struggling not to give the game away
with my heart jumping up
out of my throat onto the field of death he begged me with his eyes i
sliced across his palm with the great tree knife i pulled it back swift he
clenched his trembling fist he held high his red right hand for all to see
he said here is the hand of peace
here is the blood that will end our chapter
of the immemorial feud of worker versus boss
we will forge ahead united in our common interests
he offered his hand but i stepped backward
he walked toward me but i retreated another step
he shouted why will you not shake my hand
i prepared in my stance with my blade ready
he yelled what in the hell are you doing
shake my hand goddammit
or i will thrust this dagger into your neck i
will dig my thumbs into your soft eyes and pop them
if they put the coin in your mouth i will steal it before
you reach Charon i will spend it on Cracker Jack
you are testing me at precisely the wrong time boy
i thundered back i will not shake your hand after you have
murdered my man Marvin and our lady Lola in front of our eyes i
did tell you i trick tricksters
right now i am hog-tying you in the desert of your mind
you are dying of thirst
the fatal poison in your blood
that is also why i would not shake your hand i
have lost my memories of living indoors i

have dreamed the Locksmith fox-masked playing the
cello bare-chested laughing at death i am the nightmare of Noah's ark
sinking and you are the last of man and beast going down with the ship
there is nothing here for you with your greed and sad stupid vanity
you have spoiled the garden so we will tend to it ourselves i
am coming to my quest for the spirit rider i am so close i can taste
the dust and dirt of the hoofbeats of death that is where i will leave you
to fall upon the earth i shudder to think of your ghost it will be lonely
Alf growled like he might have had some wolf blood in him
he lunged left-handed and swiped his dagger
his right hand was wounded i
had the advantage my left hand was cut so my blade was in the
strong hand i bobbed and danced around him i knew that poison
would be taking effect sooner rather than later but i
still had to muster a bit of offense i sliced his forearm
no one with reasonable eyesight would have called me slow
but he caught me with the counterattack
of experience no young talent can match
he nicked my knuckles enough that i dropped my blade
he stepped over it chugging after me i was backpedaling i
slipped on the dewy grass and fell to my ass
his shadow covered me like the tsunami blanketing some small village
he pulled back his arm to stab my heart all i could do was
hold my hands forward and pray for a stigmata miracle like Violet's
but he was denied his strike
kicked off balance into a battle for the blade
Tomás had his hands gripping Alf's fist with the dagger clutched i
rose to aid the struggle but Alf threw Tomás against me we tumbled
to the earth Tomás was laying on me on his back and Alf got his
clean stab with the left hand he was an ambidextrous motherfucker
with severe fury he buried the blade into Tomás' belly
two deep stabs before he himself collapsed
heaving
death dimming his lights finally
i was twice pierced like by the fangs of a cobra i crawled from under
the rock of Tomás and saw to him he yanked the dagger from himself i
tried to dam his stomach but the river of blood was flowing
Tomás cried aw shit he got me good i am afraid he really did
i said we have you

he said my guts are leaving me
i shed my shirt to plug his wounds
i yelled bring needle and thread we need a stitcher
Tomás said you are bleeding too
i said it is not bad
the dagger tip exiting his back had pierced my abdomen
smiling he said i die as your blood brother
i pressed my forehead to his i said yes you are my blood brother i
have two now i do not know what i did to deserve knowing you
he said will you sing a song for me when i am across the bridge
i said yes i will write one just for you death will hide when he hears it
Tomás grinned in pain he said our brotherhood laughs at death
i said yes our brotherhood is so strong death feels our laughter as
thunder and earthquakes we will laugh in an Irish pub across the
bridge with death's upper torso taxidermied over the fireplace
the whole world had vanished but for Tomás
he said that is good Sloman keep fighting for me and the workers
this circus is ours our labor makes everything let my ghost walk
upon the road of solidarity of men of all colors
and Sloman
i said yes
he said you are beautiful but you do not have much on my lover i
will see you across the bridge let me see her a bit now 'fore i go
i had not even realized the Manxwoman Mary at my side
i had been so gripped i was hogging his deathbed time
i said few have the courage to die for the people
you are the bravest i know fare thee well brother
Mary kissed him she let her black hair fall around him
she said i will not forget your face i will come find you
they kissed in their tears i was misty-eyed myself when
i saw the crowd scatter with the police whistles
at least a dozen of them one on horseback with
the newspaperman in toe Newt must have tipped them
Frederick placed his ear upon Alf's chest
he set the cobra dagger on the heart and clasped Alf's bloody
hands across the stomach like for a fallen king lying in state
Mary was covered in dead man's crimson
she lifted her full wet eyes to me and said will you stay with me
i said yes ma'am this is partly my doing i will face them with you

i collected my knife and cleaned it on my pant leg
Mary said we all had a hand i would do it again i
know Tomás and Marvin would too
Frederick drew his blade he said we cannot let these cops take us
alive nor seize the equipment if they do
our worker-run circus will be dead in the water before we set sail
i said let us stay close i will be proud to die fighting alongside you
we gathered near Mary as she held Tomás the police surrounded us
the old captain on horseback in a coonskin cap shouted
one of you care to tell me
what in St. Peter happened at this circus of death
Mary gave me a jolt rising bloody-faced with tears she explained
there was a dispute and he shot her and him and we thought
there would be a truce so him and him cut their hands but he stabbed
him and we are pretty sure he dropped dead from the shock of it
so the only criminal here has died
the cop eyeing me said you got nipped by a snake in the grass did you
i smeared the blood trickling from my abdomen i said i reckon i have
he lit a long cigar
he said Alf Jackson was a man of considerable influence
his family will want his body and the circus equipment
Frederick said we are a contractor circus sir all the equipment and
the animals belong to us the silver caravan is Alf's you cannot miss it
the police captain puffed smoke with a dubious countenance
he had a quiet word with one of his lieutenants
to us he said how do we know you are telling the truth
i said i can show you my tiger Babou i will prove she is mine because
i am the only man she does not attack she has killed three in her time
he swirled his cigar and eyed Alf's body
he said do not let me catch your kind in Salem again we
will give you the witches' welcome that means fire and hanging
he tugged his horse's reins
Frederick kept his silent eyes watchful the whole time his blade
concealed but ready he would have made a good samurai in another life
the undertaker came and loaded Alf into the covered wagon and rolled him
away i was lying on the blanket with Nadezhda tying rags to my stomach
wrapping my hand she had cleaned my wounds with whisky soap and honey
Mary counted the ballots bloody
and wept when she totaled four votes to keep

things the way they were
and 136 in favor of joining the ranks of the IWW
i could not play my guitar with a bandaged paw
but we buried our dead
with songs in the night after we all had reached the Cedar Swamp
i could feel their hoofbeats galloping among the spirit riders
the Gypsies burned all that was Lola's
i had a finished vision of the ceremony i
had been driving toward all my life
i dreamed it that night
i dreamed Walt Whitman's beard blowing in the wind
i dreamed Tomás and Marvin in a field of rye with Lola and Rosa
Lola had her aunt's cards
she shuffled them and turned one over
it was the man hanging upside down
by his ankles she said this man is in limbo
i thought of my mission and the seven long years that had passed
i said yes it will not be long now
guilt gnawed i lay in the rye and slept at her feet
i dreamed the wildcat sniffing my leg i woke to find it was
Professor Walnut i pet him we passed back through Boston
the city of dead faces the newspaper said in big fat letters
CIRCUS IMPRESARIO ALF JACKSON DEAD AT 48

פּוּפֿצנט

three days had passed since the Gallows Hill killings
when we all assembled
on the Boston beach with a gray sky
like the one that had sucked up Flossie and Prince Triangle
i had said maybe ten words
in my shiva mourning for my Irish blood brother and Marvin and Lola
Mary found Frederick and me in the crowd
she said i never wanted to be a leader
but i also do not wish to be a coward i
chew chaw i
wear this beaver pelt upon my head i
killed it myself
you young men are strong your brotherhood
shines out to the workers they have seen your bravery they like
your parade and your songs i would like you to help me lead this union i
will do it at least to start but i cannot do it alone
we three crafted an itinerary down the east coast
and presented it to our fellow workers
mostly familiar stops with a couple new ones
Baltimore
Richmond
they ratified it
we traveled by the Seaboard Air Line Railroad
ratcheting our caravans upon the flat cars
we left the tribesmen in the care of a Bowie State anthropologist
who said he believed they were Chadian rock people
he said he would be heading to Africa after the New Year
we bid them fare thee well with 500 dollars for the journey

Wildcat Dreams in the Death Light

The Wildcat Circus had kicked off as a stunning success we made money
with that parasite off our backs we were drinking gimlets down by the pier
every razorback and performer
with a new sense of pride and dignity in his labor
we rose to the occasion of our new stakes and the eyes upon us
Fat Ali accepted our appointment to keep the books
we broke for the off-season with
our new headquarters in Thunderbolt Georgia
a mile from the Wilmington River and the Honey Park
good gusts of ocean air at our backs
i said to my three friends
hell how about we all go to Key West for the off-season
i had had some gravedigger i gambled with
tell me about the damn Overseas Railroad
Nadezhda glued her gaze upon all that water rolling by
a shimmer in her eye
we rented ourselves a couple of solid beach bungalows
Frederick and i fished for our dinner with a sun-leathered Cuban
who steered the 19th-century pilot cutter with hooch in his hand
he said i lit off a bomb in Cambridge one fine winter day
and was never caught
he laughed so hard with the boat swaying in the warm salty sea wind
i said why in the hell did you do that Rodolfo
he said i have the balls of a wolf
he was laughing he
said i fucked a woman in the lobby of a skyscraper i did not know she
was another man's girl her man shot me in the leg and spit on my face i
was lying on the street in Midtown with people passing by i asked him
why in the hell did you shoot me he said i know you fucked my girl i
saw you two through the glass doors of the skyscraper
did you not hear me pounding outside i told him i am sorry
the spirits of ecstasy must have swallowed me whole and he said
do you want another bullet in your leg i said go ahead he
fired one more into my leg the stupid ass did not know i have a peg leg i
saw her the next day at her reception desk with a black eye she said she
could not ever see me again or he would kill her i followed him all the way
up to Harvard University he was studying to be a banker i was standing
in the snow i saw him leave his house at five i broke down the door and
shouted in every room to make sure it was all clear then i rigged the

satchel full of TNT on his kitchen table i
blasted that sucker to kingdom come
Rodolfo doubled over laughing before he
said he came back from his seminar
and his whole house was smoldering rubble i
was sitting on a park bench i got to see the monocle dribble
from his eye i approached him in his stupefied shock on his knees
in the street i said remember me i made a honest mistake but your
girl she chose too she chose me so forget about her and forget
about me you can still have a nice life as a bloodsucker but if
i see you again there will be no warning i will subdue you and
tie four sticks of dynamite to your hands and feet you better
shoot me first or you will be force-fed by soft-handed singing
monks who secretly resent having to wipe your ass
hey i got one
Rodolfo lunged for his pole
he reeled some giant sea beast with all his strength we leapt to help
because it appeared the fish might yank him overboard
it is after all the right of all fish to desire the death of man
Rodolfo in his fighting shouted holy fuck it's a Lemon Shark
we had a beach-fire feast in the evening with our women and two of
Roldolfo's neighbors i leaned over to him in the dark by the smoky fire
the five women danced in the sand to Frederick's mouth harp i
said so you never did say what became of that New York woman
Rodolfo laughed with a slick of butter smeared down his chin
he chewed his shark and said you see that pretty little white woman
with the seashell necklace dancing among them that is my Mildred i
came back to her i said i have money saved
how about we quit this cold ugly shit city and go
to Havana where the sun is shining every day i
know it like the back of my wood foot
Rodolfo laughed slapping his peg leg
he said so she came down with me we stayed in Cuba for a year but i
could not work those sugar fields forever not with a woman like that
my life changed when this Spaniard beat me outside the bar he was drunk
and asking me if i had killed his brother in the war i
said how in the hell should i know i
killed so many of you Spaniards i lost count i
will tell you if he visits my nightmares some of you do

he knocked my tooth out and stole my leg i scurried after him
thinking of my woman the whole time i
sniffed his tracks like a bloodhound i
found him sleeping in the boat cradling my leg lovingly in the
    moonlight i
crawled down the dock and hopped back to my woman in our sea shanty
i woke her and said do you trust me
she said who knocked your tooth out
i said a drunken Spaniard who mistook me for his brother's killer he
also took my leg
she eyed me in the doorway on my crutches and said yes
i said yes what
she said yes i will trust you but only
one more time i did not come down south to be awakened by
a drunk man with his tooth knocked out i can go back to New York City
i told her i understand i
will take us to Key West this morning our final destination for
the good life i know where i can get a boat and become a fisherman if
i fail i will rob a bank and send you back to New York with the money i
will keep none i
will serve the time i
will hang myself in my jail cell
she said hopefully that will not be necessary
Rodolfo laughed at that
he said well she packed her things i gathered mine
we returned to the dock as the sun was rising i said
honey darling i do not want you to see this
i crept aboard the vessel with devil's stealth i lit the Spaniard's hair afire
he woke slapping his head and jumped into the water i
commandeered the boat with my woman hopping aboard i
yelled to the Spaniard anytime you are thirsting for a drink
from the bottle of death you come see me we
will raise a glass together my cup it runneth over
Mildred sucked my ear on the morning sunrise ride to Key West if
you find a woman who stands by you if
you can defend her from yourself in the dark moments we all have
when she has her troubles and lashes out and vexes you then
i say you should ask her hand do you hear what i am saying
i recalled Nadezhda's mother and her request of the three years

that had passed also her pillars i kept them the best i knew how
i said i reckon i do Rodolfo i appreciate you helping us find some
food down here i thank you for your good company
he said well i have seen a wild hog strolling through town i
have seen three women dancing naked on the street in Italy with
six men in top hats reaching into their pockets evidently jacking off i
have even heard the pope tell a balding bishop to go fuck himself
yes i tended the black garden in the mountains for some years
so i know when i see two men
claiming to be brothers from other mothers
and it rings true i
get a good feeling
he stirred the fire
i took up my guitar i said are you ready to dance
he said you bet your ass this peg leg works just fine in the sand
we joined them in their nighttime merriment
i held Nadezhda upon the shimmering seashore all the way
to the warmth of our bed i made her an omelette in the morning
and got down upon one knee the ocean waters lapping my bare feet
the sun rising in her eyes i
am a simple man
she kissed me with the gulls screaming in celebration
she said what do you think about a ceremony by the Monterey
Cypress in San Francisco i dreamed of you there on Tu BiShvat
when i was a girl i wrote to you in its shadow
i hugged her kissing her neck i said it shall be there
she said the spirits of our kin will ride out to bless us
i knew because one lifetime with her would not be enough i
needed to find a wedding present
that also could not be fully experienced in one lifetime
i set myself to it before we reconvened with our comrades
in Thunderbolt at the start of February
to give ourselves several weeks to map out the 1913 season
the year of The Wildcat Circus

זעכצנט

we had received no news from Alf's family making claim
to the equipment we rode free and clear that year with
the best of our selves shining like the eyes of rabbits who
if only for one afternoon have outrun the falcon of death i
came to rest in the gentle rhythmic movement of walking
everyone upping their game not with the whip-crack demand
for more mind-numbing spectacle but with the challenge the
artist feels unto himself and with the encouragement and healthy
competition from his peers like that one foreign book the Bible says
iron sharpens iron
for example Alexandre acquired a couple more monkeys to join
RT and what he did was juggle those three monkeys
and the monkeys themselves were juggling grapes all while he
rode the big-wheeled bicycle
Nadezhda got herself some new chalk for her hands she
was doing twisting flips on the trapeze that i could not have even
dreamed i could barely watch for the danger of it Fyodor threw
his blades blindfolded upside down he seemed death accurate but
i was not going to let anybody William Tell me anything Laura
got to curating a collection of some pretty nightmarish jars with
specimens she had stitched together like a shark with the eyes
of a deer there was a dead baby monkey with lobster claws
her work was impressive
she was always going to be a big-boned woman but i
was glad she had stopped making herself sick overeating
at least a few times i had seen her eat so ferociously that
she leaned over and vomited she
set her jars up in a tent where you could look at them

she was also inside sitting in an ornately carved wooden chair
spinning the barrel of a pistol with one bullet inside
softly singing some German song
putting the gun to her head every now and then and pulling the trigger
but she had removed the gunpowder from the bullet
the world's smallest man his name was Dominic
he dressed up like a postmaster and was selling tiny envelopes
for a quarter and inside there was a tiny letter with words so small
you would need a magnifying glass to read them i
did once and the letter was about 16 little people like him
who all meet in the woods to fuck each other
i had a band to play my songs i
wrote 20 that year on the road i sang one in Chicago
when we had all the Wobblies of the headquarters
come see us under the big top with the band backing me up i sang
guarding all the goods of the dead
mine is junk
drinking liquor in the shade
the trees all in bloom
i've been a wildcat howling in the dark
and in the fog
singing all the sweet songs sung
over my grave
good luck
without grace
invites the darkness
i am the darkness howling in your head
our general strike it'll haunt you 'til you're dead
roses coming up through the concrete and smog
the governor's brain turned to glass and it shattered
i saw the viper plunging its fangs into the city
the spirit of the end-times is starting to begin again
the spirit of the end-times is starting to begin again
good luck
without grace
invites the darkness
i am the darkness howling in your head
our general strike it'll haunt you 'til you're dead
i had many outside telling me they appreciated that song

one gambler said she would be singing it with her friends
and the fire knocker said he would be singing it in his sleep
we brought the crowds from Baltimore to Bakersfield
there was not any men and women floating away to
their death and no killing men with poison upon my blade
there was only sweat solidarity muscle and magic
Fyodor was a fine ringmaster and every performer
hitting their pinnacle with the vine-ripened taste
of the fruits of our labor the mood of the crowds even
grew in cheer trailing our disposition
we marched our parades with a hopeful step
out from under the profiteer's yoke
Nadezhda had picked the location of our wedding
so i got the date it had lined up on Halloween
i dreamed of a mule the night before i kept trying to get a look
at his face and that of the rider the path was colorful like
Joseph's coat all the fall leaves fluttering onto the road i
lagged behind but i picked up my step i shed my guitar
off my back and my knife my boots and my hair i tugged it out
all my earthly vanities left in a trail like bread crumbs so some
other could find me with a lighter load i caught up to the mule
and it was Leonardo i hugged him our faces grazed i
kissed around his eyes and wept i dream kissed his nose i
rubbed his ears i said to the rider upon him i am sorry mister
but this mule has been a brother to me
the man tipped his straw hat
so i got a better look at him he said i know
it was Frank the spirit rider
he said you might not have known but from the exact moment
the pistol burst skyward birthing our horses from the starting gate
death was upon us i must have eyed him funny because he
gave chase to me like a crazed starving hunter
he meant to end me on Sweet Kiss' first stride but he
was not prepared for the work we had put in he
was not prepared for the ten thousand honeybees
of desire teeming in my gut he
had no clue Sweet Kiss had been dancing on his hind legs
and balancing on his front ones i spied him do it once through
a crack in the barn door around midnight he and i were spurred

by a lifetime of slashing night knives the fiery swords of a ghost army
there is a special danger that arises in a man when he finds something
he wants more than his own life it is the terrifying wolf's howl that
could never be answered not even by the president praying on his knees
they could not catch me i was riding with you i meant to deliver you
this mule and be a champion in your eyes and the eyes of your Aunt J
i gripped his rough hand with my other arm hugging Leonardo's
soft neck i said wherever you go Frank
you have a championship star in your pocket
you have opened a door for me i would have been locked out of life
i found my woman
i would ride a blind tiger into a castle of flames for her
i would die for her
i have given her brother every cent of mine
400 dollars i presented him with a bottle of brandy
wrapped in a silk scarf the color of these fall leaves i
wished you could have been there to take the father's first pull
and place the necklace of gold coins upon her
Frank said yours is the hard-earned love of the pilgrim
he handed me two roses and they bloomed each one with
Nadezhda's eyes in the middle
i woke in my tent next to the silk scarf
mysteriously returned to me as i slept i
examined the garment and there came money fluttering
with a note from Ahimoth
my thanks brother
with your part we will make a fine feast
and i am pleased to know you will give it all for her
he had returned 300 dollars to me
he rubbed the ritual spices upon me outside my tent
he said when Seth lifts his arm Merripen will bring her we
asked him last night though he said Lola was right i
have lacked the spine to protect my daughters
Nadezhda told him then i hope you find redemption
in the niece who needs you
we fly through the air risking everything
you may honor your daughters yet by saving a life
by standing as our pillar reborn
well i heard him weeping in the night

and in the morning he said he would walk her to the altar
alongside our father's wandering spirit
i buttoned my shirt over my spiced body
i said you know your father's greatness has shown through
in the way you Nadezhda and your mother have spoken of him i
can sense it when i strum the guitar that was once in his hands
you had big shoes to fill in your time i for one see you as a pillar
of our lives now it is you who leaves the trail of giant footsteps
you honor all your kin Ahimoth
he embraced me like a brother
he said i thank you and all the forces that brought Wu's violin
to your ears that day as you traveled the woods
for today i found you a special band of musicians i
have met them once before in Montreal i will see you
at the ceremony brother
Ahimoth departed as Frederick was approaching
in the distance in a fine suit of clothes
he had a pair of spotted mules
he petted the fluffy one and said hey say hello to Pumpkin he
is your ride to the wedding i rented them from an almond farmer
i finished getting my suit on
i said i have not been upon a mule in seven long years but i
had been dreaming of Leonardo last night matter of fact i did tell him i
would think of him on my wedding day he is a spirit rider
Pumpkin his animal kin will help me honor him i
should have known my best man would be giving me a lift
Frederick produced a wooden box from Pumpkin's saddle bag he
said here is my wedding gift to you and your bride he handed it to me
i opened it to find a fine compass with the day's date engraved on the back
October 31, 1913
i said we will cherish this you know i would be lost without you
    brother we
have traversed oceans we
have had death weeping the whole seven years we have known each other
Frederick said i had been wearing a mask for so much of my young life
you helped me learn how to take it off
we still have many miles to go i love you
we embraced i told him i loved him
i have something for you as well brother

into my tent i fetched for him and returned
with a bottle of 1900 Tokay wine
i said i won it off a Hungarian outlaw
in an all-night poker game in New York
he had stolen it from an imperial cellar and told me
typically these bottles cannot even be uncorked without a royal decree
Frederick eyed the bottle closely and said hot damn now this
is one of those beverages so fine it could stop a war
i said and there is one more thing i
have hired a photographer to take five pictures and one i
give to you i have a feeling if you get yourself and Violet in the frame
your grandchildren will glimpse a handsome couple in their youth
Frederick shook my hand at the forearm he said i
was baptized in a creek but i have never felt so good and new i
remember the first time we met you asked me about Nadezhda i
could tell destiny had an eye fixed upon you two i
wish you both the joy of beehive honey
may this day be an island to which you always return
i smiled back at my brother holding his gift
i said well now i will always know the way
we mounted our mules and made a slow steady step
there was beauty in that beast
the great Cypress in the distance and about a hundred gathered
in their frightfully dazzling Halloween costumes
they had been sipping whisky and nut roasting i
could smell the delicious air in the late afternoon light
it was dimming and the carved pumpkins lit our glowing path
i brushed Pumpkin's neck and leaned forward to pet his ears
the misty mystical mystery of Leonardo's spirit washed against me
i saw the faces of the dead among our guests
the hunter who had shot his friend and himself i
was glad to see him in peace
also the camel pushed overboard
the hobo of the Battle Creek library steps
the woman eating rhubarb pie who had sold me my bet on Sweet Kiss
she must have crossed the bridge
Lola
Rosa
Prince Triangle with Flossie too

there a crabapple lump hatched in my throat for Marvin and Tomás
dressed as the card kings of heart and diamond who had carried Frank
in his champion's slumber he was at the front with Aunt J in a velvet
bonnet and across from them the good poet Vernon costumed as
the anarchist Ravachol i could tell by the mustache
he was penning a poem about the Gypsy band
five men and five women whose known origins begin in Chișinău
they were standing ready stage left of the tall chuppah shelter
where we were to say our vows
the ocean sloshed below our vast overlook
the only golden gate bridge in San Francisco at that time
led to the land of the victorious dead
Frederick and i dismounted our mules
his was called Spinoza
i was grinning at my brother while we tied our beasts
the tailor had sure known his craft we
stood next to Seth in our fine suits his cape rustled in the salty
brisk breeze one hand upon his cane the other holding a book
he eyed me from above and winked with a glow like
the pumpkins and the whole west coast on the crest of twilight
ready to break and tumble into the peace of Shabbos
the band struck up with the accordion the violin the guitar of passion
and the way they all vocalized
it was like Jewish Gypsy music emanating
from the secret Moldovan forest of my dreams
Lai-Lai Lai-Lai-Lai-Lai
she appeared in a crimson cloak atop the silver moon horse
her red lips smiled beneath the precious stones shining with
the love that overflowed the wildcat cup of my stolen life i
marveled hard even the ocean calmed with the crowd in awe
Merripen brimmed with wistful pride striding alongside the bride
Violet a stunning radiant jewel herself trailed upon Scotch Castle
so smooth i suspect they had all bathed in buttermilk
the daughterless father helped the fatherless daughters down
and passed the moon horse's reins to Curtis they
tied them nearby while Nadezhda circled me seven times
the Jewish way to form the spirit fortress we joined hands with
her eyes delivering me all the strength i would need in my time of
dying they shone like a village of refuge for a man gone mad with

great raving lapses of what he has convinced himself is poetry
Seth began he did not slur or blur a single word he
said dear friends we gather this fine dusk to join
in marriage two young souls of two ancient peoples
who had once traveled as one tribe and so it shall be again
among a new family we forge here in strength and holy matrimony
do you Sloman take Nadezhda to be your wife
do you promise to love her no matter how old or ugly she gets
even if all her teeth fall out
and her fine face is overtaken with sores
i said i do
he said do you Nadezhda take Sloman to be your husband
do you promise to love him no matter how fat or bald he gets
do you take him even if he is mauled by a bear
she gazed deep into my eyes and said i do
so sweet was the honey of those words i
had become reconciled with death
in the distance down the aisle of pumpkins dividing the crowd
Meriwether Cloud in thigh-high deerskin boots
led sweet lumbering Babou to the chuppah where i
unsheathed my knife and kneeled as they arrived i
pressed my forehead to the beast's i said i love you
more than the outlaw loves the shelter of a good cave i
love you with the wild kindness of a stranger
your fur is more magical than a unicorn's plumage i
will come visit you with good food
during the party i love you forever
i brought my blade to her neck and sliced the string around it
the rings fell into my hand Babou chuffed and rubbed her
empty eye sockets on my chin i scratched her
i said you are the ring bearer of my wildcat dreams
i returned to Nadezhda under the chuppah
drinking every stray drop of love in her eyes like i
had been a poisonous-snake-bit fool released into the river of life
the false king with the crown of regrets was that day guillotined
by her beauty and warmth she marked my soul and showed me
my birth was actually good
i can be Robin Hood
she is the forest the green heart of earth

we slid our rings upon each other's fingers
Seth said i now pronounce you man and wife
Sloman you may kiss the bride
i kissed her like a ghost ship drifting into safe heavenly harbor
with the arrival cheered by a multitude
i stomped the cloth-wrapped glass with the joy of my life
mazel tov they shouted
Seth said ladies and gentlemen with the power vested in me
by the ocean below
the great Cypress tree behind
and the sky above
it is my great honor to present to you the newly married couple
Mr. and Mrs. Mort Sloman
we raised our joined hands with the circus roar of
our comrades washing against us we strolled the pumpkin aisle
with Frederick and Violet arm in arm striding after us we
all met at the end of the path i
did not expect my brother would be gushing with tears
but it was also with Violet
Nadezhda
and plenty of friends and spirits gathering in the crowd
i shed a few tears in the strange euphoria i was laughing
we dried our eyes for the pop flash pictures
we feasted in the Gypsy spirit of so much food the weight of it
bends the tables i could not converse a word with Mónika but
i kissed her foot to say thank you she had the combined powers
of a thousand fine chefs with assistance from Guinevere
Fyodor
Laura
Titus
Curtis
even both bands lent their hands and played songs 'til dawn
we danced 'til the moon went blue in the face
i had a second dinner of apples and smoked salmon
my bride was feeding me upon my lap and laughing
we turned the night to day with our light so strong and good
a chill in the breeze felt to me like death on his knees
feverishly begging forgiveness of people and beasts
i did not forget my sister Babou though it was near daybreak when

Nadezhda and i saw her with a roast chicken she was glad to see us
Nadezhda said her breathing is like a soothing thunderstorm
my bride and i ran hand in hand to the caravan
upon the beach our new home she had known
rolling her whole life
she kissing me furiously said i want to make this place different
she pulled her underwear down on the Sabbath and i
sunk it in and held her we did things to each other that
may not have been legal at that time
we hollered our lungs out i pressed my ear to her
breast and heard the holy heartbeat of the promised land
my bride kissed me to sleep in our afternoon cocoon i
dreamed the bed so warm and good i wept i
dreamed the Locksmith's womb i
dreamed eating melon with my bride i
dreamed the *Pittsburgh Gazette*
and i am talking all of it from editor to paperboy i
dreamed the ghosts of dead cows returning
to the slaughterhouse for vengeance i
dreamed the goats of June i
dreamed smoking the peace pipe with Red Cloud i
dreamed Babou dreaming hawk eyes i
dreamed the Gypsy lips too holy to kiss i
dreamed the friendly posse waiving upon the wharf they
had a ship prepared for us the Locksmith was among them
ready with the bottle of champagne to break upon the bow
i slept like a baby tree i
awoke alone in the evening my bride upon the beach with
the fire fluttering i draped a quilt around her and sat in the chair
next to hers
she said i did not want to wake you from a slumber so tranquil
i said did you find good rest
she said yes though i admit you woke me several times
talking in your sleep
i said sorry about that i do not believe i do that often
she said i cannot imagine what you were dreaming
i said what did i say
she tended the fire and said well you mumbled quite a bit but
i did hear you make mention of the secret treaty of Antofagasta

i said never heard of it
she said yes and you did say time is a hard-hearted bitch
i said i beg your pardon
she said but what you kept saying several times was i have
the skeleton key in my hand now
her saying those words sent me contemplative eyeing the
ocean with my mule and young dogs in the deep blue i
heard dissonant cellos and troubled barking the kind that
usually means the hound has witnessed a murder i
mindlessly sifted sand through my hand with the fading
sun in her eyes she said what are you thinking
i said my murdered mule
she came over to caress me she said he was a good one
she vanished and returned with my ritual gift of marriage
a greatcoat of warmth to the knee she draped it upon me
i had planted her a tree in Key West i said it is a Cypress
like our love it will keep growing after we are dead
she straddled me in my chair and with my coat upon her
she said will we return to see it in our off-season
i said yes if you want we can make the island our refuge
when you are done dancing with death and i am too old
even to lift my guitar i will write a poem of our lives
we will renew our joy into the sand where i asked you
she invited me inside under stars with the taste of sweet
repose we rolled from gold to sagebrush across the land
back on the tracks to our constant labor and travel
the air was cool and good the leaves had crunch i had
my own bed warmed by Nadezhda and Professor Walnut
no more damp earth sleeping until i went to take my rest

זיבעצנט

our circus had a honeymoon too even in the cold we
laughed by our evening fires after the show was done i
had a half dozen people mistake me for a young doctor
in Philadelphia because my coat was so long and stately
we had a grand finale Christmas show for the 1913 season
at Madison Square Garden The Wildcat Circus took New
York City but when the dazzling was over and we had
returned to our camp a couple miles away in Turtle Bay
Nadezhda
Violet
Frederick
Seth
and Duncan the braid-bearded razorback
of Panther Burn Mississippi we were spinning yarns
deep into the wine-soaked night with
the season complete and the day ahead for rest
before our trip down to the warmth of Thunderbolt
an ancient hobo drew our eyes limping toward our fire
on a tobacco stick with his worn black anorak he
had a chewed-up New York City face of scars
with a chunk of his right nostril missing
it appeared a wolf may have bit his ear off he
ripped his tooth out like some scurvy sailor and upon
our gasps he spoke with blood brimming over his lip
he said now that i have your attention i will perform
a feat that will haunt your dreams not even you circus
folk will have seen the likes of it
from his pocket the hobo produced

an apple and a hundred-dollar bill
he said i bet you this money i can hypnotize one of you
into eating this apple
he slurped and wiped the blood off his mouth
Frederick piped up he said i will take that bet
i glanced him with surprise i knew my brother
had been riding in the same world of tricksters with me
when you see a traveling hobo waiving cash and pumping
some hot bet you best check your wallet or grab your blade
i said to my brother are you sure
he said we have six against one he will not con me
Frederick stood and said let us set the terms traveler
the hobo said you give me 15 minutes i will have you so
hypnotized you will imbibe this fruit core seeds and stem
i said wait a minute where did you get that c-note
he said well i have hypnotized half this borough
i said do you have a gun
he chuckled and rubbed the tip of his tattered nose i
rose drawing my knife i said i am sorry old friend that
will not do for an answer i need to check you
he lifted his arms and said do what you must i
need no pistol not with the powers i have
i patted him down and found nothing
i tucked my blade away and said alright then
Duncan and Frederick hefted the hallowed tree stump
we used for a table and Violet handed the man a
mug of whisky she said swish this in your mouth
and do not go pulling your teeth out ever again
the hobo accepted the cup with a bow and plopped
into one of the two chairs Seth had placed across
from one another with the tree table between them
the hobo said much obliged ma'am
he covered his hard-luck face and began to weep
Nadezhda eyed me like to say
something is very strange about this hobo
i said say sir would you like a plate of beans
he gargled the whisky spit it out and moaned in agony
holding his mouth he said this is the stupidest thing i
have ever done you are kind people

he crumpled the hundred-dollar bill and chucked it
into the fire Frederick lunged after it kicking with
his boot but to his dismay the burnt bill was unsalvageable
the hobo cried leave that Judas money it is the
silver of betrayal i was paid to distract you because
you stay awake laughing all through the night they
had wanted to sabotage your circus while you slept
you should secure your animals at once
i whirled around to the menagerie tent
and caught eyes with the bandit keeping lookout
he had a bandana over his face and a gun holstered
in the distance he bolted inside with the frenzy
beginning i told Nadezhda go wake Fyodor
i unsheathed the great tree knife once again and
Frederick's was already glinting in the moonlight
we dashed our asses to the menagerie but were
arrested by the streak of flames jumping up the tent
Dorothy the elephant burst through them
with a masked outlaw on her back
the other four saboteurs spilled
from the tent choking on smoke
and with a stealthy step Frederick and i each
grabbed one with our knives on their necks
i yelled who are you
Frederick shouted to the two others drop
your weapons or we will open their throats
the masked men shot at us wounding their accomplices
one of the shooters caught a flying blade to the belly
doubling him over
the other did not see where it came from he
fired a shot into the caravans but another one
of Fyodor's knives pierced the man's neck he
could throw them to a bullseye in his sleep
my bandit dropped dead with his bullet wound
Frederick's drew his pistol and pointed it behind himself
to shoot my brother's head
but he missed by an inch the gun blasted off
into the night and Frederick with his
free hand buried his knife several

good inches into the man's eyeball
he fell over as Fyodor arrived to deliver
the coup de grâce to the man he had first
struck the menagerie was burning behind
us Fyodor pointed his blade to Dorothy
galloping across the field into the city
he shouted do not let them get away
Frederick and i gave chase flying
like spirit riders in the home stretch
we gained on him sufficiently as they
rampaged down E 50th i was nowhere
near retracing the chain of events that had led me
to pursue a loose elephant through Manhattan
i was footracing with a single thought to get our
beast back Frederick was on the left of them i
was to the right and the bandit atop her fired
his pistol at Frederick who dove out of the way
onto the pavement and at that moment i leapt
like my boots had springs i
stabbed the bandit's leg in the dark he twisted
toward me and shot three times but i had sneaked
too far under Dorothy he was pistol-whipping
her head to make her run faster the city had been
a ghost town at that hour with winter's chill
until the shattering train whistle announced
the lumbering locomotive floating down the track
having just departed Grand Central Station a half
mile south the bandit and i saw it and he leapt from
her but in her fright our sweet Dorothy did not stop
a five-car Mohawk steamer even if it is crawling
has plenty enough power to crush an elephant i
learned in my horror with Dorothy's searing scream
a stone's throw from my face the railway engine
barreled off the tracks along with the next two cars
they crashed onto their sides i pulled my watering eyes off
the carnage to the bandit stumbling dazed to his feet a couple
steps from me and equidistant to us was his pistol glinting
in the streetlamp he had dropped it flying off her he dove to it
in a headfirst home plate slide and with my shadow upon

him i was cobra-poised to strike with the knife
but he flipped around and *bang*
i might as well have been clavicle punched by the Galveston Giant
gripping the great tree handle i brought my fist to my left shoulder
there was a hint of smoke rising from the barrel of his gun when i
fell upon my knees to the hard street
steam leaking from the wreckage
with the cracked-rib broken-leg final breaths
of Dorothy the elephant she never harmed anyone
the bandit scrambled backward with his gun on me
he got up and stared me down
in his sights the dim sky foretold the imminent morning
blood soaking through my sweater
i said upon my knees who are you why did you do this to us
his face still concealed with the bandana his eyes
called to me like to ask forgiveness
and as a token of his apology he did not kill me
he lowered his revolver
and staggered off bleeding from the calf
i leaned forward to get up and blood dripped from me
like the black paint i had slathered upon the casket of
the poet Vernon i crawled upon my hands and knees
to the silent ruins of the future
a hush crushed by Dorothy's anguished grunting
she had her back bent in an unnatural direction
and her legs were so broken she was weeping
i pet her head with my guitar-calloused fingertips
i said this is the second time you have made me cry with
your pretty eyes do you remember when you took that
peanut off my hand
you are invited to stride among the spirit riders in
the ceremony of light i have been preparing my whole
haunted life there comes a day death pops his whip
on us all i am sorry you had to cross the bridge so soon
yours is a legacy of beauty and joy
your death is a crime for which the world will never atone
i will keep a peanut in my pocket for when i cross the bridge i
will offer it to you we will run and laugh now fare thee well
Dorothy barked like she could not believe what

had happened to her body the prison of torture it
had become i sang a hymn of peace cutting her throat
i sang with my head upon her trunk caressing her cheek i
fell over like a hawk had knocked me off a ladder i
lay in elephant blood eyeing my bride arriving with
a band of horse Gypsy healers to tend to my wound
her tears fell upon me with death upon her lips she
was weeping my name Mort do not leave me Mort
there was Fyodor too and my limping brother hoisting
me onto the wagon bed of my dreams sailing unto the
Basilica of the Holy Blood
the eyes of virgins carved into the corners of their homes
the taste of ash
the crown of chocolate
the sun of Jerusalem
the underwater city of refuge for the politically oppressed
guarded by the bare-chested ocean woman swimming with
legs of fish scales she had three heads of animals
the wolf
the eagle
and the dragon
Alf as a centaur upon the sea floor gorging Corpus Christi
he said you think you are making love
when really you are licking the widow's vagina
you earned an enemy who will give beyond the last dollar
it will be my life of fire to unite you with your kin
he vanished when someone wet my whistle
with a cool glass of grass dew
collected off the green blades of an upside-down world
i woke on my back in the cold dark lantern-lit sick bay of
a ship with the maritime doctor's long-nose pliers fishing
in my shoulder i balked yelping he twice said easy son
and smiled satisfied with his white mustache
when he pulled the pliers out and said voilà
he clanged the metal piece in the tray i
felt some relief until he pressed the antiseptic-soaked rag
upon my wound like a ripping hot bear claw from hell
in my grimace he quickly said you will be quite alright
while he bandaged my wound i

said are you British where am i
he belched and said you are aboard the *Beardmore*
we are set to reach Liverpool in three days

אַכצנט

the doctor left me in the room of steel with
some sleepy-eyed old moaning man in the other bed
there was a prostitute kneeling
giving him a Kentucky handjob on the sly
i had returned my gaze to the ceiling when he grunted
she departed grazing Nadezhda on her way out
my bride rushed to me she said i was so scared i
slipped you your card again
i touched my pocket for the good wishes of
Saint Michael i said hazily what is happening
what of my brother Frederick was he wounded too
Nadezhda said he banged his knee but is doing fine
we had no choice but to flee
the iww lawyer said we could all be held liable
for the deaths of the men and the train accident those
men killed all our animals with poison and fire we do
not know who would want to hurt us so bad it is like
Alf's ghost haunting our circus from the grave it had
been going so good
i said he is alive i feel it in my bones he did not die
those star-struck newspapers print the rich man's lies
Nadezhda said if he is alive we will surely be out of
his reach we cannot go back to New York City maybe
even we will be old before we can return to America
i had to shut my eyes for the pain and deep sadness
sinking in i said the ceremony of light i was so close
she embraced me in warmth i was shivering cold
she said i am sorry i believe you will still make one

worthy for them
i said what of our workers how many have come
she said all told with you and me we have 64
the others did not want to roam as outlaws in foreign lands
even the band has gone
they and the departing razorbacks seemed to think
our circus was finished with no animals they said
there would be no crowds
i asked if not a single animal had survived
she said Alexandre's three monkeys and
your sweet Babou she got lucky with her tent set aside
i said oh Lord praise Hashem
i pondered a moment further i
said perhaps in the long run we should
ride without the menagerie i see how those animals
are acquired i see how they suffer in bondage i have
had to slice a throat every now and then when some
accident befalls them i say we keep Babou and have
her live out her days with us but from now on
aside from his monkeys and the horses we need
we should leave the animals living in their fields
Nadezhda said but what if those razorbacks are
right what if the crowds will not come back to us
i said well long as you are flying upon that trapeze like
some falcon's ghost i am not worried for our circus
she touched my hand with a glimmer in the eye
Frederick limping with Violet joined us in the room
i could barely feel my wound my friends brought
such a cheer to my seasick sloshing stomach
Frederick said any time i am down i look at these
he held the wedding pictures to the lantern
they appeared to me as images of a holy pilgrimage
i said to my brother i am sorry to hear
you banged your knee
he said well it is not much compared to a bullet i
have been walking ok and will regain my speed soon
the old man in the bed across the room stirred
drawing our eyes he spoke in a French accent
with his gray beard he said so you have been shot

i said yes sir i was
he said did you shoot him back
Frederick studied the old man in silence
i said well i am a blade man i stabbed his leg
the old man coughed he said that is good
there is honor in the blade most all men
with guns do not have the courage to look
into the dying eyes of the man they have shot
i said yes i reckon that is rightly so for many
and even worse are the cowards who give others
the gun and send them on their dirty work that i
believe is the case with the man who shot me
the old man sprung up in his bed with bugging
eyes he said that is the future i have dreamed
the whole of France exploding in flames i
smoked opium with dwarf whores
on the banks of the Neversink River
one last celebration before i meet my end
in the tsunami of death that will envelop Europe
and the whole hemisphere we are sleepwalking
into the age of frightened pilgrims who
with their guns follow rules of kill or be killed
a pestilence of insane orders and mass obedience
America has been gun crazy from the beginning
but what will happen in Europe will not be some Wild West shootout
it will be more like the Laki eruption of 1783
do you see what i am saying i am talking about fat rats
feasting upon the dead as far as the eye can see
Frederick said if what you say comes to pass
what then is a fellow to do
the old man said he must live and die with honor
you may have seen me in every brothel in America
but i will never pick up a gun for some rich swine
snapping his fingers i have heard your problems your
departed razorbacks are right the crowds will not
come to your show without animals they will not
come to your show because the politicians and
profiteers who grind the common man into the
dingy and mean streets want it all for themselves

Wildcat Dreams in the Death Light

and nothing for others and most importantly
the people will not come to your show for
they have been seduced by the nickelodeon i
know my brother and sister used to make
pictures in Hollywood but they have been
exiled like violent outlaws for the crime of
incest well i say it is their right to fool around
if you take me to them in Paris they will make
you a motion picture that will bring back your audience i
am too ill to travel on my own
the shell of a man you see before you will be you someday
have pity you will think of me at the end
you will say my God that old man
that was me
that was me
that was me
my friends and i all eyed each other unsure
Nadezhda said sir we would take you down
to Paris if it was our road but we had to leave in
such haste that our accommodations on this ship
emptied our coffers we will have to tour
England for at least one month i do not think
that would be agreeable to you
he lay back on his back wheezing he
said three shows if you perform three shows
and you find success in one you can leave me
in some hospital and tour England as planned
but if all three go bust how about we all then
head directly to Paris i bet we will
i spoke on deck with my friends Frederick said
should we trust this man what do you all think
Violet said it seems unlikely he has some posse
in waiting to ambush us again
Nadezhda said i agree what have we got to lose
we gathered our remaining fellow workers after dinner
and coaxed them into giving the old man's deal a try
their mood echoed our women
they said what the hell it seems unlikely
we would not draw a crowd in three tries

but without our animals anything can happen
we frolicked in our small parade with my guitar
Frederick's mouth harp
Seth wheeling Wu with her violin
Fyodor's khromka accordion
Alexandre on the bike with his monkeys
one riding atop Babou's back
Nadezhda walking torch in hand
it was like back in the early days
but in the fire-breathing industrial desert of Liverpool
they did not have two pence to spare
nor hardly a crust of bread
that poorhouse country dined upon crumbs
smoke
and socialist hope
we traveled on with the sick old man
his name was Charles-Auguste
he had a nose for the future we had not been able
to summon more than 150 under our tent
striking out zero-for-three like he predicted
i stayed up with him by the fire and played a song i
wrote thinking of his words i said this one is called
That Was Me
he had an eyes-closed smile lying on the ground
in the flickering firelight while i sang him to sleep
i bid him a quiet goodnight and joined Frederick
by another fire
we talked about our imminent return to Paris
and what we might do in this motion picture
i said say when that New York hobo
came to our camp i have been meaning to ask why it
seemed you were so awfully hot for that hundred dollars
Frederick sunk into his chair he said well now i am
embarrassed about it but i had a mind to set myself up
a little better for my life with Violet i was fixing to find
a fine ring and throw her a wedding party with all the trimmings
i perked up i said did you ask her
he said not yet
i said well when you need that hundred dollars

let me know because i would like to offer you a trade
he said for what
i said i need your metalworking expertise i
know you have some from working with your father
he eyed the fire and said that was a long time ago
i said i bet it will come back to you if you get the tools in hand i
only need a simple sturdy structure of bars on wheels i dreamed
he said now what do you need a simple sturdy structure of bars on
wheels for
i said for the ceremony of light
he said you have been talking about that for a long time
i said that is true but i will do it
he said i bet you will
i said i will give you a hundred dollars tonight if you just promise
you will help me give it a try
he said i did not know getting shot makes a man lose his mind
i jumped up out of my chair i said i will take that as a yes
he called after me saying are you even serious
on my way to my caravan i saw Charles-Auguste lying on the earth
next to a small fire with a prostitute sucking on his limp tallywhacker
she flicked it with her finger and it just flopped over
she said have you gone to sleep on me sir
she rubbed his belly but he did not move
with some panic in her voice she said wake up sir
she turned to see me stunned like i had been betrayed
by some slick-talking angel she contorted her face
in trembling horror saying oh i am certainly damned now
sucking on the penis of the dead
the more she wept the more beautiful she became
she might have even been Italian
i checked his breath to know for true
i said now dear he was walking the tightrope
since i met him you did not do anything wrong
did you get your money i know you are not sucking
on some withered tallywhacker for the fun of it
she eyed me like we had gone in on a secret
she softly said yes i thank you sir
a pipe-smoking man on horseback appeared
she climbed up with him and they vanished

into the wild dark of night
Frederick and i wrapped Charles-Auguste in a blanket
we smuggled him upon a wagon and inside a ship
i searched for my money before we boarded and
discovered Nadezhda had given it away to help
keep our circus afloat she told me in our caravan
Mary had bribed two policemen to let us leave New York
she had to buy out some beekeepers who had already
booked passage on the vessel it was all hands on deck
Nadezhda poured me a mug
of huckleberry mountain wine and asked if i was angry
i said no your brother returned that money to me in
generosity i say we help our circus in the same spirit but i
do know i need to find the incestuous siblings
of the dead prophet of doom
when we landed in Le Havre i had to tell my brother i
actually did not have a hundred dollars for him at that moment
he looked up from pounding a tent stake he said oh
that is alright i had guessed it was campfire talk
i said it was truthful campfire talk i
will follow through on my promises they
are just on hold 'til we find those siblings
and make our motion picture
he hit me with a dubious eye
i said now do not go getting skeptical on me
we will find them
he said alright i hope we will
but the next day there was the razorback Duncan digging
a hole with Fyodor on the edge of camp
next to Charles-Auguste wrapped in his blanket of death
i said now what in the hell do you two think you are doing
Fyodor wiped his brow saying i am sorry comrade
but this body is beginning to stink
i said well i know it is i
just think we ought to deliver him to his kin is all
as a show of respect which might sway them
to make the motion picture he was talking about i
worry for our circus if
we do not have some new way to draw the crowds

Wildcat Dreams in the Death Light

Duncan leaned against his shovel and spit
he said goddamn those nickelodeons
i said i say the same but people flock to them
all i ask is two days for us to reach Paris and one day
for me to find the brother and sister in the city
after that i will bury him myself
they hesitated in their response but i said if you
remember it was our past master Alf who did not
allow the dead their due he kicked camels into the ocean
Duncan said well alright i will keep the razorbacks at bay
Fyodor handed me his shovel and said you have 72 hours
i wrapped Charles-Auguste in another blanket and sprinkled
some of my bride's perfume on him and we traveled on to the
City of Lights i ran the gauntlet empty-handed all day i had had
12 hours of walking talking and seeking with nothing
i sang for my supper
i was wolfing a crêpe in Montparnasse when i stood and
announced to the whole restaurant well where in the hell
are the goddamn filmmakers around here
they all laughed especially this table
of five dandy-dressed young adults my age
i marched up to them and said is there something funny i
should know about do any of you even speak English
the woman in the peacock-feather hat said you have some luck
this woman here by this time next year
will be the most famous actress in all of Paris
it turned out that dining there with her friends was
Musidora
like the strange dangerous beauty of magma flowing at night
she knew the brother and sister Jean-Jacques and Juliette
she wrote me their address in my book
she said they have been exiled from America yet
they still long for the dream of its big wild spirit
if you can give them America they will give you the world
before i left Musidora leaned back and said how about a song
with your guitar
so i played one in gratitude and of the three men
with their suits and ceaseless cigarettes the one who was the son of
the Greek ambassador was snapping his fingers and Musidora put a

peacock feather in my cap saying your music is strange and good
i arrived to the siblings' manor by ten o'clock it was
like a small castle on the edge of the Parc Montsouris
i rapped upon the door and said hello i have news i
do not have time to waste
the door creaked open by the butler's hand a Spanish man
with olive oil flowing in his veins i said i am here with some
tough news for Juliette and Jean-Jacques may i see them
the butler motioned me in to the living room where a naked
young woman lay upon a mink carpet before the roaring
fireplace the butler said wait here i will summon them
i sat in the chair with the woman eyeing me she rose
with her breasts and nakedness taking my breath away
she said are you American i said yes ma'am
she said i am an actress i dream of America i
dream of the boatloads of migrants
the New York City hoopskirts
the Texas oilmen limping in thousand-dollar suits
one day i will take Hollywood
and America will dream me
she prowled toward me like a puma and bit my ear
i said hey lady
she laughed and said i am the feeling you got when
you peered over the edge of the cliff
my tallywhacker swelled in my pants
i said oh dear Lord i want the death by the mountain
she grazed her cheek to mine and said but why are
you horny for death when you could have me now
the devil was a shit tempter compared to this woman
until i eyed the dead mink fur behind her and the fire
i said fine as you are i have sworn an oath to the Gypsy
aerialist she is waiting for me with my circus kin they
will bury Charles-Auguste at midnight
with no goodbye from those who truly knew him
the young woman recoiled in fright
she said Charles-Auguste is dead
i said yes child i am here to summon
Juliette and Jean-Jacques if they have
horses or a couple stout mules

that would help we must make haste
this wide-eyed woman took my wrist
and led me in a streak upstairs past
paintings of buffalo and the marble bust
of a man who must have done something
in the hall she threw open the bedroom door
to halt the butler fucking the wrinkliest old
nude woman i had ever glanced she was
Juliette the sister they were shining
with olive oil i had thought i smelled it
the brother Jean-Jacques was slathered too
dangling like the others
puffing a pipe and stroking away for dear life
the young woman shouted in the French tongue
snapping them to action and finally i was
not the only one in the manor to be clothed
Jean-Jacques appeared downstairs in a giant fur
greatcoat even bigger than mine he had goggles
and a gleaming Grand Double Phaeton it was
my first time ever riding in an automobile i
sat in the back with the bundled actress
who gripped my hand and appeared younger
than she had first seemed she shivered nervous
in the night wind with Juliette up front and
Jean-Jacques behind the wheel whipping
around the leisurely striding equines of Paris
we reached our camp in the Bois de Vincennes
and the young woman ran from the motorcar
crying où est Charles-Auguste
she caught the eye of some razorbacks with
me and Juliette and Jean-Jacques trailing
Frederick and Fyodor stood from their fire
with Nadezhda Violet Guinevere
and Seth on his cane
i yelled have you all buried that Frenchman
the grave look on Fyodor's face was a yes
he said i will take you to him
he lit a torch and led our party to the dirt mound
whereupon Jean-Jacques fell above his brother below

and sobbed is there no human road
that does not wind its way to death
the wind the sun
even water kills people
drowning in it
drinking too much
Juliette next to him moaned like
a 17th-century warship breaking apart
the young weeping woman
squeezed her arms around me
Nadezhda eyed me like who is she your new buddy
i patted her back sheepishly and said there there
and there an awkwardness lit in my comrades
Fyodor rubbed his neck he said we are sorry to bury
him here but it had been several days we
did not know if our man Sloman would find you
Jean-Jacques rose from the grave he said i will
return with a stone but now let us say our words
for his rest
the brother of the dead spoke for some ten minutes
about when he and Charles-Auguste had rambled
westward with strange poems of hunger and laughter
and how they had stolen equipment from a film studio
holding it for ransom until they gave them jobs
he concluded with Charles-Auguste's belief that the tide
of history will reveal life to be a parody of meaninglessness
Juliette spoke fondly of her brother saying
he had been born from the womb of time
she wiped a sad tear of laughter after she said
she had once caught him spilling seed into a glove
she said she wished him to dwell in castles of splendor
built by mad poets of architecture
the young weeping woman said when i was a prostitute of 12
Charles-Auguste said i will not fuck you i
will give you bread books and a room in my home
none have been so kind to me as he and his kin
she kneeled and kissed the earth above him
with a tear landing and the whispered words
je t'aime pour toujours Charles-Auguste

my people and i sang him a hymn
and the kin of Charles-Auguste made their procession
back to the Grand Double Phaeton
i broke off behind them saying well wait a minute
with the hymn concluding in moonlight i
said Charles-Auguste spoke of your films he
struck a deal with me
if i would see him to you he said you would lend your talents
to help revive our circus the crowds have thinned
Jean-Jacques said have you seen him to us
i said in a manner
Frederick arrived behind me
Jean-Jacques fastened his goggles on his head
he said i would not say you have though
because he was already buried underground
so you will have to get in line behind 500 others
who wish my sister and me to make their film
Juliette said your countrymen scorn us but
we are making a film that will show America
its true face they will cry delirious and rip
their hair out when they look in the mirror
the young lady kissed me upon the cheek with
farewell eyes of mourning longing and regret
they climbed into the car but before it was
rolling Frederick came to the driver's side he said
now wait just a moment my brother has written
a song inspired by Charles-Auguste i heard him
playing it for your brother and it pleased him
you give us two minutes we will show you
the side of America you did not know you knew
i did not wait i began strumming
and in the back seat the young woman in fur
told the brother and sister i wish to listen
Frederick had drawn his mouth harp he wailed
by the time the rest of our comrades had arrived
i was singing
split town when my whole family burned down
that was me
spoke of doom and damnation all night

that was me
sun fried my skin picking them mustang grapes
that was me
quick bright flash hot hand gambling man
that was me
crying out for more morphine in my bed
that was me
stranger to myself my whole haunted life
that was me
in America the song is the singer
i'm rambling in these waves
in America the song is the singer
i'm rambling in these waves
a version of yourself drinking wine on the curb
that was me
lost a tooth fistfighting a crooked dentist
that was me
limped up a mountain stole holy fire
that was me
met a white-haired villain in chains
whose freedom was mine
in America the song is the singer
i'm rambling in these waves
in America the song is the singer
i'm rambling in these waves
the song is the singer
Jean-Jacques lifted his goggles to his forehead
he consulted his sister in the shotgun seat he
said i have a vision for this song we will return
tomorrow at noon with my filming equipment
Frederick elbowed me
i said good deal Jean-Jacques
they drove off
i hugged my brother saying now here is a man thinking on his feet
our five comrades with us were buzzing with excitement as well
i lay in a field
bundled with Nadezhda in the frosty air
she said she was pretty
i said who that young woman

Wildcat Dreams in the Death Light

Nadezhda said yes she was eyeing you
i said i did not even catch her name i
may never see her again in my life
she said does that make you sad
i said well perhaps when i am old and ill
upon a ship i might regret that i
would never hear her voice again
she said i should kick your shin for that
i laughed i said you know you are everything it
does not matter what side of the bridge i am on
you are the nourishing rain of my fields we
will see this circus revived i will never give up
soon there will be more eyes upon us than ever
with our film they will see the spark of our secret
we know the heartbeat of the volcano inside
a world that wants to kill the idea of dancing i
have failed more than most people have tried
yet here i am laughing in the face of death with
my traveling companion to the mountain
she said i want you to make love to me like
a band playing a slow waltz during a murder
i put my fingers in her mouth in our warm bed
it was a session like hand-to-hand combat
i dreamed a lacquered upholstered train
and a century of peace in the valley of the monks

נײַנצנט

they filmed my songs with Babou roving
Frederick Wu and Fyodor playing they
filmed Nadezhda dancing with death
and Dominic flipping on his horse they
filmed and spoke French with Alexandre
who hailed from Bordeaux they
interviewed Laura and filmed her creations
and i knew she was happy about it because
she yodeled in her sleep that night
Jean-Jacques and Juliette had special
technology to play the sound of what they
had filmed they set the world afire with
Wildcat Dreams in the Death Light
Parisian crowds flocked to the theatres they
stormed our show in the Bois de Boulogne i
myself played my songs under the big top with
my friends we rambled all over France having the
time of our lives with our footing firm and the
summer weather warming when the assassin's bullet
pierced the neck of Archduke Franz Ferdinand
no one i know had ever held brimstone but
a fellow could just about grab it out of the air
with the ominous talk swirling every rumor of war
like a viking's dagger into the heart of hope
men on foot and horse carrying tools of death
i lay before a dentist in Lisbon who
yanked the hot rotten tooth from my head
even he had seen our film

it was rolling ahead of us through
Portugal Spain and other parts of France
creating a sensation reflected in our big crowds
we returned to France
with men not thinking for themselves
a soldier put me in a headlock and told me
one Frenchman was worth ten Huns i
did not fight back i let him and his buddies
pass like spirits drifting everlastingly i
had Charles-Auguste's prophecy in my head
at our final show a woman tickled my nose with
a feather and asked me why i was not in the army
i was awakened by a bugle the next day and
our parade was superseded by a military parade
i saw a man pissing in his boots
ammo packs on the chest
gas masks and the Mad Minute
Seine pleasure boats full of soldiers
bags of bombs
seven men grunting their bare asses on a pole
which snapped and they were laughing in shit
when the fighting caught us by the river Marne
at the end of August we folded our tents to flee
the death was complete you could hardly believe
anything had ever lived there at all with
the awful stench of dead horses and men
the fat rats feeding and
the horses riding up riderless
the old priest weeping in the garden
i held Nadezhda at night i did not sleep
she said maybe they will finish tomorrow
with my eyes closed i said i hope so
she said i have read the most significant battle
in Japanese history lasted for 15 minutes
perhaps tonight the soldiers are sleeping
like babies sucking wisdom from their thumbs
i dreamed my promise to Frank and Aunt J
and followed the road to Belgium until September
people had said it was a neutral country

but before we could prepare our evening tents
in the university city of Leuven there came marching
a dozen German soldiers with long guns arresting us
on the stone road by the tall church tower
they surrounded Fyodor at the head of the line
i told Nadezhda to wait in our caravan i
said if i do not return you can find me at the
ceremony of light they will not take us alive
we kissed and she hid a dagger in her sleeve
my brother Frederick had poked his head
from his caravan he said let us go see them
Fyodor hollered for Laura who moved slow
and breathed heavy we walked with her and
the German soldiers were laughing when we
three arrived Laura spoke their tongue she
said they say we are to surrender our arms
and our money or we will be committing
illegal civilian resistance
Fyodor said tell them we have no arms
we are a traveling circus
we entertain
that is all
Laura spoke to them
they guffawed and sneered
she said they say what about your knives
i said can you ask them to let us pass
and there will be no trouble we will
leave them in peace to fight their war
Laura pursed her lips saying i doubt
they will be inclined to agree
i said please just give it a try
she asked and set them laughing
the commander pushed his nose up
and was oinking mocking poor Laura
her tone grew more fierce with them
but the more angry she got the more irreverent
they appeared in their pointed helmets
she must have been cussing them when the
commander drew his Luger and pointed it at her

Frederick and i crouched on instinct and Fyodor
pushed his hands forward saying bitte bitte bitte
the officer cocked the pistol and leaned to his men
cracking one last joke of his life before the spray
of his brains blasted out the back of his head
freezing us all with the smoke
rising from Laura's tiny single shooter she
had tucked away in her breast she had aim
the commander's pierced cheek hit the stone road
leaking red at their feet they trained their rifles
upon us like we had been instantly put before the
firing squad i did believe we were fixing to cross
no blindfolds it would be a death quick and hot
like the blood of a wolf
one of the soldiers' hands exploded
he screamed with just a couple fingers left
and another doubled over clutching his chest
Fyodor did not waste one second flinging a knife
from his belt into the neck of a young man i
rolled on the road with a bullet whizzing above i
plunged my blade so deep into the man's thigh
he dropped his gun and bled out on the stone
curled up like how he had come into this world
Frederick slit a throat and grabbed one of their guns
stabbing his knife into the man's stomach
Seth's arrow pierced a soldier's heart i
did not even see in the distance he
had been lurking with a compound bow
Fyodor stuck another through the ribs
there had been a sniper in the church tower
like an Angel of Death passing over us
and visiting them we made our exodus
miles outside the town we could see
black billowing and burning they torched
all those years of labor and creation
the homes dashed to ashes in an evening
many mothers murdered with the men
and the stone road we had trod
salted with tears of widows and orphans

we rode due south through the night
Fyodor in our 30 minutes of fireless rest said
those Huns have been scorching and looting
the continent whether you put up a fight or not
they are vicious i am not sorry
some of them have died by my hand
Fyodor i could see was feathering our morale
like the one-winged falcon it was
back in France where their
green and gold grain fields could have
you thinking you were in the 15th century
Mary diverted us into the woods
off the dirt road because
she said she had seen a tank ahead
it did not make sense to me
all i could think of was the dunk tank
of a clown nothing to be afraid of
but the metal beast prowled past like
a roving tomb marking the death of humanity
where are the giant patches of quicksand
when you need them i
saw the sleepy-eyed elder swaddled in blankets
driven from his home with the starving families
pain in their faces
the long line of blinded British soldiers
their hands upon the shoulders
of the man in front of them
Duncan's horse fell over from exhaustion
she had seen many years of work and wonder
Duncan left her a bucket of water
and a couple apples he said you rest up
and take your retirement as a wild horse
you roam where you please
you run from Germans
his voice cracking saying
i love you forever Molly
Duncan bunked with Seth and we traveled on with
the horse breathing heavy on her side watching us go
we had death upon our tail

like a fly that would not leave Jesus alone on the cross
after days of ceaseless riding and shaking hunger
we and our beasts caught a break in Metz
they had a train to Geneva
we loaded up and passed out on the journey
the circus of silence
the circus of sleep
down to Switzerland
down through Italy to Sicily
i learned a strange thing from a Belgian who
had escaped Leuven he said the sniper in the church tower
was a German who had confused his troops with the enemy
we continued southerly and caught a boat to Tripoli
when Nadezhda was chewing peanuts i
swear it sounded like Duncan's horse galloping
through the devastation afoot
the death light in their eyes
we were guzzling Tripolitan wine
drenching the notion that everyone we
had known in France was dead or in danger
our women were sleeping by the beach fire
in the moonlight
my brother on the sand said have you heard
there is a killer chicken hawk terrorizing Chicago
we laughed with our beards
i said how much money do we have
he said with all our hit film drummed up i
reckon we could make our funds stretch for a year
i said shame that picture is probably lost to history now
even their sound technology
Frederick said well we are living without justice
in a world seeking to execute all the lazy dreamers
you could be one of the grand artists of Paris
sculpting in dolomite
you could scribble your poem in ink on the page
or chisel your songs on the side of the mountain
it does not matter where you write in this world
you are writing upon sand
i said you might know more than all philosophers

put together
he swigged wine and said suck an egg
we laughed with the dark sparkle of the nighttime sea
i had drunkenly teased my brother
but i dreamed what he had said
like the warmth of Walt Whitman's last breath
and the feeling you get when you see yourself
weeping in the mirror
with the knowledge
you can never be famous enough
you can never be rich enough
you can never get goofed up enough
the volcano of time is spilling into your village
and all you can do is light a cigarette off the magma
and laugh and struggle with your brothers and sisters

צוואַנציקסט

we followed the coastline my gift compass pointing east
all water that touches the ocean is to me
a cenotaph to my mule
we thrived on sardines and olives
not a single one bruised
all the way to Egypt
with traces of a senile Ottoman empire
in the rich soil of the river Nile
the stirring of ancient memories
the sun was down but not out
we had been men and beasts craving for water
fighting sandfly fever
advancing into heat and emptiness
to the elders of the Arab mudtown
bartering for melons and mangoes
my wife savoring the taste like it
was the last mango on earth
i shaved my beard
with a piece of volcanic obsidian by the sea while
a hunting party of Negro dwarves watched in silence
with swords tucked behind them
they showed my brother and me the night market of
ghosts where they trade at the root of humanity when
there were no different skin colors or languages
i had been a part of the voices pushing us eastward
it might have been the Hebrew in me
and the words echoing next year in Jerusalem
as the floodplain silt of the Nile punished our path

we rode through hell with the Desert Mounted Corps
i raked in dead money at their poker table
on past the Suez canal with the riverboat of
wounded British soldiers some writhing on the deck
and their Turk enemies with broken limbs
crawling across the desert on hands and knees
but the fighting in Egypt and Palestine
was a war of small armies and large spaces
my wife and brother had given me letters
to feed the holy Wailing Wall where i wept
with the dead and the dream
the light of the mountain prayer
the Shema spilling from my lips
so many miles to go i doubled over and
the three-toothed Jew who had laid my arm tefillin
said i have run with black deer in Poland i
have tripped over a dead hawk in a field of barley i
am not joking when i say three nights ago i
drank wine with the man who invented basketball
now what whirlwind of travel has led you to this wall
are you a pilgrim
i composed myself saying i am the pilgrim
who travels with the no-eyed tiger
and The Wildcat Circus that vanished from America
he repeated the word wildcat sounding surprised
i said yes we have vanquished our murderous boss
we run the circus ourselves
we toil in brotherhood
he said your circus sounds a sister to the kibbutz
my nephew and his friends have undertaken
they are 215 strong a four-hour ride from here
you might not know Hanukkah begins in three days
you should gather your comrades and follow me
you can delight the kibbutzniks and their children
they will feed you from their fields
have you recently had a good hot meal
i said my whole life i have done much with little
but as it stands now i could take a bite of this wall
he chuckled saying now you do not want to do that

you will crack your teeth and have less in your head
than me i am Ephraim i will lead you to my kin
i persuaded my circus comrades with talk of
food rest and the festival of lights
in a year darker than horses feeding upon horses
which i saw in the great ruined plains of France
hounded across the Suez by the smell of death
we made camp
performed our stunts
sang our songs
worked the fields
and kindled candles with
Ephraim and his nephew Goose Herman
i could not speak with half the kibbutz
in the Russian Polish and Yiddish tongues
but Nadezhda's entrancing dancing broke
all the language barriers like Fyodor's knives
and Mary spinning six hoops on her arms and legs
Babou running obstacles with Meriwether Cloud
who had been blasting himself skyhigh
on a spring stilt i bounced on it while honking a shofar
the children marveled upward at Seth and his cape
Goose Herman and his people had invited us to stay
i said to Goose at the nightfire i
was not sure you would embrace us with this being
the Holy Land some see the circus as sin and decadence
he was a corn whisky sipper he said i know the true evil of
this world and it is chess
they pit black versus white
they worship feeble kings i
have seen queen sacrifices that would make a man stab
his eyes out checkmate formations haunt my dreams i
used to be heavy in the throes of addiction myself
but i shed that snakeskin working the land i
think of the madness in Europe and ask
how many played the war game chess in their youth
the paranoia of the board spilling into the player's life
i said you are making me glad i never touched the stuff
i will keep strumming this guitar instead

he sipped and said wise man wise man
Mónika birthed herself a screaming baby boy
they called him Herman in honor of our host
we stayed upon the kibbutz for 14 months
like it was a shelter against volcanic fallout
with the magma of death scorching the earth
we worked the sun fields sweltering with our hosts
they fed us three square meals at the long dining tables
where i played guitar to an elderly Polish Jew who
beckoned me to his ear and with a solemn whisper
said tell the little black man to stop it with the unicycle
apparently Titus had been riding a unicycle at night
loudly jumping ramps and bothering people i
had thought the old-timer was about to compliment
my song but that is close-knit kibbutz life for you
Fyodor taught me and some others how to whip knives
my friends and i boiled our socks in a cauldron
some kibbutznik youths stitched Babou a quilt
it had been a long time since the sound of
fighting had reached my ears
one night i dreamed the cold sword of Samuel slicing
king Agag to pieces and stretching across
the desert to scatter the pawns and bishops
the last Shabbat of February 1916 my wife
and i fucked in the shade of an olive tree
we lay upon a blanket noshing in our underwear
when she said Mort i have to tell you something
i had a mouthful of challah bread i said uh oh
she said i am sad
i chewed and chewed until i could say
what is the matter angel face
she said i miss the world we knew i miss my home
upon the rope rings and trapeze
through the air
i said outside this kibbutz oasis there are men
cooking horse meat in a violent struggle to survive
should we not stay a while longer
she said i know the danger but one year of my prime
has slipped away in idleness i will be 23 soon i

kick death in the balls with each sequence i land i
wish to drop the jaws of the ropewalkers of Rome
like a sweet kiss delivered across the bridge i
know you yourself have a mystic mission of light
our ancient people may have taken their first steps
upon this sand but we cannot stay we must ride with
a struck match burning between life and death
she straddled me with my back to the tree
the warm wind tumbling with Frank's spirit i
kissed her i said oh my Lord woman you are right
what do you say we gather our forces and see who
else might be ready to kickstart this Wildcat Circus
it turned out Alexandre was with us around the fire
assembly he said i have built a little bed for RT i
taught him how to blow out a candle and tuck himself in
Juan Carlos said i have learned how to have someone
take a sledgehammer and bust a rock over me
Olena the strongwoman said i have been mastering
my horse stunts balancing a wine glass on my head
Wu said she could now floss her teeth with her feet
Merripen said he could jump rope on a highwire
ok ok Mary said we have been sharpening our acts
but with the world as it is where will we take them
i said i would put forth we roll our caravans over
land and across the sea all the way to Australia i
will return to the Holy Land as a pilgrim once again
but i would like to speak my native tongue and
see their kangaroos and perhaps a Tazmanian tiger
Duncan said but in Australia they have cannibal tribes
who will kill you with a boomerang and eat you raw
Frederick said they sound compassionate
if they kill you first they could just as easily eat you alive
i laughed and Duncan swatted the air saying aw c'mon
i said we have already spilled the Germans' blood i
do not fear the cannibal tribes
the day they see me they will skip a meal
my fellow workers echoed my defiance a few laughing
Mary said well our money satchel has only shrunk
and we are due to buy a couple goats for Babou

Wildcat Dreams in the Death Light

Frederick said i say we shove off in ten nights' time
after i marry this blazing beauty at my side
i leapt at them and hugged him and Violet my siblings
Frederick and i rode single-hump camels to the altar
in our fine suits shepherded by torch-bearing soldiers
from an obscure sect who believe
it was actually Ezekiel who was the son of God
there were neighboring Arab elders and their kin
farming friends of Goose and his father who
joined the holy hands of Violet and my brother
at the great conjunction of Saturn and Jupiter
not seen for 800 years they said their joyful vows
Violet sang a melodious tear-jerking song concluding
in uproarious cheering even the camels were screaming
with the sun waning we danced under the stars in the
waves of Jews and Arabs playing their music of peace
Frederick and i had them laughing and whooping with
our boots on our hands pulling respectable handstands
there was death sulking in the corner bent out of shape
about the legendary timelessness of our brotherhood
the newly married couple spent one week in a villa
in Jerusalem reappearing as we prepared our journey
with a fare-thee-well final feast among our true friends
Ephraim Goose and the kibbutzniks who welcomed us
we made our exodus from the Promised Land with
the British scattering their promises like seeds of poison
Fat Ali wept on the banks of the Tigris he said i was born
here i did not think i would ever look upon these waters
we began to perform again our skills sharper than ever
swept city to city through rain and sand
bartering with people whose tongues we did not know
lighting their eyes with stunts and songs
we stirred the Sultan's soul in the Sublime State of Persia
but he had a letter delivered to us saying if we did not leave
by sundown he would arrest and lash us all for performing
for free to several hundred weary peasants threshing grain
we departed hastily with Fyodor saying this is why i warned
you all not to go picking up any stray asses they will foot
whip you over a simple misunderstanding about a melon

our road unfurled long across the desert-strewn land i
am one of the few people in world history who was born
on Fire Island and turned 24 in the Emirate of Afghanistan
i have shared unleavened bread on the path
to Dehli with a blind begging holy man
who had lost his voice reciting mantras
we met the starving
the mad sufferers
but also the young man lounging by the lagoon
who could basically walk on his head
bouncing with no hands upside down
my jaw dropped while he did a dozen good hops
i said you are invited to join our troupe
we are en route to Australia
rightside up he said thank you friend but my home is here
i bought a whole gunnysack of crisp apples off him
we hit the pinnacle of our Indian summer
dazzling them in a giant Portugese-style amphitheater
near the golden shores of Goa
there must have been 4,000 people packed in
with at least 119 maharajas and their brides
keeping us fed to our Ceylonese September
i saw a giant whale skull on the beach of Colombo
i feared the ocean voyage to the Dutch East Indies
like a fireman's nightmare of burning alive
but Nadezhda taught me to eye the horizon
the sea that was typically tougher than a forest hog
with tusks finally showed me her merciful side we
carved a path through the lush tropical vegetation
of Northern Sumatra finding
ten-thousand-year-old fossils of tribal warfare
and the soul of the nation in a single royal codex
after three very hungry days i wolfed salvation
in the heat and crunch of Javanese cooking
and i can honestly say i have been in a shoving
match with the Sultan of Yogyakarta after he
shorted us when we put on a damn good show
but we sorted it out before anyone had to get
stabbed through the cheek with a pencil

אײן און צוואַנציקסט

Nadezhda traded the Javanese princess a porcupine handbag
for a cow with a face full of flies we milked all the way
to Australia when it came time to feed Babou i
fixed a glare upon the heifer and said not this one
we landed in Perth harbor into the arms of a young
exhausted nation on the verge of a breakdown the
homefront women and children seemed to appreciate
the circus distraction we brought i was not sure with
few animals and no hot film if they would come
but our parade with Babou who had grown old
enough to be rather harmless and adorable
had them lining the streets and filling our tents
1917
i hear the year and think of the mother sow bellowing
for her piglets who have been taken and slaughtered
the broken holy ghost weeping on his knees
the arrow through the chest of the fearless explorer
the long shadow of death stretching into now
every breath was stolen
every breath was a storm
across the new Trans-Australian Railway to Adelaide
with war posters plastered all over the city
would you stand by while a bushfire raged they said
but the Aussie's struck back against their Napoleon-sized
ruler who traveled to this room and that in a cloud of
blue tobacco smoke with a gun in his pocket he
wanted conscription but the people said no and there
were even a few iww posters around Sydney

To Arms!
Capitalists Parsons Politicians
Landlords Newspaper editors and
other stay-at-home patriots
your country needs you in the trenches
workers follow your masters
i never did see the man-eating tribe of headhunters
but i did box a couple rounds with a prize-fighting
kangaroo and after i hit a lucky poker hand i
bought a round for the prostitutes of the bar
the true ambassadors of this world
i was strumming my guitar on the corner
outside the post office when a red lipstick young woman
said excuse me good sir where is your uniform
i said well ma'am i am wearing it
all my life i have worn a striped shirt i
could not tell you why it feels like home
she drew a scene exploding shame on you coward
she stuck a white feather into the neck hole of my shirt
yelling let it be known a coward walks among you
i pulled away saying hey lady there is no need
to poke my shoulder with a brittle quill
she said here he is complaining about pokes
when our boys are fighting and dying
i said and coming back armless legless and insane
do not forget about them
her eyes blazing she spit in my face
hurling the word coward
one last time before she stormed off
i called after her thank you for the feather i
shall wear it as a badge of honor
i addressed all the rubberneckers eyeing me stunned i
said i tip my hat to your country for rejecting conscription
now if the workers of all nations could find the courage
to lay down their weapons and fight the class war instead
we would have a much better world on our hands
do you not think it so
there an old man and his wife approached he said
this is a clean handkerchief son i liked your remarks

i said why thank you i was about to wet my sleeve
the woman said feather girls are a general's invention
if there ever were one i would not pay them any mind
i wiped my cheek and returned the man his rag saying
i would bet money you are right about that ma'am
not long after my encounter with the feather girl
and the kind old Aussie couple
flowing like a river of death America joined the war
and fireside with Frederick a fortnight henceforth
he said oh my God you will not believe this bullshit
i was pan-sizzling vegetables i said what
he folded his newspaper and holding it out to me said
Eugene V. Debs imprisoned for his sanity and integrity
i had trouble finding sleep that night but when i did i
dreamed a wild mule weeping with a crown of thorns
and my blood brother Tomás slowly dying in my arms
i loved him like a poet loves the word honeysuckle
he caught me by surprise coughing the question why
have you not orchestrated the ceremony of light
you have been taking forever
the feather woman appeared in the gray Salem field
repeatedly piercing my arms with a thousand sharp quills
until i was weeping with wings i
said i will tell you my blood brother Tomás i
have lacked the courage to let them go i
am the feather bird coward she said i was
he said i do not believe that for one moment
you who has never paid rent taxes or read *Hamlet*
you who has shit in the sunlight like an animal
you who has walked alongside the blind tiger
you who has heart and head lines running together
Tomás was reading my palm
he said you have seen the nets of American justice
catch only minnows the wild whales swim recklessly
gorging upon the good and green land belching out
all circus and no bread America the circus of death
with profiteers at the helm the forked-tongue talkers
you know they say the grave danger is to die while alive
but they are wrong

that is the strength of untamable lions
i know you
you are Mort
i squeezed his hand saying you are a dagger into the heart
of meaninglessness you have strength and charm to spare
he said i have one more thing to tell you
i said what
he said i have met a Slovenian doctor here across the bridge
you will not believe his name
i said what is it
he said Tit Pigman
i laughed saying you have got to be shitting me
we laughed so good Tomás' wounds healed
he rose to his feet i said where will you go now
he said i will be swimming upside down in a sea of mystery
writing ten-thousand-page poems i circulate anonymously
and preparing rooms in my castle for when my guests arrive
i cannot help but still dream of that Manxwoman she
will be coming round the mountain when she comes
now you pump your wings and see what happens
i flapped and flew viewing the world from above
like the falcon of the bridge and there i saw
boys whipping stones deadly fast in a rock fight
a stable of horses escaping the Wizard Prince of Arabia
my father pushing my mother in her wheelchair
i landed before them upon the road i said
i wish i would have known you folks better
my father said i am sorry son but who are you
i said i am the one who has the courage
to love without being loved
my mother smiled reaching for her hidden blade
she cut off both my father's payos and stuck them
to the sides of my head with their blood
my father removed his black-brimmed hat
and placed it upon my head
i said what do you think
they laughed but i did too
we three embraced laughing and weeping
my mother said your second name is Raphael

it means Hashem has healed
and they vanished into ash over the sea of mystery
i woke in the arms of my lover she said are you alright i
heard you laugh and weep in your sleep
i said my dear
there is something i have to do you will not like it i
told Eugene V. Debs to his face i would stand with him i
swore an oath to myself i would honor Frank and Aunt J i
would have been homeless without them i
would not have abided the orphanage
and i have promised my mule
the elephant Dorothy
my blood brother Tomás
the good man Marvin the worker of light i
do not wish to lose myself upon the sinking ghost ship of regret i
hope you and the troupe will return to America with me
but i know you have been born to perform i do not quell your talents
she said you have gathered our comrades for me i
will try to persuade them it is our time to return
if they do not agree i will travel the ocean with you
the performer's passion still burns in my heart
but i could not be parted from you we ride together i
shall put your letters inside my coffin like flowers
i held my bride with the smoldering kiss of passion
we assembled our circus comrades i must have pulled
a mood from the air they were ready to confront America
Frederick floated a well-received plan on the ship he
said i say we make a benefit show for Eugene and the Wobs
we completed our journey from Sydney
to Auckland
to Suva
to Pago Pago
to Honolulu
to Los Angeles
i did it like a veteran mariner
well-prepared with lemon ginger and water
with my supplies i even helped a young man of 13
return to health he had a wife and two children
we stepped upon American soil as flat broke as we had left it

צוויי און צוואַנציקסט

i hovered over our five-night stand in LA like a hawk ready
to fly away with a doe in his claws Alf's ghost lingering in the city
every Angeleno i asked said that Alf was a dead man they
had not heard hide nor hair since my blade slit him in Salem
we scraped together enough to live and ride the iron highway
for the summer upon the Grand Canyon Route to Kansas City
we performed our first benefit show for the KC streetcar strikers
they had the scabs stuck baking in stifling coaches amid August heat
propelling the union to a quick victory of full recognition the next day
the law did not hassle us on the road but our IWW comrades
were catching clubs to the jaw in Chicago
i was sniffing my way there like a lynx
Woodrow Wilson with marbles in his mouth and blood on his hands
set his goons loose on Wob offices across the land seizing everything
that was not bolted down i am talking furniture and paperclips
a dozen of us sat upon donated apple crates at IWW headquarters
with Big Bill Haywood who said i have been dreaming of madness
and of choking to death on Wrigley's gum we are under siege like
never before in the history of this union the nation is teeming with
unchained cops and the unblinking private eyes of the profiteer class
our lawyer has told of the sabotage you experienced in New York i
am grateful you soldiered home bravely we need every scrap of help
in this fight when do you propose to orchestrate this benefit spectacle
Frederick said how about October 3rd a fortnight from today
Big Bill said that is a good one gives us time to spread the word
Mary said we will prepare all the grandeur we can muster i
know Olena has been completing equestrian feats with birds on her
and Nadezhda has been double flipping with the one-hand catch

Frederick said my man Sloman and i will parade through town
all day before the show with music and a sweet old blind tiger
Big Bill eyed my guitar he said i have something for you guitar man
he rummaged his briefcase and said here is one they did not get
he passed me the IWW songbook i said is this for me to keep
he said it sure is if you play a song from it during the show you
will be leading a singalong of several thousand i bet i even know
where we can find an amplifier i have used for my speeches
i said would you give one the night of the show to fire them up
Big Bill consulted my comrades he said does that sound like
a good idea should i say a few words
he stepped to the microphone under our big tent by the lake
the night of the show every performer in the ring even Babou
before the sardine-packed crowd of three thousand he said
good evening comrades and fellow workers i am Big Bill Haywood
and The Wildcat Circus has a big evening
planned for the One Big Union
they cheered
he said for those of you who do not know
we call it the One Big Union because it is big
enough to take in the black man
the white man
women and mothers
big enough to take in all nationalities
we are a union big and strong enough to obliterate state boundaries
to obliterate national boundaries
to obliterate the death machines of war
Big Bill had everybody roaring on their feet
and when peace comes he said
we will forge new bonds among the ex-fighters
who in all their suffering will turn against the politicians
the bankers
those who profit from the labor of others
and we the IWW will lead the way to a new society
built upon respect and solidarity thank you
Frederick and i stepped to the microphone the instant Big Bill
waved and departed our cue had been spoken in the applause i
struck up on my guitar of spirits Frederick and i singing together
solidarity forever

solidarity forever
solidarity forever
for the union makes us strong
when the union's inspiration through the workers' blood shall run
there can be no power greater anywhere beneath the sun
yet what force on earth is weaker than the feeble strength of one
but the union makes us strong
an army of sweet mules emerged from the ocean waters
of my heart as the multitude rollicked and sang with us
their cheering upon our final note hit me like a powerful
administration of cognac to have you skating around
maybe even knock you off your feet except no vomiting
Dominic backflipped upon his black horse while Meriwether
somersaulted through the air overtop them with his spring stilt
there was Olena the majestic rider and Fyodor winging his blades
blindfolded from a great distance against the board with Wu
grimacing to make it look like he was piercing her arms but when
she stepped forward to take a bow the crowd gasped to see
the arms were fake and she had none
Wu played her violin with a cellist we hired
while we dimmed the electric lights and RT tucked
himself into bed with a spotlight on him there was something
moving about the way that little monkey did that with the music
and Babou appearing from the dark to kiss him and lay by his side
some of our toughest razorbacks
Tex
Duncan
Wolfgang
and Little Jesse
watching from the standing room wiped their eyes
our circus bloomed transcendent with roots in the ground
and blossoms in the sky i did not think there was a single thing
that could choke out our hope when Nadezhda ropedanced
and flew like a multitude reborn from trials
with a symphony of dreams
until the flickering finger of flame mounted the canvass
ceasing the music
shattering our world into chaos
Frederick opened the tent and led them stampeding out

Fyodor did the same at the other end
i dashed into the ring where Nadezhda and Merripen
were caught in the bird's nest with the fire nearing
and the panic spreading slowly then all at once
when a pistol report rung out into the crowd
a fellow worker fell wounded
pop pop pop three more i
traced them to the source at the edge of the ring
the top hat and the hammerclaw tuxedo
Alf had returned for his fire
a newspaperman flashed a picture of him
and a gunshot from elsewhere drew my eye
it was Frederick wrestling an armed bandit
who had been blocking people from exiting
a man lunged to help and Alf shot him
i bolted to them in dumb instinct yelling no no no
after the bandit had shot Frederick in the chest
but he did not know my blood brother was a lion
battling for the people with his grave wound
Frederick thrice stabbed the bandit in the stomach
dropping him disarmed and bleeding to death
Duncan had rushed Alf and Alf shot him down
men tended Frederick pulling him outside
and there were piercing screams from the hundreds
left struggling to escape the smoke rolling in
the man to my right had his shoulder explode
speckling me red and Alf's gun clicked empty
he did not have the chance to reload with me
and the great tree knife buffalo-charging him
Alf unsheathed the cobra dagger i knew it well
we slashed around one another in a deadly dance
i said now you went and fucked up everything Alf
he swiped at me trembling in his rage he
said everything is nothing less than you stole from me i
have been forced underground i
could not return to my kin for the shame of it i
hunted you all the way to that shithole New York City i
spent years in the bottle in a shack in Maine i
was near to killing myself i

had even chosen the method until i
received word you all would be in Chicago i
have come like death to take back what is mine i
will take it wrapped in flames with me to hell
Nadezhda screamed from the nest with Merripen
the fire burning the canvas and lapping closer
i said Alf what did you think would happen
the first time you tasted our blood
you bullwhipped your ambitions into a class
that could only devour the world i
am a gravedigger with a lust for life i
must murder you now or go to my woman directly
you choose
he tucked his dagger with defiance he said go to her
i tore off underneath them stuck 40 feet in the air
Merripen took off his pants yelling i will lower her
as far as i can you will have to catch her
i wrangled Zinnia
Olena's frightened horse who
had been searching for an exit
i had a mind to stand upon her to get closer
Merripen wrapped his feet in the nest rope
and dangled upside down lowering Nadezhda
she was gripping the pants between them
cutting the distance back to earth by a fourth
but through the haze Alf was loading his pistol i
said oh you must be shitting me that lying demon
he fired upon me i hid behind the mare who
was struck repeatedly with Alf approaching
pop pop pop
he lifted his shooter upward toward my bride
as Zinnia tumbled over falling like
death's robe dropping to the dirt to reveal me
there winging the great tree knife with all my might
it thudded into Alf's chest stunning him to his knees
Nadezhda let go and plunged with a scream
into my arms nearly ripping them from the sockets i
had broken her fall enough to keep her in one piece
she grimaced with all the wind knocked out of her i

dragged her behind Zinnia seeing as Alf still had
a gun in his hand i yelled upward jump Merripen
i peered over the still brown horse to Alf contentedly
eyeing his revenge his smile burning with inner peace i
hollered how about you pull my blade from your chest
and bleed to death a little quicker Alf
he cried out gutturally i will not die by the knife
of a hook-nose son of Abraham
bang
he blew his head off and tumbled over
my bride coughed in the engulfing doom
part of the big top caved in and i yanked
her forcefully over the horse
Merripen fell flailing to earth breaking
both his legs and his left elbow he howled
Nadezhda and i choked on smoke in the dirt i
crawled to Alf to claim my knife i
said this way Nadezhda
she said my uncle
i said let me see you to safety i will come back for him
the blaze brought down another pole blocking the exit i
had had in mind it probably would have crushed us in fire
i said my God woman let us get him and go
we scurried low with a million tiny daggers to the lungs
the roasting heat of hellfire
Nadezhda kneeled to her uncle she said we will not leave you
he strained in pain saying you must
there were chunks of flaming debris falling i
could not see two feet in front of me with the smoke so thick
i could barely breathe enveloped in that coffin feeling like
when they had buried me alive
my coughing bride said i am scared Mort
i said i know my dear let us stay low
slither like snakes and be born again
i pulled Merripen in his agony for a few crawls
but as soon as it felt like progress
some punishing flame wall repelled us
in despair with the blanketing smoke
burning my mouth and eyes i shouted in frustration

i am blind
but the sound of roaring reached me
and it was not the fire
it lit hope in my heart
i said Nadezhda that is Babou she will lead us out
we dragged Merripen together to the blind tiger in her cage i
seared my hand unlatching it
and Babou commenced her vigorous sniffing
our sister of light
our eyeless Moses leading our exodus
through the obstacle course of a lifetime
i retched and spit drooling with the dark closing in
when Babou had led us to the wall of canvas i
slit and pulling Merripen by his arms
we rolled in the fresh air like the first breath
after being submerged in an ocean of smoke
the whole tent collapsed consumed in flame
lighting the night as workers helped us away
from the first appearance of fire it did not take long
ten minutes that broke the back of The Wildcat Circus
Duncan was lying on a wagon someone had carried him
out but he died with four others
Henry Oswald the Wobblie barman
Newt the Pinkerton agent of death
tragically seeking money for his ill son
Sophie Honeyball the suffragist unionist housewife
who had been born without fingers
and Alf Jackson the murderous profiteer
the venom dripping from the fangs of America
my bride and i were hoarse-talking
coughing up magma
while the medics loaded Merripen
i wheezed to Seth where is Frederick
he said on his way to the Negro hospital
i gave him a thumbs-up and climbed inside
the ambulance with Nadezhda and her ailing uncle
the doors slammed and they had us sucking oxygen i
demanded they take us to the Negro hospital
the medic said but you are white

i croaked the words thank you for the newsflash doc i
have a brother there and as a matter of fact i am Hebrew
the driver said i bet he means Provident they take all races
i said yes please take us there
my wife squeezing my arm silently wept in the dark
they performed surgery on my brother all through the night
i prayed soot-covered in a chair in the hall with Violet
her hands clasped outside his door into the early morning
we thanked the doctor profusely when he said
they had removed the silver bullet a millimeter from his heart
crossing the tightrope he woke
to the gray day
the big block letter Chicago newspaper headline
THE CIRCUS OF DEATH

דרײַ און צוואַנציקסט

alone with him in his room later in the afternoon my brother
showed me the silver bullet he said i am going to sell
this bullet for ten dollars and treat my baby to a fine dinner
his lip quivered he said this was supposed to be a time of joy
Violet is carrying our child
i came alive in my torpor at his bedside i said whoa mazel tov
that is a beacon of heavenly light when we need it the most
his tears spilled he said but now with our lives in ashes
we do not have anything i will be a sad scrambling father
i touched his forearm i said you are a good worker
we will find our way
all you have to worry about now is healing
you are on a good road
he wiped his eyes saying it feels mighty dark now
Merripen had had his bones set
Nadezhda was at his bedside caressing his cheek
she said you have honored our kin
i kissed the top of her smoky head and left her with
her uncle and Ahimoth Mónika and little Herman
i rode Scotch Castle north to camp i
kissed Duncan's forehead in his casket of wood
i said whatever is growing in your garden
may it grow wild with your horse in France
fare thee well brave fellow worker Duncan
his eyes popped open startling me backward
Fyodor closed them saying that happens sometimes
our camp of mourning was diminished
the razorbacks and half our performers had already scattered

concerned about the law but Mary said with the photo
of Alf in the newspaper and the eyewitness accounts
those nettlesome police passed all of us over like
our door had been marked with shankbone blood
Fyodor closed the coffin lid and said it is finished
Guinevere has delivered all our money
to the two families of the slain workers we
could not reach any known kin of Duncan's we will
bury him in the morning and travel our separate ways
his cold words shattered me upon my feet as he trudged off
but before i returned to the hospital of my mending kin
i summoned the 13 remaining around the late afternoon fire
i said i will give each of you a warm foot bath if you stay with me
please for the love of Hashem i still have half a soul it is true
a part of me vanished when i saw Marvin die for the people
when i learned Rosa had fallen
when i saw Prince Triangle and Flossie float over the bridge
when i saw Lola and our comrade Duncan mortally wounded
when i saw Jaymus and the caretaker reach peace
when i saw Tomás defend us from the dagger of death
when i saw Zinnia cloak me in grace to blind the eye of death
when i saw our tent and equipment consumed in flame i
know i am not alone when i say i
have passed some golden championship years
upon this circus we stole from
an arrogant murderous profiteer who robbed us first
the ones he killed guided the great tree knife into his heart
as he was taking aim upon my bride they ride with us still i
have seen roses open like the eyes of the dead
the profiteer vanished into his revenge yet we steal still i
would have never been part of this journey with you all i
was the stolen hog who at daybreak was due for slaughter
my Aunt J and my uncle Frank sailed with me so i
could play the guitar and laugh with you all so loud
blood trickles from the ears of death i
have a sacred ceremony to orchestrate for them i ask
who among you would do me the honor of taking part i
would have never known how to gather the Locksmith keys
without this circus i do believe i have them jingling now

at precisely the time we need some meaning in our grief
some manner to say farewell even though it will fall short
if you allow me to represent us to the iww i will ask of them
train fare for all of us plus the cost of food and land to camp
in the city of my youth Battle Creek for the rest of October i
will consecrate the ceremony at dusk on Halloween who
among you will travel one last lost road with me the moment
my brother quits the hospital with a silver bullet to sell
Seth with the aid of his gold-knobbed cane lifted himself
in his black cloak drawing our eyes upward he said i am
not shitting you i had a mind to take my life tonight i
am 32 and my walking ability was not like i remember
there is not much else i can do on this earth except circus
work all my kin have cast me aside my best friend is dead
but hear me Sloman i accept your invitation as a gift
i scooted our small picnic table near him and stood upon it
hugging him like i would a man closer to my height
i said you are my friend
that means i would feed you eight meals a day
you can choose solitude but if you wish you
will never have to suffer loneliness so long as i breathe
he said do you ever dream of the German soldiers we killed
i said every now and then i wake in sweat gripping my blade
he said i dreamed last night they were all convalescing
in a grand seven-story hospital of magisterial architecture
and the whole building burned down cause of a cigarette
Mary hopped upon the picnic table and draped her wool
shawl over Seth she kissed his cheek
saying i had the same dream
Seth wept eyeing us all with just two words he said my friends
we sealed with spit handshakes their word to join me in Battle Creek
i played a song for Duncan the next morning as they lowered him
i trotted upon Scotch Castle to the world headquarters of the iww
deep in the heart of infinite Chicago
hat in hand i demanded a word with Big Bill
i said i am sorry our circus did not go as planned
Big Bill seated in his shoestring office under siege said
yes it was quite a tragedy i am sorry as well
you see the base viciousness to which they stoop

but i commend you and your comrades
you acted quickly and saved lives
i said i myself would have died smoke-blinded with
my bride but our tiger's magic whiskers sensed the path
Big Bill narrowed his eyes he said what can i do for you son
i said well through it all we have been current on our dues
since the end of 1912 when we all became Wobblies
almost five years ago
i showed him my red book i said here i have the stamps
we have hardly ever asked this union for much of anything
but now we are in need
all i request is a modest loan
so that we may regroup and perform the ceremony of
light for my kin who have crossed i will pay you back
he said how much do you have in mind
i said 150 dollars would see us through
he said how do i know you will not skip town with it
i laid my knife upon his table i said this is the blade
of spirits who have been my guardians all my life
this is my compass a wedding gift from my brother
if i do not repay the loan by the new year they are yours
Big Bill said do you think you could arrange a photo
of this ceremony and mail it to me for the *Industrial Worker*
i said i reckon i could
he said then you may keep your knife and your compass i
hope you and your comrades regroup and continue fighting
with us for the future of respect and dignity we will win
a fat man in the corner began playing the hammer dulcimer
Big Bill unlocked his safe and counted me out 200 big ones
he said this is not a loan this is solidarity
i rode Scotch Castle into the palace of the imagination
reciting poems that arrive upon the page without labor
50 lines at a time
my bride was face down upon the hospital bed weeping
while Merripen was shut away on the toilet
attempting to shit with broken legs
i said my dear
she said if i had some i would flood my belly with knives of
moonshine the world is boiling with war strikes fires and riots

what do we have left to do but get old and beg in the street
i said do you want to know where Babou's eyes went
she lifted hers troubled and bloodshot with
a tiny spark of curiosity and agitation
i said you are looking upon them right this second i
am the tiger who has emerged from the mist
bearing news of a final mission for our circus
it is my whole life on the line i
cannot abandon the spirit riders who
led me to your door you contain multitudes
and i need you the dancing Medusa
who tricks death into gazing your glory
i wiped my bride's tears she whispered in my ear
shall we gather our forces once more
i said my dear they have sworn an oath to ride with us
we have the means to prepare for October's remainder
with more than mortals to dazzle the spirits of Halloween
we shared news of the mission with Frederick and Violet
Frederick eyed his bride like oh my Lord do you believe this
he said Violet and i had prayed not five minutes ago Lord
send us a sliver of light now here comes a whole ceremony
with the strength stirred in me by my wife child and friends i
will be quitting this hospital bed on the morrow
later Merripen said i will not be one to hold up the troupe
wheel my broken ass to Battle Creek

פיר און צוואַנציקסט

i presented myself to Bob at the country store
with his white hair and beard i said hello Bob
it is Sloman the guitar player if you remember i
have never forgotten your kindness
as far back as my memory will take me
you have always been a pillar of this town
Bob's cigar fell from his slack mouth
he said holy shit the Scottish schoolteacher who reads
all the newspapers of the nation at the library
brought me one years ago clear out from Los Angeles
with your picture it was written you had died
i said yes i have been mixed up with death
for a long time i have been traveling lands
where reality evaporates and legend becomes truth
Bob yelled to his back office Luke get your ass out here
you will want to see who has returned
we three had a moment of merriment with their sweet tea
Bob told me Frank and Aunt J had been buried at Oak Hill
Aunt J's step uncle had made the arrangements bless him
but the funeral was not quite befitting them Bob said
i said well that is ok that is why i have returned
Bob put me in contact with a metalworker
Frederick and i rented his tools constructing the
simple sturdy structure of bars on wheels i had dreamed
one of the Locksmith keys i had gathered
i spread the word busking on street corners the week prior
while my bride prepared her feats swinging and twisting
upon the bars of our big contraption

the ceremony of light commenced with the bright pop
of the photographer's camera capturing all 26 of us outside
Kellogg's sanitarium smack in the middle of town
300 onlookers had gathered
some in their costumes of animals and spirits
the Halloween dusklight dimming upon
our troupe rambling sacred cities of the soul
there was Olena bearing a torch upon Scotch Castle
there was Dominic the postmaster to the other side
standing upon Duke Delano the Arabian stallion
there was Alexandre upon his bicycle with the three monkeys
RT Jules and J. Paul Bundy nestled on his shoulders
all four of them in black tuxedos
and in the three seats we had welded to our rolling contraption
there was Wu in her ornate high-necked Mandarin gown
her feet gripping the violin
there was Titus in the gold-and-black-sleeved garb of
a Kentucky colonel with his big buffalo drum
there was Merripen in a vest of fine buttons
he too had a drum on his lap his good arm clutching a mallet
and with me on foot
there were four strong steady country boys known to Bob
each standing by a wheel they had volunteered to push the contraption
their names were Homer Quincy Allen
and the last one to shake my hand said my name is Frank
there was Bob with two caskets upon a wagon drawn by two stallions
there was Seth with a dancing flame shining high
there was Fyodor in a suit of corduroy with his khromka
there was Guinevere crowned with flowers wrapped in a snake
there was Juan Carlos hunched in his suit cradling a block of concrete
there was Fat Ali in his long tunic carrying a sledgehammer
there was Ahimoth with black paint around his eyes and the violin
there was Mónika with the flute and Herman upon her shoulders
there was the warrior Laura in a red bonnet her lips upon the tuba
there was the Manxwoman Mary in curls with ruby ribbons
she had dusted off her trumpet
there was my brother Frederick at the ready with his mouth harp
there was his bride Violet in a black dress and velvet gloves
her vocal cords warm we had been practicing

there was Meriwether Cloud in a fine shirt of buckskin
holding the thick rope tied to our aged eyeless elder
the lovely lumbering seer through flame and smoke Babou
and perched 12 feet high atop the metal structure there was
my bride like a falcon of beauty nesting in the Belfry of Bruges
the crackle of fire and the silence of the crowd fell upon me
with the guitar of the dead unknown poets in my hands i
addressed them in as loud a voice as i could muster saying
this is the ceremony of light for Frank and Aunt J
Aunt J embraced me
a youngster soot-covered from fire
shivering in the snow
she lives in the vines and the taste of wine
Frank was a spirit rider
he won the eternal championship
the love death cannot touch
he saved my foot and won me a mule i
have been preparing to honor them for 12 years
this mission has been a blessing to me
it has led me atop mountains of joy
it has kept me seeking
the poems of simple and plain language written in mystical trances
the secret words of yogis and holy men
the deep sadness in Abraham Lincoln's eyes
the submerged castle on the sunken continent
the touch of insanity
the deadly dreams of good and evil
Frank and Aunt J have taught me
to wield the glowing hot strength of dying in life
and i am proud to be indebted to you all
the people animals and ghosts gathered here
as we celebrate the spirit riders of light
the natural bridge between us
the hope of solidarity
the Locksmith keys of Walt Whitman
the key of softness
unlock the locks with a whisper
set open the doors o soul
i strummed with my fellow musicians joining

we commenced with a slow step
the contraption rolling with us
i sang the glowing words with Violet and Frederick
i had a map of poems and i was looking for the way
but i was too blind to see
my brother riding muleback he found me in the rain
with the levee bound to break
he said death's the natural bridge but you'll be crossing it with me
and i was feeling like a king
Frederick hit the mouth harp solo
Nadezhda pirouetting in a handstand high above
the crowd moving in wonder
a hive of pilgrims
my heart tasting the river of prophetic visions
wine from the land in a bottle is beautiful
he passed to me we were falcons in flight
i left the banker bleeding in the street
rig all the rules and your darkness you'll meet
further up ahead we met a widow with no eyes
she was asking for the bridge
lines upon her face they were rivers at the crest
falcon feathers in her hair
walking with the mule we were all three singing bright
with the thunder close behind
the sky darkening we strolled down Champion Street
and paused after crossing the Battle Creek River bridge
our music hushed except for Titus pounding his drum
some anxious anticipation spread through the onlookers
i announced this light is dedicated to Leonardo the mule
he has been a stalwart brother of mine swimming the sea
of the unknown with Frank
Aunt J
the victory stallion Sweet Kiss
and my sister Esther
who showed me the book of the dead i
dream them all
Nadezhda dangled upside-down by one leg as
Seth lit the rolling structure afire at two torch points
woosh flashed the flames

the crowd hollered clapping with our music reigniting
lighting the night with dancing and camaraderie
like a traveling spiritual experience of living poetry
Alexandre and his monkeys juggling with fire
Nadezhda stunning us all with the salto mortale
our procession spilled onto the graveyard grass
with our numbers having grown upon the path
Dominic handed out a hundred tiny candles they kindled
on our seventh stop deathly quiet with my silent guitar
i made pretend like i was using it to dig a grave
Fyodor and Frederick carried Juan Carlos with
coins over his eyes and laid him upon the earth
among the mossy tombstones
his arms folded over his chest
Mary and i lifted the gray cement block together
and laid it upon his stomach
everybody fixed their eyes upon him in stillness for a ten count
Fat Ali smashed the block atop him with the sledgehammer
Juan Carlos bouncing up unleashed wild cheering from all
a cacophonous finale from the musicians
Babou screamed sweetly barely keeping her balance
the country boys had lifted the coffins off Bob's wagon
placing them upon the earth
with the chill of night
Frederick and i flipped them open to reveal
each had a finely dressed scarecrow inside
a woman and a man they had heads of mule skulls
as the multitude jostled with one another to get a look
my brother and i sparked our respective fuses sizzling
all the way to the caskets startling the crowd with
the most thunderous dazzling fireworks display
my comrades all the people illuminated blue and red
by the skyward spectacle they wore expressions of awe
some so filled with emotion they wept
Nadezhda climbed down from the contraption
into my arms we sealed the ceremony with a kiss
amid the booming light
ceasing into the dark
smoke lingering in the air

i wept
and a colossal ovation rose forth for the night
the dead had filled our cups with living waters
i embraced all my troupe
in the crisp air there swirled a spirit
of all joyous holidays combined into one
death weeping among the tombstones
like a master humiliated by a nobody
moonlight gratitude poured from dozens in attendance
and a newspaperman with several others
asked me questions with keen interest
i told them i have nothing to say about this ceremony i
only hope you had the chance to see it and take part
the crowd thinned a bit people wishing us farewell
there came a man with a distinguished gray mustache
and a fine three-piece suit leading a stallion my way i
had to pick up my jaw off the grass i drew a few eyes
exclaiming Sweet Kiss oh my Lord is it really you
i rubbed his mane saying sir is this the horse i think he is
i eyed the man hard in the torchlight and he struck me
as one whose shadow i may have glanced in a dream
he passed me a ragged page as if torn from a book
he shed his suit jacket to the earth and ripped his vest open
popping the buttons off he did the same with his shirt
bearing his chest and the tattoo of the ace of spades
he said my name is Beauregard Bird i am the rider
who caused Frank's death i
did tell you i would be haunted
my shame is not chickenshit i
wish to vanish into the beauty of this ceremony
he fished a revolver from his pocket and shot himself
through the temple before i had one second to protest
he was already on the grass blood pouring from his head
the scene sent me trembling woozy barely able to stand i
steadied myself upon a young woman's wicker wheelchair
she had a little legless girl upon her lap they were screaming
i mumbled sorry shaken pawing my way to balance when
the frenzy commenced with shouting and the flashbulb
deep in the night by lantern light at the tiny table of

my caravan i read the words of the dead
his page said
92 Hatch Road
make haste to the storm cellar
the moonshine jug in the corner
should you perform for me a ceremony of light
in Louisville Kentucky the city of my birth
you may have the jug and its contents as your reward
i trust you will not betray me since you ride with Frank's spirit
you spoke truth when you said he is a good man
fare thee well
BB
i traversed the land of my youth i knew in my sleep
i obtained the jug and returned to our camp at dawn
my comrades stirring for breakfast gathered around i
busted the jug with one crack of Fat Ali's sledgehammer
there was 21,000 dollars inside
the morning edition newspaper carried the headline
BATTLE CREEK VISITED BY THE CIRCUS OF DEATH
the story said Beauregard Bird had been a notable horse breeder
my comrades and i each pocketed one thousand
and mailed the IWW a grand
plus the photo from our ceremony with the note
The Wildcat Circus is no more
but we have been reborn
please find enclosed our dues for the next five years
solidarity forever
The Circus of Death
after we had performed the ceremony for him in Louisville
Beauregard's brother Cincinnatus found me nibbling a plum
at Beargrass Creek he said i will bet you the wheelchair under my ass
my brother sleeps in peace beneath a wild cherry tree
my father thrashed me so bad i have not been walking since
but he died with rat poison upon his lips
Beauregard got him and headed north
your ceremony could make Shakespeare seem insufficiently poetic
i chucked the plum into the water and embraced the man
i said you have done me a kindness with your words
it was an honor for me and my comrades

Wildcat Dreams in the Death Light

to see Beauregard across the bridge
we watched my fruit bobbing away i said say
your brother was mighty generous with us
did he leave you some money
Cincinnatus said why yes he did i will presently inherit
the proceeds from the sale of his home stables and horses i
am heading north on the morrow with my family to see
to his affairs and collect the things we will remember him by i
myself am a horse dentist i get them to lie down and i go to work i
live comfortably so any sum he offered you keep it free and clear
my troupe and i rambled to Lexington on another commissioned ritual
word had spread of our strange manner of farewelling the dead
we conducted 14 ceremonies over the following half year with
more requests than we could possibly complete across America
but during our procession in Savannah Georgia we were attacked
by the sea captain's widow she swung her purse wildly crying he
hanged himself after making arrangements with you in Atlanta
some men who knew her pulled her off the road i was shook
guilt gnawed her suffering stung like a scorpion in the boot
i dreamed mule-murderer Coleman oceanside when he said
the more i worked
the poorer i got
because there lurking in my heart was
the more lives i honored
the more death i brought
we debated around the campfire the following morning
i said one man taking his life i thought ok
he had a hard road and he crossed on his terms
but with two i am troubled
Fyodor picked his teeth with a knife he said i have known tea
brewed in Liechtenstein that makes a man kill himself
in Japan the samurai has opened his belly in protest
those who lie in that garden are called by an unknowable voice
Mary said yes i do not understand the mysteries of that act
only the pain within the ones they leave behind
therefore we should make known we will not conduct
our ceremonies for those who have taken their lives
lest we add to the death and suffering so widespread these days
Seth said but what if the person who died has been suffering

what if they are very old or ill
Nadezhda said yes i think in some situations
some people who kill themselves are very brave
Mary said well ok if they are very old or ill that is one thing
Wu said but who can determine who is sufficiently old or ill
Titus said i am inclined to agree with Fyodor who can know
why a fella does anything
Violet said it seems to me what we have not considered
is that someone might intentionally die saving other people
should we deny them if they request us in their will
Frederick said i also have a concern that
if we publicize our view saying we do not wish to conduct
ceremonies for those who have died by their own hand
it may make us look guilty
like we know we have already caused some suicides
when i do not believe we can say that is the case
Laura said when i was eating way too much too quickly
some people accused me of committing suicide with food
and in hindsight i think i was slowly trying to kill myself
so we would need to establish a timeframe for the acts
we are willing to allow and the ones we should exclude
there lingered silence after Laura's comment and Seth
placed a hand upon her shoulder with a tender glance
our troupe was contemplating our words i know i was i
said when i first got the notion of a ceremony of light
for my uncle Frank and Aunt J it came to me
like i do not much feel like i imagined it or dreamed it
this ceremony came to me in Locksmith visions
and from the joy when i am with you all
Meriwether Cloud said then we should continue our ways
if we do not have consensus now
when the spirits speak
we will

פֿינף און צוואַנציקסט

it was only a week later when a woman from Jacksonville
advertised in the Savannah paper
she had heard we were in town and was looking to get in touch
her sister of 36 years old had choked to death on a hushpuppy
i spent a whole day searching for a public telephone i
put the horn to my ear for the first time in my life i
was connected to the Jacksonville woman on the other side
we agreed upon terms for a dusk ceremony the last day of May
my troupe and i traveled down the coast the slow old way
and conducted a fine ceremony for the departed woman
and her kin along with many Jacksonvillians well-wishing
Babou did not wake up the following morning
even when a creature achieves the remarkable age of 28
death can still blindside you like a strange bright light
when all you can do is squint with your hand up
trying not to sound afraid when you say who is there
i wept into her fur and obtained the casket of rosewood
Meriwether cut two of her claws and cleaned them
he gave me one and said i will carry the other with me
and bury it when i return to the eternal wigwam of peace
her funeral we held upon the shore with torchlight
and Meriwether saying my people believe a great spirit
dwells in clouds and smoke i
believe Babou made contact
she is a spirit rider of light
he and i swam her coffin into the ocean and set it ablaze
with a ceremonial pyre song of the warrior's good death
still not 48 hours had passed i was in the throes of shiva

when Frederick knocked upon the door of my caravan i
was red-eyed in my blankets with one of her magic whiskers
that had seen through smoke to guide us out
i opened the door to Frederick we sat at my tiny table
with morning mugs of hot tea
he said this newspaper is chock-full of bad news
he flopped it down and there was a photo of a woman
he said there was no sister who choked on a hushpuppy
this woman faked her death
enlisted our services
pulled a Tom Sawyer zinger watching her own funeral
and the next day she opened her wrists in the bathtub
i shut my eyes and saw Babou resting atop the mountain
i opened them and said did it not go by awfully fast
this circus life
Frederick said i reckon so i
will take with me much joy from our time
too much for a mere mortal
we smiled bright
i said when is that child of yours kicking free
Frederick said could be any moment
though i would not mind him or her waiting
they say there is supposed to be a big storm tonight
i glanced where that was written in the newspaper
and in the article next to it there was talk of healthy
young soldiers who had a slight wheeze in the chest
and were dead by morning
i pointed to the page i said you read about this influenza
he nodded gravely saying they say it turns you blue and kills you
they are fixing to outlaw sneezing in public and gatherings of any size
we summoned our troupe with the news
and reached consensus of our end embracing one another
with even the toughest among us like Fyodor Titus and Laura weeping
we ate a fine dinner of boiled salmon with music and light
i sang with everyone and Nadezhda backflipped over the fire
the rains and wind dashed us inside our shelters i
held my bride with Professor Walnut purring at our feet
i said you are not too sad we must close this chapter
she licked her fingers and snuffed the candle

she said i know it is time
perhaps we can continue south
and check on our tree in Key West
we fucked lovingly during that hurricane
and in the morning
we found that that night my brother's son had been born
he and Violet named their child Vernon Sloman Honeycutt
one of the great honors of my life
and an homage to our friend
the poet whose death led Frederick into the forest to find her
we all met the child in the blue sky morning
and now i can say i saw a giant tenderly kiss a newborn baby
we all shared our plans while packing our camp
Fyodor and Guinevere heading to the wilds of Montana
Dominic Alexandre and the monkeys San Francisco-bound
Mary to a cabin in Vancouver
Titus back to Kentucky
my and Nadezhda's kin blowing in the wind
with the rest of them who had a mind to scatter
i had lobbied them all to join us in Key West
and found success with Frederick and family
Seth Wu and Laura by lunchtime i was brimming with hope
we had a notion to ride out the pestilence under the sun
and earn our way street performing and fishing with Rodolfo
The Circus of Death assembled for the last time that day
but before we got to striking off upon the open road i
said i would like to say something and i hope you all
mark it good
write it down
commit it to memory
if i am still drawing breath on this side of the bridge
at sunset of October 31st 1928
ten years from this coming Halloween
you all can find me at Gallows Hill in Salem Massachusetts i
will be strumming and singing songs in honor of our comrades
Lola Marvin and Tomás their courage is a blessing and a light
Mary embraced me in the gentle whisper of i will see you there
Merripen not too old but cane-walking from his injuries said
the thought of that day up ahead will fill me with strength

Meriwether Cloud called me a pilgrim and i hugged him
i harnessed Sweet Kiss and Scotch Castle to my caravan
and bid them all fare thee well departing with my friends
rambling south we shared a meal with men from Belize City
who had arrived upon a raft of coconuts and torn clothing
they said the British had been forcing them to cut timber
we ate a shark
we saw a blind seamstress singing
i saw a man in a beak-nose plague mask walk into the ocean
and never come back
i could not say it was a time of joy with
the Angel of Death rampaging around the world
but when Rodolfo saw us upon the road he screamed
he embraced all of us laughing saying if you have brought
that influenza i will remove my leg and beat you with it
we had such fun fishing
Mildred taught us all how to make Key lime pie
we had delicious nights at the table
beach fires
the sweet baby sunshine
my comrades and i grateful to be passed over
Nadezhda and i had been renting a coastal cottage
that even had an indoor pull-chain toilet and a rainwater cistern
the fever of the world broke in the spring of 1920
we emerged with a banner year performing downtown
golden times
i cast the only vote of my life in November
Eugene V. Debs for president
Frederick said to me on the boat one June day
my mind has been wandering back to our salad days in France
we plan to head over and stay for some time i
wish Vernon to grow in the unworried freedom i knew there
i said we will miss you like hell but i understand
he said i will search for the film we made in '14
if i find it you will know by the worldwide sensation
the grand resurfacing of *Wildcat Dreams in the Death Light*
we had a good laugh and a farewell feast
we exchanged letters of brotherhood
plotting our reunion of music and light

Reagan M. Sova

Seth and Laura said their vows upon the sand
the ocean waters lapping all our bare feet
Wu married the seaman in a ceremony
of fine jade objects and the holy violin
my bride and i moonlight-kissed in bed
with the joy of her growing belly
peacefully she said i see them with my eyes closed
i said who
she said our circus comrades
the good working people with whom we vexed death
i said it is a beautiful bond we have
we will join with them again in time
we will sing poems of light
we will never give up
she said our child will know honey
i said yes
we held each other in the night
the warm breeze rustling desk pages
this poem i have written before the mountain
where i strike my match
where i sharpen my blade
words of the dead folding the past into now

WILDCAT DREAMS IN THE DEATH LIGHT

About the poet

Reagan M. Sova is an American living in Belgium. His writing career began when he was orphaned at the age of 16. At that time, Sova developed an idiosyncratic gambling method in the casinos of northern Michigan. These bets financed a flight to Paris where, at 20, he first discovered the power of literature. Since then, Sova has produced poetry and prose that have been featured in *Ghost City Review*, *Common Dreams*, and *Expat Press*. He also authored *Tiger Island* (Harvard Square Press, 2017), an alternate history novel about water privatization, soccer, anarchosyndicalism, and WikiLeaks. In addition to writing poetry and fiction, Sova serves as a writer and editor at The European Institute for Animal Law & Policy, a Brussels-based think tank that seeks to advance the interests of animals in European law and policy.

Other Books from First To Knock

☐ *Echoes of a Natural World—Tales of the Strange & Estranged*
   Edited by **MICHAEL P. DALEY**
   Translations & Introduction by **SAM KUNKEL**

   "This is the missing link between Baudelaire and the Area X Trilogy, strange, beautiful, and bizarre as any denizen of a romantic ruin, nuclear test site, or poisonous overgrown garden could ever want."
   — *CrimeReads*

   Echoes of a Natural World presents a continuum of discomforting reactions to a world perpetually out of whack. Nature—so oft considered the epitome of "order" and "tranquility" in the human mind—is herein explored at its most aberrant, absurd, and nightmarish. Through eleven weird tales, *Echoes of a Natural World* raises questions about Nature's influence on the mind and the mind's unnatural influence on Nature.

☐ *A Beam of Sunlight in the Deep Forest—Mystical Prose Works by Édouard Schuré*
   Translations & Introduction by **SAM KUNKEL**

   "[Schuré is], in our time, the sole man of persuasion for whom the few Mysteries which haunt some of us are natural and part of a magnificent birthright."
   — Stéphane Mallarmé

   Édouard Schuré was a 19th century French author and occultist who spent his life attempting to translate the ineffable realm of spiritual knowledge into literature. *A Beam of Sunlight in the Deep Forest* is a landmark collection of Schuré's prose works, offering a robust introduction to the forgotten figure. Taken together, these texts offer truths about the artistic process and the spiritual development of humanity in the face of an ever more industrialized, and secularized, world.

☐ *Bobby Blue Jacket: The Tribe, The Joint, The Tulsa Underworld*
   by **MICHAEL P. DALEY**

   "A book of history that suggests that, in the right hands, anyone could be plucked from the crowd and, in the proper hands and mind, written into an iconic figure in a wide-ranging book of history and sociology, and, inevitably psychology."
   — Rick Harsch, *The Manifold Destiny of Eddie Vegas*

Bobby BlueJacket illuminates a neglected history of American crime, identity, and politics in the 20th century. This is the extraordinary true story of a man who went from career thief and convicted killer to celebrated prison journalist—ultimately becoming a respected Eastern Shawnee activist and orator. *Bobby BlueJacket* draws upon 5 years of interviews with the subject, long-buried law enforcement and trial records, prison archives, news accounts, and interviews with others such as photographer Larry Clark and veteran reporters of Tulsa's crime beat.

☐ *How Did We Get Here?*
    by **STERLING BARTLETT**

"...a rant, a sermon against the harbingers of our pyrotechnic-insanitarium endtimes, and possibly, if enough people pay attention to the Void, an illustrated pamphlet for a coming revolution."
— *Apocalypse Confidential*

How Did We Get Here? is an interplanetary gripe session in the form of a comic book. Its target: pretty much everything. This postmodern hellfire sermon (delivered by a para-physical, ultra-terrestrial entity named Void) pinpoints the micro-absurdities and inconvenient perpetrators feeding the downward slide of contemporary culture. Hooks are thrown right and left in an attempt to halt our earthly souls from becoming completely quantified, price stamped, and sold to the highest bidder.

☐ *Brainfazer*
    by **KEVIN BARRY**

"Barry's work is a psychedelic outer space puppet show of crazy blinding colors. It's easy to get lost in these drawings and then re-emerge with your brain pulsating and your eyes dripping."
— Johnny Ryan, *Angry Youth Comix* and *Prison Pit*

Kevin Barry's *Brainfazer* is a show stopping, psychedelic art trip that stretches the eyeball to dimensions never-before-traveled. The neon color work leads to compositions of such mind-boggling visual density that the initial breathtaking shock of first sight is usually followed by hours of meditation on the page. Yes indeed, *Brainfazer* is a debut art book from one of the most exciting new American visual artists to emerge in recent times.

Coming Soon from First To Knock

☐ *Oklahoma Cockfight*
   Edited by MICHAEL P. DALEY & NICK FERREIRA
   With an essay by MICHAEL P. DALEY

It was a time of contradictions. Get-rich-quick oil gushers and men perpetually on the bum. Zig-zag architectural wonders alongside heinous racial violence and cultural genocide. Persistent venereal disease and contagious old-time religion. Unrepentant hucksterism and wide-eyed sincerity. This was 1920s Oklahoma, booming big, for some, in the shadow of a Great Depression yet unknown. And in these times, such incongruous forces coalesced around the cockpit, if only momentarily, to behold a brutal spectacle of violence—gaffs, feathers, and blood.

☐ *The Solar Circus*
   by GUSTAVE KAHN
   Translations & Introduction by SAM KUNKEL

The Solar Circus is the great forgotten masterpiece of French symbolist literature. Written by Gustave Kahn—the man whom Stéphane Mallarmé and Jules Laforgue credited as having invented free-verse poetry—the novel drips in decadent images of pastoral vistas, exotic gemstones, and a phantasmagoric menagerie. Inverting day for night and reality for a dazzling dream, *The Solar Circus* tells the story of a solipsistic, isolated Bavarian count who falls in love with the star of a traveling circus. Together, they set out from the count's castle, encountering a world in transformation: peasants in rebellion, the bright lights of London's Orpheum Theatre, and even an ether-swilling Jack the Ripper in an opium den.

First To Knock publishes books and records.

The company is based in Michigan City, Indiana.
It is independently run and distributed.

First To Knock titles are available on its webshop or at some of the finest bookshops in the United States, Canada, France, Australia, and the United Kingdom.